BETWEEN DYSTOPIAS: THE ROAD TO AFROPANTHEOLOGY

BETWEEN DYSTOPIAS: THE ROAD TO AFROPANTHEOLOGY

Oghenechovwe Donald Ekpeki
Joshua Uchenna Omenga

Caezik SF & Fantasy
in partnership with
O.D. Ekpeki Presents

ISBN: 978-1-64710-084-1
First Edition. First Printing October 2023.
1 2 3 4 5 6 7 8 9 10

An imprint of Arc Manor LLC
www.CaezikSF.com

An imprint of Jembefola Press
www.odekpeki.com

CONTENTS

INTRODUCTION TO AFROPANTHEOLOGY

The African cosmology recognizes two spheres of existence—the physical and the spiritual, between which there is an inseparable link and constant interactions. Every sphere of existence is connected to the other: the living to the dead, the born to the unborn, humans to the deities. And because many African stories (and particularly many in this collection) are a fictional reflection of the realities of life in the African cosmology, it can be a mislabel to regard them as fantasy—especially if by fantasy we mean the genre of escapist literature in which readers must suspend their belief to enjoy.

The concept of fantasy (part of the broader category of speculative fiction) used to label imaginative fictions involving outlandish characters, magical elements, and often set in created worlds, can sometimes be ill-fitting when used for many literary works of similar rendering from the African continent. Thus, the scope of literary works contemplated under this project is not captured by any extant term in African or other literature.

In view of this lacuna, *Afropantheology* was conceived to capture the gamut of African works which, though having fantasy elements, are additionally imbued with the African spiritual realities.

Afropantheology is a portmanteau of *Afro* and *Pantheology*. Pantheology is the study of gods, religions, and the bodies of knowledge associated with them. Derivatively, Afropantheology is the study of African (and African-descended) religions, gods, and the bodies of knowledge associated with them. It is a term to capture the essence of the stories in this project, and also solves the age-old problem of accurate and respectful labelling of stories based on African lore and religion. They are not mere fantasies, neither do such labels as "godpunk" serve entirely to clothe these works, as skins do bones, for these stories stretch beyond just showing the "gods."

In this collection, "The Witching Hour" reflects the apprentice system in the voodoo practice still extant in many parts of Africa. "The Deification of Igodo" reflects the creation of deities from among the ancestors in African cosmology (in which deities create humans as well as humans create deities). "A Dance with the Ancestors" reflects the interconnection between the world of the living and the world of the dead. And "The Land of the Awaiting Birth" reflects the link between the born and the unborn. There are no magics in these stories, except if by magic one means what is not provable by science. In that case, the African cosmology abounds in such magics, and all the artist is called upon to do is to represent them.

Why then the creation of *Afropantheology*? It does not suffice to merely insist that these stories are the realities of the African cosmology, especially in this era of scepticism when only the scientific is believed to be factual. This: that these stories, deriving though they are from African lore, are yet not wholly imaginative. Is *Revelation* in the Bible a work of fantasy? If one believes that it stemmed wholly from the imagination of John the Apostle as he sat on the Island of Patmos, then perhaps. But not if one believes that John wrote what was revealed to him by "God" or His delegates. So are the stories presented in *Afropantheology* and contemplated under the label: they are fantasy only insofar as the channels of their passage are dismissed, as has unfortunately been done for centuries now, when the continent's jugular was slashed with the swords of slavery and colonialism, and its history and culture and stories poured into the arid sands of theft and erasure. But not anymore. *Afropantheology* has been born to cauterize that wound, our words to sing to life what was lost, and to sift the sand for the true Black Gold that lies amidst the bones of our ancestors.

The stories contemplated under the Afropantheology label are primordial African stories inherited from priests and lore keepers who were in communication with the deities and the spirit world. Thus, the stories were viewed mostly by their purveyors as histories rather than as fiction. What may more correctly pass for the African literary equivalent to fantasy are the folklores, which are imaginative and didactic stories usually involving outlandish creatures and heroes, meant to entertain and sometimes instruct. And so, these stories are not folklores, but (fictional) renderings of the histories passed down from keepers of African culture and lores. It is necessary that the stories be recognized for what they represent.

The dystopic stories in this collection, like similar stories from the African continent, are realities, even if fictionalized realities. "Mother's Love, Father's Place" captures a "dark"moment in the history of certain parts of Africa, where the culture forbade the birthing of twins. "O_2 Arena" on the other hand, is a contemporary "dystopic" reality. To readers in other climes, dystopic stories are mere dark imaginings, but not to us who experience, or whose ancestors experienced, them. "Too Dystopian for Whom? A Continental Nigerian Writer's Perspective" captures the arguments of this segment. These dystopic stories, too, should be properly identified for what they represent: the African dystopic reality.

But the greatest reason for our insistence on the term of Afropantheology to identify stories of African pantheon, mysticism, and origin is to right the literal and literary injustice perpetrated on the continent and its pantheon by the colonialists and their writers. *Afropantheology* does not, of course, seek to resurrect the discussion on geographical colonialism or even the dark history of African slavery (except incidentally). Those are worthy aspirations, but they are already being taken care of by other forms of writings, colonial and contemporary (and perhaps even postmodernistic). Also, Afropantheology does not preach the superiority of African deities. Of greater concern to *Afropantheology* is to correct the mis-portrayal of African religion in artistic writings, and to encourage the recovery, rediscovery, rebirth, and documentation of African stories, cultures, and religions.

In this wise, *Afropantheology* seeks to assert the right—and indeed the obligation—of Africans and African descended peoples to tell the stories of African deities and mysticism in the proper manner, which were handed down from the realm of the spirits, irrespective of whether they conform to "established" literary categorizations or not.

This quest to correct the mislabelling would not be necessary but for the colonization and the bastardization of African spirito-cultural sphere. While the colonialists undermined African political establishments, the missionaries undermined African spiritual and cultural establishments. Both groups of invaders came with a similarly (misplaced) superiority mindset which sought to impose their perceived higher political and religious doctrines on the natives. They worked to usher us into a culture of dystopias in which Africans were storyless, to rip from our hearts our songs, and to steal the joy from our dances, the tales from our tongues, and the fire from our eyes that looked to the future.

Thus, on the political side, African kings were forced to rule according to Western dictates, and those who—like Jaja of Opobo and Overamwen Nogbaisi of Benin Empire—refused to deviate from the ways of their forefathers were deposed or killed. On the religious side, Christianity and Islam substituted Jehovah and Allah for the deities of Africa with approximate creative powers, and the deities which found no equivalence in the colonialists' religious labelling were eroded or demonized. In Yoruba culture, for instance, Olodumare or Olorun was selected to represent Jehovah and Allah, while in Igbo culture it was Chukwu or Chineke. Both Christianity and Islam also found ready equivalents for their shared villain, Satan, in Esu Elegbara (Yoruba pantheon), Ekwensu (Igbo pantheon), and so on in other African pantheons. However, in none of the African deities did these two major colonialist religions find worthy replacement for the benevolent Jesus, and Muhammad, despite the superfluity of deified ancestors who provide striking similarities to their roles—for instance, Orunmila of the Orisha pantheon.

Unlike these other religions, whose cosmoses were polarized into simple good and evil, the cosmos of the African pantheons is polarized into wider and varying degrees of good and evil, power and weakness, physical and spiritual. Befuddled by this smorgasbord of deities, the conquerors of the African religious space relegated all the other African deities that found no equivalent in their monotheistic deisms to the status of demons—hence the insistence that their converts abandon these deities for the "True God."

Unlike Christianity and Islam, the African 'religion' not only does no proselytizing, but also readily welcomes every creed and faith in the spirit of tolerance. In its tolerance, it accommodated foreign religions and their adherents, letting its deities stand or fall for themselves, and so was taken advantage of. For in the African cosmology, the deities fight for their people and not the people for their deities. This was amply demonstrated by Achebe in *The Arrow of God* where the native gods were abandoned for the Christian god at the former's refusal to fight for themselves at the onslaught of Christian poaching of their worshippers.

While seeking to address and correct these mislabellings, *Afropantheology* recognizes the fluidity of definition and the diversity of the Continent and its pantheons. What *Afropantheology* seeks is the freedom of the artist to express these stories in their original forms, unbridled by Western labels and terminologies and the need for conformity to defined (often limited) literary standards. For, contrary to speculations, the relative unfamiliarity of stories reflecting African pantheons is due to the weakness of form rather than the paucity of stories. These stories have always been extant in oral forms, preserved by lore keepers whose goal was to ensure the continuity of culture rather than the fame of publication, who indeed sought no glorification outside the recognition of their fidelity in passing the stories. In Africa, the oral arts perhaps predate stone and wood arts, but due to its very nature, oral literature is not a subject of archaeological discovery. And because of this, the forms of these stories are fluid and not readily conformable to standards of storytelling in civilizations which commenced their storytelling in written form. In view of this, and of the diverse nature of African pantheons, any attempt at documenting these stories must take cognizance of the various histories and cultures behind them. Hence, the stories in *Afropantheology* are varied in artistic forms and themes. This, perhaps, is too obvious to require iteration.

In *Afropantheology* we provide a label which we believe more correctly identifies the stories of African deities and mysticism. We have not set out to create a new form of African literature (even if we incidentally did create one) but merely to expose extant lores of African mysticism in the form intended by the deities and ancestors and lore keepers of primeval African societies. For too long, the stream of stories of African mysticism has been held by the dam of incorrect labelling and forced terminologies. Through *Afropantheology,* we hereby open the dam to release the pent-up stream of African mystic stories into the sea of global literature, to swell and enrich it!

In the words of Chinua Achebe, "Until the lions have their own historians, the history of the hunt will always glorify the hunter."

And so, our stories are here reformed and reborn in the throes and strength and fires of our words, an unbroken chain stretching through an endless cycle, leading us down that dark road of dystopia, guided by the light of recovery, into Afropantheology.

OGHENECHOVWE DONALD EKPEKI
JOSHUA UCHENNA OMENGA
Lagos, Nigeria, January 2023

THE WITCHING HOUR

by Oghenechovwe Donald Ekpeki

I stood balanced at the top of the oldest palm tree, the one that grew at the south end of the village. I was in my element—pitch-black night. This was my dawn. The murmurs of glowing spirits mixed with the chitter of living insects.

The hoot of an owl reminded me there was work to be done, battles to be fought—silent, undeclared, but raging all the same. And old Mama Ishaka was on the other side of them. With a sigh, I leapt from the tree, fell free, and caught one of the power lines that led to a human spirit. The link was strong. The call of this spirit sang the music of its soul to me. It called me back home.

We sat in my hut, bare as it was, Ejiro and I, on the even barer floor. The kerosene lamp hung from a nail on the wall, its flickering yellow light the only illumination. I didn't need much, being a creature of the night.

I had chosen my apprentice for her goodness. Shy and quiet, she was my sister's child. Like other old-world witches, I was glad to recruit from family, where they were cut closest to us. Blood was more than just a symbol.

She was still learning to maneuver the delicate currents of the other side.

I rubbed the ori ointment on her eyes to ease the transition and make visible the other realm—the beauty of it along with the denizens that drive normals mad with fright. We moved freely among it all—the souls of sleeping humans, shining shape-shifters, headless spirits drifting along upside down.

I took hold of her hands and invoked the deep-black sleep that let us travel to the other side. Our bodies slumped, and we passed over. We floated, translucent and unbound by gravity. We had power in this state. A power that was intoxicating.

Ejiro moved toward the door. I smiled and pulled her toward the wall. I flowed through it, and she followed. Outside the protection of my hut, we felt the pull, the dreams, the thoughts of sleeping normals. Those souls connected to us pulled the most, sending out strong lines of power.

There was one we set out to find. I had established a connection with her in the physical world and could see her soul cord faintly shimmering. We flowed along it, shifting shapes—I an old, brown owl, Ejiro, a nightjar. We sailed swift and sure, alighting on a palm tree beside a darkened house.

I shifted back and floated to the roof. My fledgling followed. We sifted down through the thatch. I looked at Ejiro. She nodded and threw a shroud over the home's sleeping occupants, to keep them still until our work was done. She fastened on their sleeping forms, and they choked, gulping for air, struggling vainly to wake. In the morning they would say they had been pressed and they would shiver.

I drew close to the one we were here to help, a girl of eleven. She tossed and turned, feeling the energy of the other side but unable to wake to it. I slipped my hand into her chest and cradled the pulsing spirit heart of her being. She gasped. I gathered my energy and pulled. Her body convulsed, and she held back, frightened at the pull to cross over, though this crossing was only a hair's breadth, not the faraway world of the ancestors.

I pulled again. Her body heaved, its hold on her loosening. Again, I pulled, and the body's grasp slipped away. Her translucent spirit form came away. Initiation. The newly freed form floated gently, looking at us curiously.

My spirit energy was depleted, a danger especially as I rarely fed on others. I glanced at Ejiro. She was flush and glowing faintly, without intention having drained energy from those she subdued.

She had not yet mastered the art of fastening and holding without feeding. She started guiltily.

We sifted up through the thatch, leaving the newly awakened one floating quietly about the house. She would explore the new realm we had opened her to. Before a coven found her, we would be back to teach her and bring her into the fold.

We flew on. Owl and nightjar. We awakened other young ones. Each time I was left weaker. Ejiro unintentionally drank in life energy and spirit consciousness. If she drained too much, their spirit flame would be extinguished, and they would die. But as her teacher the guilt would be mine.

Dawn was near, and we were far from our bodies. We could not survive long here without the clear spiritual focus the night imbued us with. Weak and tired, I set a course for home.

We glided along the spirit currents. I didn't notice I was falling until I hit the ground and rolled roughly. The nightjar alighted beside me, shifting into the shape of a wild cat and picking me up in her jaws. She could so easily have crushed me, leaving my contorted body bereft of spirit. But she bore me safely home.

I slept for two days, waking only to gulp down water and a morsel of food.

I awoke in my hut. A blanket covered me. Beside my mat was a cup of water and food covered in a clay bowl. The hut was swept and arranged. I smiled. Ejiro had taken great care of me. I took a long pull of water. Though I wondered sometimes at the rightness of what I did, if I was any better than those we battled, Ejiro did not doubt. Perhaps I could trust the innocence and goodness of her heart if I couldn't trust my own.

I stretched and got up. I had business to be about. My small farm did not tend itself. We all had day work. Like everyone else we needed to survive in the physical world. This was why Ejiro was with me, although my sister thought her daughter helped me tend my farm. Well, she did. She just also helped me cultivate souls.

Ejiro had gone to our food stall in the marketplace. The market was a good place for recruiting, and mothers often warned their young ones not to touch or take anything from strangers. But recruiting mostly came through relatives.

Every young child had a tendency toward the spirit realm that waned as they grew and got more settled in the physical world. But giving them food saturated with the substance of the other side strengthened the connection, and in sleep the spirit strove to break free from its body and rejoin its natural home. Often, the help of an initiating witch, such as myself, was needed.

I wondered sometimes if it was right, taking them this young, without their consent, as I had been taken by Mama Ishaka. She had been a family friend. She liked her recruits sweet and kind and young. So did I. But our motives were as different as palm oil from groundnut oil. You could fry with both, but only one was good for yams. The old one exulted in corrupting innocent apprentices, warping them into bloodthirsty hags who fed for the pure joy of the misery they inflicted.

Witches like Mama Ishaka had a craving for evil, came to it of their own strong, iron will. Such ones allied themselves with like-minded dibias and medicine men, prophets and healers, the strongest of the othersiders. They lived in both sides, and with keen balance accessed either at times and ways that made us feel like normals. The dark dibias sometimes sent their witch allies to carry out assassinations and other such work. My time with Mama Ishaka left me prey to the pull of their ways.

Another haunt. A night for Ejiro to train in practices of power, skills to help turn the tide in our silent battle. I let out a hoot to signal the haunt's start, sending shivers through the spines of any beings still awake, setting them praying.

We sailed through the night in our favorite forms, owl and nightjar. We could take any shape we conjured, but the more time in one form, the more powerful we grew within it. I led the way, swerving to avoid a copse of trees—a coven's meeting place—surrounded by a haze cloaking the coven's activities from other creatures and night users: prophets, healers, even worshippers of the white Christ. They each followed their gods or god and drew power from the other side. Just power. Like a knife, it was what you did with it that mattered. But I knew what many did with their power.

The nightjar's call drew me out of my thoughts. We had arrived at our first stop. We perched atop a mango tree beside the house. Normals knew a tree beside one's house might bring hauntings from creatures of the night.

I led Ejiro through the art called *sendings*. She fed to the point where the soul's hold was tenuous, at the cusp between life and death, then I helped her establish a spiritual connection, to see this person's life threads, and move them gently, guiding their fate and fortune to their benefit in the waking world.

The one who turned me, Mama Ishaka, she taught me this, but she gave those she haunted terrible sendings, tortured them with nightmares and visions. Sometimes she toyed with them, gave helpful sendings they came to trust, imagining them from ancestors or kind spirits. Then she sent visions pulling her victims down to ruin and death. And so, witches and dreams were feared.

She did not always take the time to be this creative. She might simply feed until their heart gave out or their organs failed. The more one fed, the more powerful one became. Seeing further into the future, taking the shape of more powerful beasts, influencing people and events more. Living longer. So, some of our oldest witches radiated a powerful malevolence.

Mama Ishaka took immense pleasure in corrupting her apprentices, whom she chose from amongst the goodliest and kindest hearted. These were the ones she enjoyed breaking, pulling the good from their souls. On our haunts she pushed me to feed until our quarry's life force gave out. But I would not. I was a most difficult one to corrupt she would say, then cackle and fly off in search of our next victim. But feeding is addictive, and my craving grew. She was a patient one. She knew it was a matter of time.

Earning my freedom would require giving in to that which I hated and feeding until the victim died. But this owl outplayed her twice over. When I saw souls in difficulty, as I had their life threads stretched before me, glowing white lines leading toward good, darkened lines pulling them toward misery and ignominious decease, I went down their white threads, through a cascade of images, and gave them positive sendings, visions, and warnings for the future. I set many on a safe path out of the claws of Mama Ishaka.

And from another witch I learned a second way to earn my freedom—wake a new witch, create my own apprentice. Mama Ishaka had been enraged and tormented the one who taught me this.

So Ejiro and I followed power lines, sailing swift and sure; agents of the night, searching out the wretched of the earth, the ones that most needed good in their lives. We provided them this while feeding, an unholy exchange, rendering help to these ailing ones through a power feared and known only for misery and death.

Eventually dawn neared, and we needed to return to our bodies to cross the veil back to the world of normals. We flew for home. And into an ambush. The nightjar was pounced upon and sent careening off to slam against a tree. I was held fast in the strands of an otherside web. A spider's web. Large and thick and strong enough to hold a goat. Only an old witch with much power could do this. And there was something familiar about that aura …

The spider dropped down before me, its huge head twisting and writhing into the shape of a human face. It was she, the one who had initiated me, opened me to the other side. Mama Ishaka.

She swung around me cackling, hanging upside down with her full glare on me. Even with a human face, her maw was rich with venom that flew out, scathing and burning me. I would wake sick and wounded, if I woke at all.

She lunged for my throat and pulled back, toying with me. Then she held her pincers to my head, and in that sharp vise a tunnel of dark visions and memories swallowed me. Her memories. Of people. They looked familiar. I stared. They were the people I had helped while her apprentice. But she had found me out and carried out her revenge, tormenting and killing them.

She laughed, shrill and mocking. She had undone all I had devoted myself to, all that allowed me to live with the evil I felt inside me. My anger was a fire. I tore free of the vision.

She slid a claw down my cheek, telling me that now she was content to finally let me go. "Or," she said, "maybe I'll stay close, watch you save spirits, watch them flourish, then pull them apart, rip them to pieces." A crooked smile laced her face, and she turned to sidle up her web.

But the old one made a huge mistake that night. Perhaps to her, goodliness only meant weakness. Perhaps she underestimated the value of those souls to me, underestimated the power of my rage, failed to see I might freely do what all her power had never forced me to. I struggled in her web of body and heart and mind, and broke free. As a lion. Fangs, claws, wings, power. I shredded her strands like gossamer. She turned to face me, and I leapt upon her. My claws tore into her as she tried to transform, tried to cast me off. But I held fast. Held tight with the power of my hate, my grief, my love for what she had destroyed.

Eventually she fell still. I felt the tremors from her body dying in the physical world. Her spirit form floated away and came apart, dark dust in the wind of the nether realm.

I shrank down into an old, sad owl and flew to my wounded apprentice. I transformed and cradled the small body. I wept. I had lost myself and everything I had tried to build. The old one had triumphed. She had made me what she wanted, in the end. I had run away from death-dealing all my life, never knowing I was running straight to it. I wept, Ejiro's broken body in my hands, my hated enemy regrettably dead, and the dawn closing in on me.

One could be a certain thing, but not be bound by it, so long as one never gave up fighting it. I would keep fighting this thing I was, this evil Mama Ishaka saw in me, that she tried so hard to make me live out. Evil never wins, until you stop fighting it.

Ejiro survived that night. I recovered my heart and resolve.

We stood at the top of the oldest palm tree in the village. The night was alive around us. Two realms open to us. I meant for us to change things. Two women, one almost too old, the other maybe too young and inexperienced, two witches against a world, the set way of things. But we were all there, and if we failed it wouldn't be for lack of trying.

My apprentice looked to me.

"Perhaps good can never win," I said. "But maybe evil not winning is enough. Enough to keep us going each day. I will train a cadre of good witches. You are the first."

Ejiro nodded, and without prompting, we leapt off, following the call of souls, connecting to the lines of power, soaring into the living blackness to carry out a dark goodness.

THE MANNEQUIN CHALLENGE

by Oghenechovwe Donald Ekpeki

My name is Obaro, which means forward in Urhobo. True to my name, I was always moving forward.

I walked along the University of Lagos Road in Abule Oja. It was nothing serious, just a morning stroll. I loved to take these kinds of strolls, with headphones plugged in and music blotting out my thoughts. That helped me think. It was around 7 a.m. and shops were mostly closed. The Lagos speed day was a myth, in Abule Oja anyway.

I passed my favorite food shop, Shop 10. The shopkeepers were gathered outside, doing "morning devotion"—a clap-and-dance worship session which they used to start the day, believing it ensured a good business day more than any exemplary services they could render. I huffed and shook my head. I thought to myself: why don't they go set up shop early and attend to workers leaving for work too early to prepare something in their homes? It annoyed me that after squandering their own opportunity with their religious and superstitious attitudes, these shop owners would turn to blame their semiliterate and near brain-dead president for how bad the economy was.

I shook my head and turned to look thoroughly at the road before crossing. It was a one-way road, but you had to look carefully at both sides before crossing if you did not want an Aboki okadaman to usher you into oblivion. These commercial bikemen were mostly always high. The alternative was worse. Bus drivers were not only high but also slow. At least the bikes were quick, and if they didn't take you to your final destination, they would get you to your current one, in time. Such was the public transport system in Lagos, the "mega city." Get there late or get there late.

I crossed the road and continued my walk. Along the way, an older woman was saying something to me. I took off my headphones to hear her but returned them to my ears in annoyance. She was one of those "Mowa stranded"; people who claimed to have suffered some unfortunate mishap and got stranded on their journey somewhere important. They just needed a little help to get there. Meanwhile it was a profession—not getting somewhere important, but being stranded.

I stopped at a Mallam's shop to buy gum. There was an old man in front of me purchasing something. Probably snuff or cigarettes or something else not good for him at his age. He was bent almost double and taking an awfully long time. I waited impatiently. Eventually he finished his transaction. As he turned, taking an infinitely long time, I caught sight of what he was buying. It was indeed cigarettes. I hissed and, in my annoyance, said in pidgin, "Oga comot from road na. This one wey you just stand for road like mannequin. Them dey do mannequin challenge for here?"

He turned and, looking me in the eyes, said, "You will hend up as a mannequin." His Yoruba accent was heavy. I saw him fully now. He was a very traditional-looking old Yoruba man, likely uneducated, old, complete with tribal marks on his face. The slashes highlighted his red eyes. He must have been drinking already this early in the day. I took all this in in a moment. I paused my music and noticed he had gone on a tirade. I didn't understand the words he was saying, but I could understand clearly from his tone that they were invectives. He was cursing me. I shivered a bit. Of course, a modern man like me shouldn't believe in things like that. Curses are words which have no power to magically hurt you.

But I knew better. Jazz was real. By jazz I didn't mean a brand of music considered classic. I meant real, dark magic that was used to harm people and influence events in the real world. Why, my maternal grandmother in Ughelli had been a powerful ATR practitioner. I still remembered the space in her wardrobe where she kept what my parents later came to call her idols. There had been a big bowl of red water in front of it. I always wondered what was in the water. Probably palm oil. I always told myself it couldn't be blood. There had been Fanta and Coke bottles and kolanut, Cabin biscuits, and other oddities offered in sacrifice to the god(s). My parents hadn't always considered it idolatry. Before their conversion to the modernity of Christianity, they had been ATR worshippers, both of them. That was how I knew enough not to take jazz or the old man's curse lightly. My grandfather on my father's side had been a great jazzman too. He had been blind in his old age, but they had said he saw more than those with two eyes. Therefore, being from two great lineages of jazzmen, I knew enough to be afraid of curses.

I still had memories of my father cutting us with razors on our wrists and forearms under the direction of my grandma, after which he sprinkled some protective charms on the incisions. That was before my parents became Christians and turned away from those barbaric practices. But I had confirmed the potency of those charms long before they stopped. One day, I had gotten into an altercation with someone. He swung a cutlass at my head. I wasn't in time to dodge it and had instead foolishly attempted to block it with my arm. The cutlass bounced off, to everyone's amazement, myself included. I would later call it Metal Bending. It wasn't all magical, though. I felt the pain—sharp and loud, as if I was being hit by a blunt instrument, although I later confirmed the cutlass to be as sharp as my sister's tongue. Yet my skin wasn't broken. I didn't tell my parents or grandma, since we rarely went to the village anymore anyway. I did tell one of my aunties, who confirmed for me that the charms my grandma made were still as potent as anything, even after two decades.

It was against this background that I felt trepidation at the old man's curses on me to become a mannequin. And of course, everyone knew the story of Bode Thomas, the then colonial minister of the colony and protectorate of Nigeria, who had been cursed by the Ooni of Ife and had barked uncontrollably and continuously to death, like a dog. The Oba was later deposed and sent on exile. Wikipedia said Bode Thomas was poisoned, but we all knew better. The Ooni had cursed Bode Thomas for disrespecting him, saying he would keep on barking like a dog for yelling at him. That very night, Bode Thomas started barking in his home and died shortly after. So, I knew curses were real, and shivered as I walked fast from this man's curse.

I suddenly froze, unable to move. I was stuck, by myself. The world was moving all around me, but I was stuck in my body, like a mannequin. I remembered all the stories I had heard about curses and felt a sudden sweat break out on my forehead. I felt a palpable fear take me over. I wanted to piss myself. I shook within but couldn't move without. I called on my grandma, her gods, and my grandfather's spirit to save me. I didn't call on the Lord. I had seen MFM worshippers call on the lord and fire countless times without any fire actually showing up. But I knew, and had seen, my grandma's magic work before. So, I called on her. At the same instance, I felt my body begin to transform, a brittle, plastic feeling. My arm began to change. I was becoming a mannequin, truly. Then I felt something else in my blood. My grandma and father's blood magic fighting it. The effect of the transformation continued. It took over me, although I wasn't a mannequin yet. My transformation hadn't been stopped but merely neutralized. That was the effect of neutralizing jazz.

I had heard of acid-to-water jazz; a jazz that turned acid to water when your enemies poured it on you. I didn't feel like a mannequin, though, I didn't feel like myself either. I felt *different* but thought nothing of it. I went home, had my bath, and went for my 11 o'clock class. I was on my way back home, in front of one of those shops along the road, when I saw a woman with a child tied on her back, crossing the road. She was casually, unconcernedly crossing the one-way road. An okada was speeding down from the other side. She wasn't looking that way because it wasn't supposed to be there. I wondered for a split second what possessed her to let her guard down like that. This is Nigeria. What worked the way it was supposed to? Why would you expect anyone to obey road and traffic rules? Weird. She was totally oblivious and going to be hit by the car. Everything was slow, or rather, still—like in a mannequin challenge.

I didn't always think myself a hero, but in that moment, I felt it. I launched myself at her, trying to push her out of the path of the speeding bike. I was in the air, then everything unfroze. My hand shoved her away. But I was now fully in the path of the bike. I was completely airborne. In front of my face was a women's fashion store. What a thing to see before you die. Shouldn't my life be flashing before my eyes? Well, it had been an unmemorable life thus far. That would have been a boring last thing to see, scenes of my uneventful life. Instead, I saw women's clothes, which wasn't any more exciting. Women's clothes worn by a mannequin. I looked at the face, the eyes. It seemed to suck me in. Then the bike hit me. The force was crushing. I felt myself hit the concrete. Snapping, its back tire ran my skull over. Then darkness.

I woke up in a store, wearing women's clothes. The salesgirl burst out screaming. I later walked out to find a crushed mannequin wearing my clothes on the road. The bikeman had sped off without stopping. Typical, I thought, standing there in a woman's pants and bra.

They later called it a prank, but I knew better.

I was standing at the top of the senate building of the University of Lagos with a naked female mannequin. I was over ten floors high. I wore the mannequin's clothes and tied the thing to a pole there. I wasn't sure how this worked yet (or if it worked at all), but that was why I was here—to run some tests. I had developed powers late, but they had come. Better late than never as they said. Though I say better late than late. The power had come not in the ways I expected it. It hadn't been a radioactive spider biting me or an explosion in a lab from an experiment. I was a law student. Anyway, what was I doing in a lab? I would just get myself burnt for nothing. It had happened, a little unorthodoxly, but it was what I wanted. No more uneventful life. With my new mannequin powers, the possibilities were limitless. I could do some espionage, infiltrate, and obtain valuable information, even if I didn't think much of my fighting abilities. Something like Antman. It wasn't what I would have chosen, but it was something. So, the mannequin was tied, wind wouldn't blow it/me off. I figured I could shift my consciousness into the mannequin and it into my body and the transference would end once it was destroyed.

I watched recent superhero movies and read enough fantasy novels to know how this worked. A leap of faith, like in *Into the Spiderverse*. Here was I, to take a literal leap of faith. That moment you were in danger was when your power activated. It had activated already. But I needed to be sure again. I stood at the edge and turned around. I was naked. I looked at the mannequin. I had chosen a female one because the first one had been female, and I felt more connected to the female mannequin. I hope that didn't sound creepy. I was about to connect with my inner woman. That definitely sounded creepy. Especially staring at a female mannequin wearing my clothes and being as naked as I was.

Leap of faith, right? I looked at it one last time then dove over the edge.

The rush, it was exhilarating. I should change now. Then I realized something was wrong. This hadn't happened the last time. My life was flashing before my eyes.

OGHENECHOVWE DONALD EKPEKI (ESSAY)

by Oghenechovwe Donald Ekpeki

It's been a harrowing year for all, especially for Black people and Africans who have borne the brunt of the pandemic, from being the demographics with the highest casualties in Western countries like the United States, to lacking vaccines altogether on the African continent due to global vaccine policies and hoarding. Yet it has also been a year of triumphs and successes. A good number of literary magazines—*Lolwe*, *Isele*, *Iskanchi*, *Open Country*, and others—sprung up, publishing both established and amazing new voices on the continent.

Speculative fiction anthologies like *Africanfuturism* and *Dominion* were nominated for the Locus awards, a first time for African editors. The *Dominion* anthology was, along with its stories, nominated for the BSFA, BFA, Nebula, Sturgeon, Locus, This Is Horror, and Subjective Chaos Kind of Awards—record firsts for African writers and editors on the continent. These are in addition to making several Year's Best anthologies and recommended reading lists.

The triumphs of people of African descent have cut across the fields of sports, literature, and entertainment, with Jamaicans taking gold in track and field events in the Olympics, and the Nigerian basketball team beating the US team in the preliminaries.

All these outpourings of African excellence have sparked a lot of joy. But along with African excellence comes mockery, jeering, negativity, and a staunch refusal to recognize the value of the African name and any excellence attached to it. Africa has been known by a lot of names that detract from the excellence or value of its people: the Third World, the Dark Continent, and recently by the previous US president Donald Trump, "shithole." It continues to be known by anything but the names that it and its people define themselves by.

When the Nigerian basketball team achieved an unprecedented feat to become the first African team to beat the United Sstates in a pre-Olympics opener game, the US sports commentator, Stephen Smith, made a mockery of the victory and refused to believe that people bearing African names like Nnamdi could beat an American team.

One is forced to reconsider the clichéd question: what is in a name? Does the value of a name lie in its familiarity, or the simplicity of its pronunciation? So that, alas, Nnamdi and other African names fail to elicit value from the Westerners who mock them for this reason. Does a name, for its being unfamiliar or difficult to pronounce, remove from the skills and abilities of the bearer? And if the mockers believe that names represent the value of a person, do they then think that denying a person their name, or misspelling, mispronouncing, or mangling their names, devalues them even further? Is the purpose of this deliberate distortion of identity to devalue the bearer of the name?

Names possess value and power to their bearers. Like misgendering a person, failing to honor what someone chooses to be called disrespects that person's definition of their own self. This is just as important in sports, entertainment, and the arts, where many practitioners use different chosen names or variations of their birth or legal names.

In the publishing industry, there was a debacle at the 2020 Hugo Awards with the mispronunciation of *Fiyah Literary Magazine* and other names. During awards and conventions this year, in 2021, African names have been misused and disregarded in much the same manner. It is a menace that continues because people fail to recognize the value, the importance, and the roles that names play in defining a person and respecting those definitions.

The constant refusal, malicious or not, to pay attention to and respect the African name, comes from the same place as the current wave of anti-Africanism that has been blowing lately, both sharing roots with colonialism and even slavery. It is a failure to recognize Africans and bearers of African names as people capable and deserving of humanity, individuality, and excellence.

So, whether to an African athlete, entertainer, creative artist, or to any African at all, endeavor to call them by their correct names. Learn the name, say it, write it, use it well—in a manner that represents the personhood, acknowledges the identity, the power, and excellence it represents.

Oghenechovwe Donald Ekpeki. Say my name.

THE CITY OF THE DEAD

by Joshua Uchenna Omenga

The mechanic's error and my indiscretion decided my fate.

I had not checked my tires as usual because I was in a hurry. A few miles outside town, as the car was climbing the steeps of Konden Mountain, the front right tire gave a thunderous sound as it burst. Before I could make any effort to keep the car on track, it somersaulted and plunged into the gaping valley by the roadside.

. . .❖. . .

It was dark when I came to myself. I wandered in the darkness for a while before I saw a beam of light ahead. I walked toward it, afraid that it would vanish if I looked away.

Suddenly, the light flickered and went off. Fear came upon me. I turned to retrace my steps, but I could not tell whether I was moving forward or backward. I heard incoherent voices coming in my direction. I was torn between running away from the voices and running toward them. Maybe they too were lost, and their company would be a consolation. I was still pondering over this when I felt several sets of fingers close on me. I was lifted from the ground.

"Who are you?" I asked, terrified.

My two captors made no answer. They bore me forward as if I was a piece of wood. The darkness started to dissipate, so that I could make out the things around me. My captors were giants and moved like automatons.

We came to an immense gate which seemed hewn from a single rock. It had no visible entrance point anywhere. One of my captors rested his palm on it. For a while, nothing happened. Then a rectangular line formed on the gate and the marked area slid open.

Inside the gate, everywhere was resplendent with the sort of brightness that had no focal point. The sky overhead was like an interminable piece of glass work that glowed at all points. Crumbling columns stood majestic and daunting. Dilapidated mansions jutted in every direction. Signs of a civilization, hurriedly abandoned, pervaded everywhere: hotel signposts, debris of canteens, half-obliterated school names. Everywhere I looked, an interminable stretch of ruin confronted me. But there was not a sign of life anywhere, though I had a feeling of being watched by eyes I could not see.

My captors stopped and bound my hands and feet with thin, white strands. I became dizzy, and all was dark again.

...❖...

I awoke in a dungeon where all was white. I tried to break the strands, but they dug deeper into the folds of my skin and stung me with excruciating pain. I leaned on the wall and closed my eyes. I only needed to wake up from this nightmare. But my effort to wake up was in vain. I was trapped in my nightmare.

The tunnel door opened, and a figure in a white robe sailed in. He was tall and lean, and his snow-white beard grazed his chest. His wrinkled face was expressionless. He looked at me as if I was an object that needed close scrutiny. Then he bent and touched my binding strands and they melted away.

"You have come a long way, Duriki." His voice was light and lyrical.

I regarded him with distrust. Had we met before? I could not remember anything about him. How did he know my name? "Who are you?"

"Call me Ven Sanuwa, because our destinies are intertwined."

"I share no destiny with anybody!"

"Everyone here shares destinies, Duriki."

"Where is this place?"

"This is the City of the Dead."

"The City of the Dead?"

"Yes, Duriki. That is what it has become."

"Are you dead?"

"For a while."

"Am I dead?"

"That depends on you."

He conjured up a seat and sat facing me. He did not seem to notice that I was trembling. His face was calm.

"Listen to me and I will tell you about this city."

I nodded. He caressed his beard before he resumed.

"This city was once a thriving civilization. It was called Havwen, which means the Land of Peace and Prosperity. It was filled with happy and contented people. Everything was going well with them. They had machines for doing any kind of job. They had adept physicians who cured all kinds of diseases. Only King Jallo was unhappy.

"He was unhappy because despite all the advancement in his kingdom, his people still grew old and died. He wanted a kingdom where none of his subjects would grow old and die. He therefore summoned his scientists and physicians and asked them to make immortality for his people. After years of research, they told him it was not possible.

"The king did not give up hope. He would not be stopped by the limits of science. He summoned the magicians and priests and tasked them to provide immortality to his people. But even they too had no better answer than the scientists and physicians.

"'Is there nothing in the holy writs that can give immortality to my people?' the king asked in dejection.

"'No,' said the Chief Priest. 'The gods have decreed death for all that lives.'

"'Yet the gods do not die.'

"'The gods are wiser in this affair. Man is fated to receive only what the gods have given.'

"'Is there no price at which I can buy immortality from the gods?'

"'The price of immortality,' said the Chief Magician, 'is higher than the joy of immortality.'

"'What price must I pay for immortality?'

"'Immortality can only be purchased with blood. The length of life in the blood is the length of life to be received in return. What blood will pay for the lives of your citizens to keep them alive for eternity? To be truly immortal, only the dead can show the way.'"

Ven Sanuwa went on. "The king was troubled by his failure, but the words of the Chief Magician kept ringing in his ear: *To be truly immortal, only the dead can show the way.*

"Age was already telling on the king. He desperately needed immortality. One day, he summoned the Chief Magician to his secret chamber.

"'I am old,' he told the Magician. 'Can you make me young again?'

"'Yes, my king. But only with the blood of the young.'

"'Take the blood of my youngest son and make me young again.'

"The Magician rejuvenated the king at the price of his son's life," Ven Sanuwa continued. "The king was troubled by the sacrifice of his son, but he told himself that it was better for the one to die in order to save the many. He had to find immortality for his people. And time was against him.

"He became immersed in the mystic arts. He read all available books in necromancy. He secretly constructed a laboratory underground where he carried out his experiments in the mystic arts. He allowed no one into his laboratory. He took counsel of no one. When he was convinced that he had learnt enough for his purpose, he announced that he was going on a journey of which he did not know his day of return. He set his son, Jaeffa, to rule in his stead. The people protested because they loved him, but King Jallo told them to transfer their love and allegiance to his son.

"Jaeffa became firmly established on the throne of his father. But he was unlike his father. In two years, he brought to a halt all the progresses that his father had made in Havwen. He maintained no diplomacy with other kingdoms. He threw wild parties and bragged about the achievements of his father. He displeased all those whom his father held in high esteem.

"Jaeffa's folly estranged all those who had helped build Havwen. The enemies of Havwen welcomed them and paid them handsomely for their services. In turn, they helped to plot the ruin of Havwen. Their hatred for Jaeffa had overshadowed their love for Jallo.

"The enemies now knew the strengths and weaknesses of Havwen. In his vanity, Jaeffa still believed Havwen to be unassailable. He made no efforts to maintain the army. Jaeffa's new advisers were not better in their reasoning than their master. The few wise ones, who could have helped in averting or mitigating the impending ruin, were working secretly against Jaeffa. Nothing stood between Havwen and her enemies."

He paused. There was a look of misery in his eyes. Then he continued.

"The day of reckoning for Havwen was like the judgment of some vengeful gods. All the surrounding nations coalesced against her. They brought all their forces and their wisdom to bear against her. They plotted her ruin with ingenuity. While the people of Havwen went about their activities, the enemies secured their position round the city.

"They rained fire on Havwen from land and from air. She offered no resistance. The enemies kept firing long after Havwen was in ruins. Not a house was left standing. Not a tree was left standing. Not a man was left alive. The destruction was total.

"But the enemies were not done with the people of Havwen. While the soldiers and the scientists wrought destruction on Havwen, the enemies' sorcerers and magicians wove a magic trap around the precincts of Havwen. The dead of Havwen could not pass to the land of the dead. The dead were made to suffer in the land of the living."

...❖...

I asked, "Did Jallo not return to his people again?"

Ven Sanuwa shook his head. "Jallo had traveled to the land of the dead in search of immortality. When he got there, he was sorely disappointed. Not one of the dead had the answer he sought. They gave no thought to the lot of the living. All he had learnt in his necromancy books were useless. His sacrifices had been in vain. There was no hope for his people.

"While Jallo was lamenting his failure, he saw the spirit of an eminent man from Havwen. It was painful to meet a kindred spirit in the land of the dead, yet Jallo was cheered at the prospect of news from Havwen.

"'What brings you here, my noble countryman, when you have not grown old?'

"The spirit bowed. 'My king, I had not thought to see you in this land of unreturning. We have waited for your return year after year.'

"'But I have only been away for three days!'

"'No, my king. You have been away for seven years in the reckoning of humans. Much has happened in your absence. Evil has befallen Havwen. I, who you see in this land of the dead, am the lucky one.'

"Jallo was afraid of what he would hear, but he was eager to know the fate of his land. 'Please, tell me what has happened to my Havwen.'

"The spirit related to Jallo all that had happened to Havwen. Jallo's sorrow was great. He wept for his lost city. He wept for his lost people. He blamed himself for all the evils that had befallen Havwen. If he had not left Havwen in search of immortality, none of this could have happened. He wished he had listened to his counselors. He wished he had not heeded the equivocal words of the magicians.

"When his sorrow ebbed, he made a vow to liberate the souls of his people. He returned to Havwen but there was no one alive to carry out the ritual to his spirit to his flesh. He took this shape you are seeing and went in search of a soul yet to descend to the land of the dead, for only such a soul could liberate him."

I drew back, terrified. "Are you then King Jallo?"

"My spirit is King Jallo, but in this form, I am Ven Sanuwa. I sent the creatures that brought you here."

"I don't understand. What have I to do with you or with Havwen?"

"Maybe you have nothing to do with me or with Havwen. But remember that you too are a form like me. Your real body is in the morgue at the moment."

I felt myself all over. There was no significant change in me. I asked, "Am I dead?"

"I have told you that the answer depends on you. Right now, you are not living. You have been in an accident and have been pronounced dead. To the living, you are dead. But to the dead, you are living, because your soul has not passed to the land of the dead. It is up to you to decide whether you will join the living or the dead. I can only tell you that it is a wiser choice to spend as much time as you can among the living."

He fixed his eyes on me. He was waiting on me for an answer. I knew what I wanted, but that was not the question. I needed to know what he wanted.

I asked, "What will I give in return if I want to be back among the living?"

"I require very little from you. Just follow me into my laboratory and do as I ask you."

"What do you want from me?" I insisted.

He was checked by my tone. "All I want from you is to read some words and plunge a dagger into my heart."

"I am not a killer."

"You will not be killing me. You will be giving me life."

"All right. Supposing I do as you bid, how will I return to the land of the living?"

"Don't worry about that. All you have to do is write your name on the parchment I will provide for you, and I will send your spirit back to your body."

I nodded and he led me out of the dungeon. So much was going on in my mind. I wanted to buy some time to think things through. He could simply be tricking me to do his bidding. How was I even to know that I was dead to start with? Even though I remembered being in a vehicle that plunged into the gulf, I had not felt any sensation of dying. Or could it be because, as he said, I had not passed to the land of the dead? But what motive had he to deceive me? I was already powerless before him. He could simply order me to do whatever he wanted.

On the other hand, if he was right—and his story seemed probable enough—then he would be doing me immeasurable good. I did not care how much he would get out of the bargain. In truth, despite the wretchedness of my life on earth, I had no intention of quitting it so soon for an eternity I knew nothing about.

Ven Sanuwa's laboratory was hidden underground. No one would suspect its existence unless the person was told about it. He swept away the earth to reveal a hexagonal enclosure. He pressed his right hand on the enclosure and muttered some words into it. It slid open to reveal the most astonishing vault I have ever seen.

While he gathered the instruments for performing the ritual, I fed my eyes with the wonder of his laboratory. It was very large, but there was hardly a space to stand on. Everywhere was occupied by one intricate instrument or another. One section of the laboratory was a library filled with antique books. I had no interest whatsoever in books of any kind, but the arrangement of the library section attracted me. I looked at a few titles. I could not read any of them. The scripts were unfamiliar to me.

He beckoned me, and I approached with more reverence, now that I had taken a glimpse into his world. He pointed at a parchment on the table. Beside it lay a dagger.

"Read the writing seven times. After your seventh reading, take the dagger and stab me in the chest." So saying, he lay face up on the table.

I looked at the writing and could not make out a word, though I was familiar with the script. "I don't understand this language," I said.

"You don't need to. It is the language of the spirits. All you need to do is read what you see. Pronounce each word as spelled. Your intonation does not matter."

"Can you not read it to me at least once?"

"No, Duriki. Once I pronounce those words, I am damned forever. Only you who have not passed to the land of the dead can pronounce them."

I was scared by the prospect of being damned for reading some strange words. I feared that if it would damn him, it would most likely damn me as well. I was still debating with myself whether to obey him, or to pull out of the bargain, when I noticed the letters beginning to move as if they would leap off the parchment. The shapes of the scripts remained essentially the same, but they seemed to convey some meanings with their movements.

"Now!"

I started reading. *Vani conde ferimi senga ribon idonisihevka to si Jallo basiki.* I read it the required number of times. After the seventh reading, I picked up the dagger and reached to strike Ven Sanuwa in the chest, but something within checked me, and I hesitated.

He opened his eyes, which had been closed during my reading, and I saw that they had become blood red. He gestured at me to stab him. My will to stall the process melted. With my eyes closed, I plunged the dagger into his chest.

The instant the dagger landed in his chest, a gale of wind shook the room. The force threw me onto the ground. It lasted only for a few seconds. When I stood up, the white figure that had been Ven Sanuwa was no longer there. Only the garment lay on the table. Then I heard footsteps coming from a corner of the laboratory. It was a young man in regal attire.

I knew immediately that he was King Jallo, because I had seen his portrait in the laboratory, though the image in the portrait was older. But then, rejuvenating himself before his sojourn to the land of the dead would account for his youthfulness.

"Where are you, Duriki?" he asked.

I was perplexed by his question because I was standing right before him.

"Are you still here, Duriki?"

"Yes, I am standing in front of you."

My heart beat in wonderment and anger. What was this all about? Why was he pretending not to see me?

He laid a parchment on the table. "Write your full name on this parchment."

I wrote my full name as he instructed. When I finished, he asked, "Is that all?"

"Yes."

"You should know that I cannot see you, though I can feel your presence, and hear your voice. I am flesh and you are spirit. Please tell me exactly where you are standing?"

I described my position to him, and he said, "Come and lie down on this table, with your feet toward me."

I lay on the table as he instructed. He placed the dagger on the parchment where I had written my name. It occurred to me that he was going to use the dagger on me. I was not prepared to have a dagger stuck in my chest even though I had just struck another with it.

"What do you mean to do to me?"

He sighed as if I had asked a childish question. "I am going to stab you with the dagger. Only a stab from the living can bring back the spirit which has not passed into the land of the dead, just as only a stab from the spirit which has not passed into the land of the dead can bring back the spirit which has passed into the land of the dead. That is why only you could return my spirit to my body. And that is why only I, who am living, can return your spirit to your body."

I understood, but still I hesitated. "Supposing you are right, won't I be trapped here with you?"

"No, not so, Duriki. Your spirit will find your body wherever it is, just as my spirit found me here, because I had left my body here."

I conceded. If I was already dead, what would a stab do to me? Or, if in my resurrection I would be trapped in the ruins of Havwen with King Jallo, what better prospect awaited me if I refused his service? I had no idea how to return to my country, even if I was still alive. In the end, I surrendered to be killed in order to live.

He said incantations similar to the ones he had made me read, inserting my name in the appropriate place. Then he took the dagger and stabbed me in the chest. I experienced not pain, but a momentary blankness.

...❖...

I woke up in a room smelling of rottenness. I felt chokey under the white sheet which covered me. I uncovered myself, and the rotten smell filled my nose. I was naked. I sprang from the bed and wrapped myself with the sheet.

The room was fairly lighted. I did not have the presence of mind to look at my environment with any degree of concentration, but I could see through the corners of my eyes an assemblage of people asleep. A piece of paper was pasted beside each bed with name and some descriptions.

As I opened the door and went outside, I was momentarily blinded by the intensity of the sun. When my vision had become accommodated to my environment, I noticed that people were running away from me. Those who did not run away stood at a distance and watched me as if I was an alien. I looked at myself and found nothing odd except the white sheet with which I covered myself.

Then my eyes rested on the signpost at the entrance of the facility: The Federal Morgue—*Caring Beyond Life*. It took me several seconds to process the information. I had been dead and in the morgue!

It had not been a dream after all. Or was it? I only know that I am alive.

I don't know what became of King Jallo after I left him. I don't know what became of the people of Havwen, whether their souls were liberated from the City of the Dead or not. I don't even know where the City of the Dead is located. All I have left of the experience is the story of it.

I have set the story in writing as I recall it. My memory of it is unusually clear. I am naturally not good with remembering things. That is why I hate books. That is why I hate those who write books. That is why I hate myself for writing this.

THE PHIAL OF OLODUMARE

by Joshua Uchenna Omenga

"Look at that, sir!" Wang Wu pointed at a shining object on the monitor of the remote excavator.

"What's that?" Jun Li asked.

"We have to find out, sir."

Slowly, Wang Wu directed the excavator's arms until they closed on the object. It was attached to a statue that had not been visible until Wang Wu increased the brightness of the underwater light. He adjusted the arms of the excavator until it was secure on the statue.

He pulled the object gently out of the water and onto the deck of the excavation platform. It was the statue of a man, on its neck, the shining object. It looked like a miniature flask carved from a bluish gem. It was secured to the statue by a chain too thin to be visible underwater.

"It's a kind of traditional relic," Wang Wu said.

"Perhaps," Jun Li said, not looking convinced.

"Maybe we should invite a native to tell us what it is?"

"Why?" Jun Li asked, turning with surprised eyes to Wang Wu. "What's our business with what it is?"

"I thought you'd be interested in knowing, sir."

"I'm interested—in this!" Jun Li pointed at the flask.

"Sir, wouldn't it be better to find out what it is first? It might be something of cultural importance that we should return to the government without tampering with it."

"What nonsense are you talking about? Did the government contract us for excavation of relics? Our contract is to erect a docking platform, and that's the only duty we owe our client."

"I'm just thinking, sir, in case it is a relic of importance—"

"Stop thinking, Wang! Whatever we encounter on the job site is no business of our client. Last week, when sharks attacked us, was it the government that warded them off? These are the perils and rewards for our job."

Jun Li held the flask and tried to draw it from the statue's neck, but it wriggled and refused to come out. He stepped back. "Remove it for me."

Wang Wu tried to sever the chain from the statue. But the tiny chain tightened on the neck of the statue as Wang Wu increased his tugging. He went to the tool compartment and brought tin snips. He slipped the chain on the cutting edge and gripped the hands firmly until his muscles bulged. The chain did not show any sign of cracking.

"Use the hydraulic cutter," Jun Li said.

Wang Wu disappeared into the engine room and returned with the hydraulic cutter. Jun Li held the chain while Wang Wu sawed at it. It took a good while before they heard the first crack of a link in the chain, and then another, and the chain broke asunder. The flask fell on the platform. As Wang Wu bent to pick it up, Jun Li restrained him, pointing at the still rotating cutter, which had started cutting into the sculpture. Wang Wu turned it off and returned it to the engine room.

Jun Li lifted the flask, held it up toward the sun, and checked it for cracks. There were none. In his hand, the flask became more radiant, as if an invisible source was polishing it right before his eyes. Jun Li rolled it in his palms and felt a strange rhythmic thrill travel through his nerves into his spine. He slipped the flask into his trouser pocket as Wang Wu returned from the engine room.

"I have an appointment to catch," Jun Li said, glancing at his watch and ignoring the questioning look in Wang Wu's eyes. "I may not return here again today. Monitor the workers. Make sure the foundation reaches eight feet today. Or at least keep them busy until five."

"Yes, sir."

Wang Wu watched as Jun Li descended the excavation platform, boarded his electric boat, and drove away. A slight spray of water from the boat touched Wang Wu's face, but he did not wipe it. He felt that Jun Li had just cheated in this transaction, and it seemed to him that it was not only the government of Lagos that Jun Li had cheated, but also him. Was he not entitled to the dividend of their discovery? He was gripped by a premonition that he would never see the flask again.

His eyes fell on the statue. There was a smear of blood at its neck where he had cut the chain. He examined himself, looking for where he might have cut himself. There was no cut on his body. He drew closer to the statue and looked at its neck, thinking it might be paint. It was not paint, but blood, and fresh for that matter. He stood up and reflected. Perhaps Jun Li had cut himself and his blood had smeared on the statue? It had to be, else why was he in a hurry to leave before the close of the workday; the Jun Li who always insisted on monitoring every drilling himself? But why had Jun Li not simply told him he was injured?

"Oh well," Wang Wu said aloud as he contemplated the statue. There was no point keeping it when its treasure had been harvested. If it should be found by one of the government's inspectors, and it turned out to be something significant, they might start probing, and who knew what they might discover? He did not wish to be an accessory to falsehood or to give his boss away. He pushed the statue into the sea and returned to the control room.

A moment later, Wang Wu heard heavy pounding at the side of the excavator and peered out to see what it could be. He saw nothing. As he was about to turn away, the excavator shuddered. Wang Wu froze the engine controls and rushed out to see what was happening. As he opened the door of the control room, he confronted the statue he had pushed into the water. It glared at him, bleeding freely from its neck and stomach. Wang Wu was too horrified to speak.

The statue took a few steps toward him. Wang Wu's legs wobbled. He could not lift them or look away from the terrifying statue. The statue raised its enormous hand in the motion of an automaton and closed it on Wang Wu's neck. He gave a choked cry as he was lifted up. His eyes bulged from their sockets, and consciousness left him.

...❖...

The plane left the airport at 11:49 a.m., four minutes behind its scheduled departure.

Jun Li had had no difficulty at the clearance desk. He took his assigned seat, 36B, between a Nigerian man in 36A and a Chinese man in 36C. He disliked economy class, but if he had to fly it, he preferred sitting in a window or aisle seat—anywhere but between other passengers. Nestled at a window seat, he could make himself oblivious to other passengers until he reached his destination.

This was an unplanned trip, and he had a feeling that he'd left some things undone. He unzipped his portable travel bag and thrust his hand into the second compartment. He felt the flask but, unsatisfied, tilted his bag and brought it out for confirmation. One never knew with these airlines and these people: important things got mixed up or swapped. Although he had not parted with the bag for a moment, something might have happened along the way. Having confirmed that the gem was in his bag, he drew it securely to himself, laid his head on the headrest, and closed his eyes.

He had been obsessed with the flask since he retrieved it yesterday. On reaching his apartment, he had brought it out and examined it. It seems to have different shades, the fully transparent outer shell, made less obvious by the inner contents, which appeared to glow. But it was too heavy to imagine the contents to be independent of the body. It weighed more than common gems, such as pearls or diamonds—he was at least sure it was none of those. He searched the internet for stones of similar colors and compared their characteristics. He could not find a close match, but he found the contact for an expert jeweler in Lagos and rang him up for home service.

On the jeweler's arrival, Jun Li took him to his apartment, double-checked the lock after him, and kept him in the parlor while he brought the flask for his examination. Jun Li caught a momentary look of awe on the jeweler's face when he first beheld the flask. It was not a look of understanding but of wonderment, and coming from one used to jewels, it was an affirmation of the worth of the flask. For more than twenty minutes, the jeweler examined the flask with his tools. Then he stood up and shook his head.

"Mr. Li," the jeweler said, holding out the flask to Jun Li. "This is a special gem. I've never seen its like before. It requires a more sophisticated examination for identification. I could find out if I took it to my workshop and examined it under better condition."

"Thank you," Jun Li said, collecting the flask. He paid the jeweler, with a tip added, and shooed him out with a smile of impatience.

At the door, the jeweler asked in an afterthought, "If I may ask sir, where did you come by this gem?"

Jun Li tried not to betray the emotion aroused in him by this question. He swallowed involuntarily, then looking the jeweler in the eye, said, "You may not ask."

The jeweler bowed and left.

Jun Li was agitated. He realized his mistake too late. He should have left the examination until his return to Beijing. But he was glad to have at least discovered that the flask might be even more valuable than he had thought. He no longer thought of the price it would fetch him. He would not let the thought of money sway him into short-changing himself as he had done with his last discovery. Only after he had confirmed the value of the flask would he think of the money it would fetch him.

Jun Li was roused from his thoughts by the departure announcement on the overhead speaker. Passenger instructions followed, and the crew went around ensuring compliance with safety guidelines. Jun Li felt rather than saw the things happening around him. His mind was impatient, his eyes closed, his heart uneasy. He was glad when the plane finally took off, and he felt the pressure of the upward thrust of the plane's twin engines against the pull of gravity, which pressed him to his seat.

The plane was beginning to level off when it experienced a momentary lurch. The jolt brought Jun Li back to the moment, and he opened his eyes. The space outside had become dark, as if someone had covered the sun with thick black cellophane. The cabin lights of the airplane were turned on. An announcement came over the speaker for any passengers who had not fastened their seat belts to do so. The darkness thickened. The plane's landing lights were turned on; Jun Li could see them penetrating through the darkness of the space outside.

Another turbulence occurred, prolonged and more intense than the first. The pilot assured the passengers that the turbulence was normal while flying over the ocean, especially at their low altitude. In a few minutes, the plane would be at a higher altitude and above turbulence. Nevertheless, any passenger who had not complied with all the safety precautions should do so. The voice trailed off, like an advertisement interrupting a good show. The voice said nothing about the darkness that had overtaken the noon sky, but Jun Li felt no apprehension. Somehow, it seemed to him as if he was merely a spectator.

Then there came a gust of wind that momentarily altered the plane's direction. A few red lights blinked overhead. The engines became perceptibly louder as the plane fought to stay on course. The wind came again. It was as if immense palms were slapping at the sides of the plane, like a mob closing in on a defenseless victim. Some overhead luggage fell to the floor and was left unattended. Jun Li's heart started in panic. He drew out his bag, removed the flask, and put it into his jacket pocket.

Suddenly, a whirlpool of black mist wrapped around the plane. From the mist came a blaze of light that momentarily blinded the occupants of the plane, throwing them into commotion. The light began to dim and then turned to a swirl of colors from which a shape began to form. The occupants of the plane burst into screams as the shape materialized into a woman. She was covered in a lambent, fish-scale dress of varying colors. In place of her legs was a fish tail.

At her materialization, the wind abated. The darkness peeled off like a blanket, and the daylight returned. She stood on the nose of the plane, her imperial face directed upward. She stretched out her hands and twisted her fingers, then brought her palms together and folded them into a ball. A wave of force swept over the plane, and it was dragged, like opposing fields of a magnet, to a gradual stillness. The engines groaned, and the plane vibrated, but remained stationary.

After a moment, the woman floated to the windshield and paused momentarily before sailing to the top of the plane. For a while, nothing could be heard but the vibration of the plane as the engines groaned louder, and the thrust propellers adjusted, to no avail, in their efforts to move the plane on its course. This was more ominous to the pilots than if the plane had been buffeted by wind. They had never encountered a force that could hold a plane motionless in midair. The cabin alarm went off; the red lights were blinking steadily overhead. This was the first acknowledgment of trouble that the passengers received, followed by an announcement over the speaker: The plane was under an attack from a strange spatial force, and everyone should put on their oxygen masks and prepare for a water landing. Quick instructions were given, and the crew started assisting passengers.

Suddenly there was a loud crash at the roof, and it caved in. The outside air rushed in, overwhelming the comforting pressure within, leaving the passengers gasping for air. Through the opening, the fishtailed woman floated into the middle of the plane. The passengers' cries of horror intensified. But to none of them did the woman pay any attention. She glided purposefully across the aisle until she reached Jun Li's seat, stopped, and faced him. The Nigerian man beside Jun Li fainted and fell from his seat.

Jun Li felt her eyes boring into him, and his heart stilled. He saw her hand coming toward him but could not move away. It seemed as though her eyes had bound him fast against any rebellion. She began to speak in a strange language. Her voice was like the howl of wind and echoed in the plane. When Jun Li did not move or react to her beckoning, she grasped him by the throat and lifted him up. Although he could not feel the pressure of her hand, its effect choked him. He struggled to unclasp her hand, but his hands simply passed over hers, touching nothing. His eyes bulged in dismay as he kicked at the incorporeal hand holding him.

She sniffed at him, and her exhalation was like perfume. Drawing him closer to herself, she rummaged through his clothes with her other hand until she came upon his coat pocket and stopped. With a slice of her nail, she tore open his jacket, and the flask fell on the floor. Still holding him, she bent and picked up the flask. The expression on her face changed from anger into triumph.

She cupped the flask, muttering some words to it, and it burst in blue light. With raucous laughter, she lifted through the opening in the roof of the plane, clutching Jun Li tightly by his throat as they left the plane's protection into the uncertain ether.

As her laughter ebbed, the plane thrust forward, and wind surged in through the open roof, buffeting the passengers. The plane veered and began to spiral toward the calmness of the ocean below.

...❖...

The sensation of choking left Jun Li, and he was overtaken by dizziness as he plunged downward. The fall seemed endless. He closed his eyes and felt the battering of the air on his body. Then he was suddenly plunged into the water, pulled deeper until he was aware of nothing else but chilled pressure amidst the palpable darkness.

His eyes opened to a sky of floating colors and a ground paved with pearls. The land was flat as far as the eye could see. There were no trees or shrubs anywhere. The weather was cool and the illumination sparse, as if the day was just breaking after the reign of a dewy night. Jun Li was tortured by the elegant blandness of all that confronted him.

He tried to wipe the vision from his eyes but could not move his hand. He became aware that his hands were tied to his front and that he was led by a chain. His eyes fell on his captor, the strange woman who had abducted him from the plane. She was remarkably different now. Her tail had transformed to legs, and her countenance was no longer as fearsome. As he looked upon her, he realized how beautiful she was, so different from the perilous figure that had appeared to him in the plane. Her chocolate skin was smooth, and her face had neither wrinkle nor blemish. Her eyes were cool like a still stream; they were no longer the hard and shiny jewels they had been when he first beheld them. Her sparkling dress was fashioned from fish scales. As she pulled him along, he noticed she was barefooted, and her feet made no sound as she floated graciously on the ground.

They came upon a mansion that seemed to have sprouted from the ground at their approach. It was solid and carved from gems of different colors. It towered, columns upon columns, until it tapered off in a tiny spike that disappeared into the misty sky. As they approached the mansion, different parts of it lit up. Its enormous door glided open at the stretch of her hand, and she led him inside.

"Did you think I would never find you, Eniasan?" she asked, tightening her grip on the chain.

Jun Li understood her, though she had spoken in the same strange language as before. He looked at her in puzzlement. Eniasan?

"Where have you been hiding, Eniasan?" She tugged at the chain to force him to attention.

"I'm not Eniasan!" he exclaimed, surprised at his own voice. He had replied in the strange language as fluently as he would speak Chinese.

"For how long will you continue to be false, Eniasan?"

He started to protest but noticed the transformation in his body for the first time. His skin had become dark, his muscles bigger, and his clothes had transformed to something scaly and shiny like hers. His mind began to conjure up memories. The mansion no longer looked strange to him, and as he contemplated her face, he discerned a familiarity of long acquaintance.

She led him to a column in the mansion and tied him with the chain. She looked hard upon him, and her eyes sparked with rage.

"Why did you steal my phial, Eniasan?" she asked with profound indignation, holding up the flask that she had retrieved from him. "Did you think you would escape me forever?"

Jun Li was not puzzled by the accusation so much as by the surge of memory that had come upon him. The events of four thousand and forty years ago played before his eyes like reality rather than memory. He saw himself as an energetic young man when Obatala had sent him, under the guidance of Eshu, to retrieve the phial of Olodumare from Olokun, who had stolen it from Obatala.

...❖...

It had happened ages ago, before Ifa devised the computation of time when, Olodumare, the Supreme God, purposed to create a race made of flesh and blood. He commissioned his chief designer and craftsgod, Obatala, for the design and creation of the race. For days and nights, Obatala worked at his studio until, at last, he created satisfactory specimens of the race and brought them before Olodumare. Olodumare summoned the gods and presented the specimens before them. The gods admired the work of Obatala, and Olodumare blessed them and called them the race of men. There were six males and six females. Olodumare gave an order to the porter of the gods to find a place in the abode of the gods for the race of men to dwell.

But this proved unsuitable for the race of men, who were dependent on nourishment and atmosphere not found in the abode of the gods. They grew thin, and their countenance became wan. The report was brought to Olodumare that the race of men would perish if they long remained in the abode of the gods. Olodumare therefore ordered for a special abode to be fashioned for the race of men. He sought counsel from all the gods, and at last, it was agreed that the abode of men should be fashioned from the ocean, which had all the nourishment and atmosphere necessary for the survival of men.

Olodumare again commissioned Obatala to fashion the earth for the race of men he had created, giving him a phial containing the power of the ocean.

Obatala set about his mission. Arriving at the ocean, he used the power in the phial to part a considerable portion of the ocean, and dry land emerged. On the dry land, Obatala fashioned the earth, creating and filling it with trees and grasses and animals and birds. The race of men was brought down from the abode of the gods and settled on the ready portion of the earth while Obatala continued in his work of creation, parting more portions of the ocean and expanding the earth in anticipation of the expansion of the race of men.

The ocean was under the domain of Olokun. She was of irascible temperament and could not abide with other gods. She alone of all the gods and goddesses had elected to live outside the abode of the gods after her quarrels with Olodumare. She chose the ocean as her home. Cut off from the affairs of the gods, she was unaware of their plans regarding the race of men and her ocean until it had been executed. When she saw how her domain had been annexed for the creation of the earth, she became angry and confronted Obatala.

"Have I ever wronged you, Obatala?" she asked in a raging voice, poised for war.

"You have not, Olokun. Neither do I have a quarrel with you."

"Why then have you done this to my ocean?"

"I have only taken a portion for the creation of earth for the race of men."

"The race of men?"

Obatala proceeded to enlighten her about the events in the abode of the gods that she had not been aware of, and how the abode of the gods had been found unsuitable for the race of men.

"The gods agreed that the earth should be fashioned out of the ocean for the dwelling of men," Obatala concluded. "I was commissioned for the work."

"Which gods agreed, when I was not consulted?" Olokun asked. "They think so little of me to decide what to do with my ocean without consulting me! Return to the gods and tell them that Olokun would not have the race of men in her ocean."

"My commission is from Olodumare," Obatala said, ignoring Olokun's outburst. "I cannot return until I have done his bidding."

"Olodumare! What have I done to Olodumare that even here, away from his abode, he would not let me have peace?"

Infuriated though she was, Olokun knew she could not pit herself against Olodumare. It had proved ill for her when she attempted it. She therefore returned to the ocean to think how best to halt the work of Obatala. From the ocean, she watched Obatala at work and discovered the source of the power with which he parted the ocean. Then she devised her plans.

The following day, she visited Obatala in his forge where he was hard at work. Obatala thought she had come to quarrel with him again and had begun to set aside his instruments to get rid of her, but Olokun smiled and spoke gently to him.

"Forgive me for my rashness, Obatala. I have inspected the earth of your creation and found it grand and beautiful. Besides, why should I be angry at you when you are merely doing the will of Olodumare? I have come to apologize to you."

"I am glad you have seen reason, Olokun," Obatala replied with much relief. "Olodumare will be happy at your cooperation. As for me, I hold no grudge against you."

"If you are at peace with me again, heed my advice. Rest a while from your labor. You have accomplished much."

"I still have much work to do. I cannot rest until it is done."

"I do not ask you to abandon your work, only to refresh yourself. Here, I have brought you palm wine to succor you in your labor."

Olokun presented the gourd of palm wine to Obatala. Obatala could not resist the urge to drink the palm wine. So, he drank, and it was sweet beyond his expectation. Olokun, finding him delighted with the palm wine, brought him more. Obatala drank gourd after gourd of palm wine until his senses left him. This was Olokun's intent, and when she saw it fulfilled, she went into Obatala's studio and retrieved the phial and returned to the ocean, hiding it in her most secret chamber.

When Obatala awoke and realized what had happened, he called on the gods for counsel on how to retrieve the phial. Some suggested the use of force, while others opposed it. Olokun could be ferocious when pushed to the limit, especially in her territory. Even Olodumare, the Supreme God, had found it difficult to bear with Olokun while she lived in the abode of the gods. At last, Eshu, the trickster god, suggested the use of persuasion. They debated who could persuade Olokun, for she held all the gods and goddesses in equal contempt.

"No god or goddess can persuade Olokun," Eshu concurred with the observation of the gods. "But a man can."

The gods were astounded by this suggestion. How could Olokun the proud be persuaded by a man?

"Olokun is proud, but she is also curious," Eshu continued. "If we send a man to her, she will be curious about him, and therein lies my design. Give me a man, and I will guide him to retrieve the phial from Olokun."

The gods agreed to adopt the counsel of Eshu. Obatala brought the most handsome and most intelligent of the men he had created and presented him to Eshu. His name was Eniasan. Eshu trained Eniasan and dispatched him to Olokun with an enchanted chain to bind the phial from Olokun's reach upon retrieving it.

When Olokun beheld Eniasan, she was taken in by his handsomeness and frailty. Oblivious of his mission—for Eniasan had pretended to wander by chance into her domain—she brought him into her mansion. She pampered him and gave him all he wanted. As for Eniasan, he fell in love with Olokun's beauty and forgot his mission. He cohabited with her for a thousand years, and gave birth to 463 Yemaja, the daughters of the ocean. Eniasan lived happily in the ocean until, one day, he sneaked into Olokun's secret room. There, he found the phial on her altar stone, and he recalled his mission.

Eniasan took the phial and left hurriedly, but Olokun felt him leave her domain through the bond they shared. Noticing that the phial was gone, Olokun realized his betrayal. She went after him but was kept at bay by the power of the chain with which he had bound the phial. At last, unable to retrieve the phial, she placed a curse on him. Before Eniasan could swim the few spans left for him to reach the earth, he was transformed into a statue with the phial hanging from his neck. Thousands of years passed while Olokun waited for the breaking of the chain that kept her from getting hold of the phial.

...❖...

The events played out before Jun Li's eyes. He felt rather than remembered the agony it had given him to bear the phial filled with the power of the ocean and yet remain trapped as a statue in the ocean. He waited nearly four thousand years for liberation.

"I protected and cared for you, Eniasan, but you deceived me!"

He had no words to respond to her accusation. The anger surged in him, and he wished he could reach her throat and strangle her for the years she had kept him trapped under her curse.

"You shall remain here until I reclaim the earth that Obatala has taken from my domain."

Jun Li watched Olokun as she went into her secret room, holding the phial of Olodumare and laughing in triumph.

IFE-IYOKU

by Oghenechovwe Donald Ekpeki

Morako stayed quiet. He was a lero—or feeler—and oversaw the hunt. On his signal the rest would move. For now, he lay waiting, careful not to alert the beast lest the intended prey become the hunter. Here, the roles of the prey and the hunter could switch in a flash, leaving the hunter to scurry for survival. But he knew that father, Obatala himself, had chosen them and imbued them with sacred gifts which, though not making them immune, offered them a measure of protection.

The Nlaagama—an enormous, lizard-like beast—slithered forward. At almost twelve feet tall, it towered over the banana trees. Its forked tongue, of about eight inches, swung pendulously and tasted the air. It bent to rip into the horned antelope that the Umzingeli hunters had butchered and left as bait. The antelope was like a horse, tall and possessing thick, strong legs, and a horn, like the mythical creatures of the old world. The Nlaagama ripped into the antelope with a savagery that made Morako swallow.

This was Igbo Igboya, the forest of fears.

With the beast distracted, Morako gave the signal. The Umzingeli, four coal-black forms, detached themselves from the trees around it. The beast only stirred before resuming its feeding. The Umzingeli merged, activating the power of anjayiyan-okan, the chameleon mind.

They became part of what they merged with and assumed their properties to remain hidden and undetectable until they detached themselves. The beast would sense them soon. Morako signaled them again. They ran toward the beast with their wooden spears extended. It stood still, trying to detect them, sensing something was wrong.

Morako shot a spike of placidity at the beast. It struggled to cast off the artificial lethargy. The warriors were closing in on it. They needed to be close enough to access the gaps between its scales. Without their skill of merging, the beast would detect them before they got close enough to use their weapons. This was not a static merging which shielded them completely from detection. It was a minute merger of their feet with the ground and the leaves and twigs and droplets of water as they ran. It was activated as they stepped, but deactivated when their feet left the ground, so that they had to consciously reactivate with each step. It was more difficult and required a delicate touch and a continuous synchronization with the environment. It was a skill that only the best of the Umzingeli could use. Properly timed, it enabled them to mask their movement as when they used static merger in complete stillness.

These were the four best hunters, the only four who had mastered the art of merging, and they had to be put on this hunt because of its importance. Nothing less than the village's best four hunters could take down this prey. They were almost on the beast. This was the tricky part: attacking while maintaining the chameleon mind, the delicate merger that allowed them to move silently and remain invisible. They were close enough now, within striking distance …

One of them lost it. Not totally, for he still managed to remain silent and unseen, but he failed to include his weapon in the merger. From where Morako watched, he saw it. Though he could sense their presence with his own skill as a lero, to his eyes, they were invisible and silent to his ears. He only saw a spear coming out of thin air while the body of the hunter remained unseen. The beast's long tail swiveled with a snap, almost faster than his eyes could follow. Its tail slapped the spear away and turned to curl around something that became visible in its grasp as the hunter lost hold of the merger. It flung the hunter at another shape that had just become visible, and both went down on contact.

The beast reared suddenly and howled, shaking its neck violently and throwing something off. The last hunter materialized some yards away, and Morako noticed the broken half of the spear protruding from the back of the beast. It was wounded, but far from defeated. He stared at it. The hunter pulled out another spear and twirled it, preparing to attack. The beast pawed the earth and roared, belching flames at the hunter. From his vantage point where he watched, Morako saw the hunter roll out of the path of the flames and vanish, remerging and blending into the environment. The beast howled again as a spear found a way into one of the gaps between its scales. It bathed the clearing with flames, turning to search if the burnt body of a hunter would appear. None did.

The beast screeched at the unseen enemy. Two large wings unfurled from its body. With its enormous wings, the beast fanned the air, spreading the fire outward. Then, in a swift movement, it lifted itself off the ground. Morako sensed the appearance of the Climbers who had been called in as reinforcement. As the beast soared upwards, the Climbers dropped a net from the trees and entangled its wings, dropping it to the ground. Flames crackled around, and the Climbers, armed with clubs and spears, attacked it. Most of their attacks snapped on the beast's thick scales as it ripped the net with its claws and fangs. The reinforcements would be in trouble if it managed to free itself. The remaining hunter materialized as from thin air and buried his spear in the neck of the beast, through an opening in its armor. As he pulled the spear free, hot blood came gushing out, scalding the climbers who scurried away. The hunter backed off to join the others who had been knocked off. The beast belched fire amidst its dying throes.

Yet it panted, refusing to die. A figure walked in, dragging a tree trunk. It was Oni, the elephant man. The climbers and hunters made way for him. He hefted the trunk and walloped the dying beast in the head. He didn't need to do it twice.

...❖...

It was night in the village of Ife-Iyoku. Everywhere was alight and alive with merriment. Children danced and laughed at the pursuit of masquerades. Palm wine and ogogoro flowed freely for the quaffing of Amala and Ewedu. A group of children gathered in front of a wrinkled but firm-looking old woman, Ologbon the Weaver. She enraptured them with the tales she spun for them. They were content to sit and listen while the other children ran around eating and playing games of Ite and Suwe.

Tonight, she spun the history of Ife-Iyoku to her attentive audience.

"This is how the people of Ife-Iyoku came to be. Long before you were born, the world was not like this. It was much bigger and encompassed different countries and cultures. Then there was a war, and all was lost. The contenders attempted the destruction of one another and ended up almost destroying us. It was a fight between two elephants in which the ground suffers."

The gravity of her voice moistened the eyes of the children. "I see you don't know what an elephant is, as none of you have ever seen one. So much of our culture was lost in the catastrophe, and with it, life itself. But we thank the almighty for sending us some things to replace what we lost." Her voice, initially grand and majestic, became as dry and ordinary as one passing commentary on a distant object.

The children followed the expressions on her face. She lifted her hand and the lights dimmed nearly to quenching. The illumination was replaced by glowing lines in the air. The Ologbon spun with her hands as she had done with her mouth. The children watched in wonderment. The light took the shape of two elephants. The elephants trumpeted and stamped on the ground, then rushed at each other. They tussled. The children felt the vibration of the earth and clutched each other's hands tightly. The Olori raised both hands and the images of the two battling elephants dissipated and faded. The ground was muddied up.

"That," she said, pointing, "is the ground after two elephants fought. Oni the brawny is named after them. In any night but this, I would go on weaving you tales of wonder and valor. But tonight is a special night, the night of the Onye Lana Riri Festival. Tonight, marks the night many years ago when the war came upon us. You must know your history if you are to seize for yourself a future. All of you are Onye Lana Riri, the ones who survived. I believe there is more in store for you than just existence. I believe that you will thrive. For those of you who do not remember or have not heard this tale, I shall tell it again. It is the story of our death and rebirth to what we are today."

As she spoke, she raised her hand to weave again. The light from the fire dimmed once more and other strands of light rose into various forms, in line with the tale she wove.

"Once we were a vast group of peoples called Afrika, peoples of special and diverse cultures and breeding. They lived in peace and unity before the war of the nations around them. These nations had developed nuclear weapons but entered into a pact not to use them against one another. Why someone would make something they never intended to use, I never got. Like the wicked senior wife that obtained poisonous charms, claiming never to have intended it for the newest wife's soup. So, one side broke the pact, as pacts are wont to be broken in wars by the desperate or losing parties."

As she spoke, the images she conjured intensified and were matched by sound. Factions launched missiles and the children watched them travel toward the raised outlines of other cities.

"Everyone launched their warheads. The pact of mutually assured destruction was broken. But the disaster did not happen now."

As she spoke, she flicked her hand. The images continued projecting. The missiles hit an invisible dome above the city and were rendered defective. Some of them jerked in the air, spiraling sporadically before ricocheting and returning the way they had come.

"America, the greatest nation in the war at the time, had prepared for this day. She had missile defense systems in place. She also had systems to seize the missiles in the air and redirect them whence they came."

She gestured to the returning missiles.

"America had the power to quash the missiles. But instead, she wanted to show her power. She wanted to punish the offenders, the Middle Easterners, from a continent called Asia, who she felt had bred trouble for countless centuries. That was how the seed of destruction that is fully grown today was sown. Hundreds of nuclear warheads were sent sailing back to the shores of Iraq and Afghanistan and their Moslem brethren. Unbeknownst to the West and its allies, their foes had obtained some of the missile-redirecting technology from their allies, the Chinese and the Russians.

"But having technology is not mastery of it. They could not manage what they were given. Their control of the technology was not strong enough to allow them to send the weapons all the way back. Their range was small, and they had friends and allies around them. So, they redirected the weapons to the closest place they could, where their friends would not suffer them, and there would be no retribution—Afrika."

She whispered this last word with sharp, dramatic emphasis. The missiles in her images of light paused in the air. There was total quietude as she continued her tale.

"Afrika was a place of culture and learning. We had no implements of war and destruction, or defense against them. We stayed out of international disputes. Our brothers in the south of Africa developed such armaments, but they disarmed them, wise enough to see that they would do nothing but destroy us and the rest of the world. However, being right didn't stop us from paying the price of the wrong. When wise ones are surrounded by fools, they often end up suffering as the fools. Sometimes they suffer more than the fools."

She flicked her hand and the missiles landed all at once. A blinding yellow light rose from where they landed, followed by fire and smoke which billowed out and spread till it covered the whole area. The children gasped. Some were weeping. The Weaver continued her story.

"Nearly all of Afrika was destroyed by the missiles of the combatants. Nothing would have been left of Afrika but for the fact that we are a special people. Our land, Ife, is a sacred ground where all life originated. We have always been deeply spiritual and in tune with the gods, with heaven and with the earth. We called on Obatala, who interceded on our behalf, as he had done when his sister Olokun threatened the world with water. He pleaded with Olorun, the sky father, to save us. Olorun urinated in a gourd and told Obatala to sprinkle the water on the affected area and all the destruction and leftover radiation would dissipate.

"The urine was not sufficient to sprinkle in all the affected parts of Afrika. Obatala could only use the urine in the healing of the land of his own people. Despite Obatala's intercession, Olorun did not care about the rest of the world. The smoke from the bombs covered the sun and temperatures dropped. All life was threatened, not just the lives in Afrika. Obatala in his infinite love and mercy decided to share the cure with rest of the world even though they were responsible for the disaster. With the sacred urine, he was able to wash away the radiation and nuclear waste. However, what was left was insufficient to totally reverse the effect of the bombs in Afrika.

"Obatala cut himself and let some drops of his blood mix with the urine in the gourd to increase its potency. With the mixture he saved Ife. Nothing was left to save the rest of Afrika. Only this small circle around Ife is clean. We are trapped, and all around us is the lingering destruction from the folly of man. The first rain that fell after the destruction affected the land and people around Ife. The sacred land rejects and repels the radiation and waste. Our blood and bodies are stronger. We adapted abilities to make up for what we lost and to enable us to survive in this new world. We became Ndi Lana Riri, the ones who survived. And what is more, Obatala left us a lasting gift. Each time one of us dies, our blood thickens, and the remaining ones evolve further, to make up for the numbers lost with strength. His blood keeps us and strengthens us further to ensure that his people endure. It is said that in the hour of our greatest need, he will return to restore us, and Afrika, fully.

"The rest of the world learned and moved on from their folly. We were the lesson. They believed that either we had all been wiped out, or the corruption around us was so thick they could not reach through. Perhaps, they refused to attempt saving us for fear of contaminating the rest of the world. They created one of their barriers to keep us away, until they discover how to undo their error and cleanse the environment. But that may not be a long time coming, because it's easier to destroy than to rebuild.

"Some may wonder why Obatala saved the world. It is because despite all that happened, survival is collective. If man would survive, we must do so together, as one. We must think of all and not of individuals."

"If we don't die out before that day comes," a gruff male voice said.

The Weaver looked up to note the presence of three people who had just joined the campfire. One was an old man who had a wrapper tied around his chest in the manner of Igbo chiefs. The other two, a man and a woman, were much younger. The man was sturdy but lean. He bore the traditional marks of a hunter: crossed slashes on his chest and claw tattoos. The woman followed him closely. She was lean too, but not as hard looking. Her softer features followed him in concern before she turned to look at the seated children with a smile. They smiled back.

The Weaver rose to greet the old Chief. "Welcome, husband."

"Thank you, wife," he said affectionately.

The children all rose to squat and greet him in the traditional manner. "Ekaro, sir."

"Ekaro my children," he responded with a fatherly smile.

"At least all is not lost. Even if gold and land are lost, our culture and blood, which are our greatest assets, still endure."

The Weaver sniffed. He gave her a curt and slightly annoyed look. She responded with an affectionate one. The children returned to their seats.

The Chief said, "The fell beast has been slain. Imade has healed the hunters and drained their bodies of the corruption they contacted in Igbo Igboya. The beast lies ready for the final phase of the ceremony, and I came personally to inform you. As Chief Priestess, you must be there to consecrate the sacrifice to Obatala."

The Weaver nodded. He turned to the children to dismiss the campfire session, but she raised a finger to forestall him. He cut off with a slight frown.

She said, "The night's session is not done. The Chiefs' Council may be your domain, but this is mine. Obatala entrusted this sacred task on me and my successor. My time is nigh, and I must do as much of my duty as I can before it comes."

Morako who accompanied the Chief stood in rigid observance of the exchange between the Chief and his wife. But Imade caught his eye with a sly smirk on her face.

Ologbon the wise, weaver of tales said, "We shall give the Nlaagama in sacrifice to Obatala in this festival. Every day before this festival, our best warriors must go to hunt these creatures which have been twisted by the corruption filtering from the outside. They are for sacrifices to Obatala. We do this to show that we are strong enough to play our part in guarding and preserving the sacred life he gave us with his blood."

Morako thumped his chest and said, "We are strong and must remain so till Obatala returns again to lead us to our destiny."

The Chief squatted to address the gathering. His wife shifted uncomfortably, but he ignored her. "I speak in my authority as Ooni, Head Chief. Obatala may return, or he may not. Whether Obatala comes or not, we will be strong and lead ourselves to our own destinies. Ife thins every day. The corruption keeps creeping in, and the creatures in Igbo Igboya grow more twisted. We have been given the sacred gifts already. We carry the power of our salvation in our blood. In our moment of near destruction, we were mutated and thus acquired resistance to things that would have killed us. Perhaps it was Obatala who had done this for us; perhaps it was not him. Whatever the cause or reason, we have become stronger than we were before. We have acquired the ability to heal and manipulate the elements. Every time one of us dies, our powers wax stronger. Let us use these gifts to counteract our possible extinction. Our powers were less when we were more. With the reduction in our population, our gifts are strengthened. The gifts call on us to use them. We must take our destiny in our own hand, whether Obatala returns or not."

The Weaver clicked her tongue and asked, "Is this another exhortation for migration? You know, beloved, that we have tried that before, and many were lost. There is no way through the corruption surrounding Ife. The outside world does not even know we exist. This issue has been raised before the council and voted down."

The Chief raised a placatory hand. "This isn't the council indeed, peace woman. I merely informed them of what they must face someday."

He turned to the children. "Tomorrow is your first day in the house of learning. You will be tested. All who are old enough will begin training on how to use the sacred gifts you are imbued with and how to take on your sacred duty of survival so that someday you may face and take on your destiny. You are no longer children. You will be great men and woman of Ife-Iyoku." He thumped his chest, and all the people did the same.

He continued, "With the permission of the Weaver of tales and teacher of the sacred lore of Obatala, we go to offer the beast as sacrifice to Obatala in honor of our sacred charge to survive."

The Weaver pulled out a clay cup and one of the children came forward. He took the cup from her, took in his breath, and dragged with his fingers as if pulling something, his focus on the cup. There was a rushing sound. He handed the cup to the Weaver and resumed his seat. She put the cup to her mouth and took a pull. Water leaked out and ran down her mouth. The Chief looked at the child and nodded in approval. The child beamed with pleasure.

The Weaver set the cup down and explained, "This is our ritual. Talking is thirsty work and Ake here keeps me hydrated. He is a puller and can pull the elements. He helps me with water after our sessions."

"That is very good, but we will need more than a cup of water to survive," the Chief muttered.

"I heard that," the Weaver said.

"Well, the festival awaits."

"One more thing," the Weaver said, as she manipulated her light-weaving gifts in complex patterns. A trail of light followed her fingers. The light glowed brighter until it became a full ball of light. She released it and it shot into the night. It exploded in a brilliant rainbow of colors and illuminated everywhere. The hitherto solemn children jumped up squealing and screaming in joy and wonder, running, laughing, and clutching each other. The Chief shook his head in amusement as the four adults went walking after them toward the festival grounds.

The Chief asked, "The substance manipulation that Ake pulled off couldn't have conjured up palm wine, could it?"

The Weaver sniffed. "You know very well that at his age, the wonder is that he can do anything at all. Besides, from what palm trees could he have pulled the moisture? He could only pull water from the moisture in the environment. It was even a bit salty, and I think there must have been some sweat mixed in it."

"What a shame," the Chief said. "If he could conjure palm wine, that would have been something."

...❖...

Later that night, Morako and Imade lay cuddled up on a mat listening to the drumming and singing from the festival and watching the stars. The corrupted beast had been given in fires to Obatala. Kolanut and palm wine flowed freely, but only amongst the chiefs. Kolanut was the food of the gods and only meant for elders and those closest to the gods. The rest enjoyed the general merriment. Children danced and played and ran from masquerades.

But Morako and Imade lay watching the stars, enjoying the festival in their own corner. She ran a teasing finger up his arm, her breath warm against his cheek. He trembled at her touch.

She whispered in his ear, "Why does a warrior of your calibre quake so?"

"Ah," he said, "my skill as a feeler makes me more susceptible to your wiles. With it I feel this ... overwhelming, enveloping warmth seeping from you, yet each time I ask you to be joined to me as a full-grown woman who has passed all the rites of womanhood, you refuse. Why do you refuse me so?"

"Not so, my strong one. I am only not sure of joining with you and bringing a child into this uncertain world."

"But it's our sacred duty to survive and that involves—"

She looked at him reproachfully. "Sacred duty, is it? You're all about duty, my dear brave hunter and feeler."

He chuckled. "I do confess my desire to be more than just for fulfillment of duty."

She nibbled on his ear lobe and clutched him tightly. "I, too, my brave hunter. Maybe someday when something changes, we will get our desire. I assure you that my refusal is not about you but about other things. I find you quite sufficient and can desire nothing more for a mate, my brave hunter." She snuggled tighter by his side.

"That enveloping, overwhelming warmth is a fire now," he said. "I am quite assured of your affections. But let us try not to burn down Ife-Iyoku."

"As a healer, I do have ways of sensing and affecting you as well. Healing is control and manipulation. When I nudge the body in certain ways, I can dampen pain receptors, and enhance and inflame other parts, like your immune system. Supposing I do this …"

She ran a finger down his belly and drew on her gift, sending a line of energy into him. His eyes widened.

"Do not wake the beast," he said, "unless you are ready to do battle."

"The beast was already awake. I was merely teasing it a bit. And who said I am not ready for battle?"

She drew his mouth to hers and kissed him thoroughly. They pulled the covers over their head and let the sounds of merriment pass over them as they created theirs.

…❖…

In the town hall the next morning, the Head Chief stood in front of the children of eligible age, ready to begin their training. He carried a supple cane which he slapped against his palm. The children were seated cross-legged on mats before him. As he was about to begin speaking, one of the tattooed hunters came in and whispered something to him. The Chief walked out with him. A little while later, another messenger came to inform the children that the lesson for that day had been cancelled and they were to return home. The children ran home in glee to have their day of fun and play. They did not know that only a dire occurrence could have led to the cancellation of the lessons.

Later that night, Morako met Imade in their usual spot under the mango tree. He pulled her close and said, "I have bad news for you."

"I know," she said, putting a finger to his lips.

"You heard?"

"No. But I felt it. The Weaver and I were connected. I felt her passing this morning. Besides, she foresaw her passing. She always said that her time was drawing near while preparing me for the role of priestess of Obatala to take over from her. She knew that this festival would be her last. I didn't expect it to be so soon, but I felt something change in my gift when she passed away. I think it is the mechanism that kicks in when one of us dies to activate our evolution and amplify our abilities."

"Isn't that a random occurrence?"

"Usually, it is. But this one was keyed to me personally. It is perhaps because of how close we were. Or because she had groomed me to be her successor. It might even be random." She looked at Morako's inquisitive gaze and sighed. "Let me show you."

She picked a mango leaf from the ground. It was withered and brown, having fallen for a while. He watched as she closed her eyes to activate her power. The withered leaf uncurled and changed in color. It stretched out and attained a soft and vibrant texture. A lush green permeated it, and she handed it to him. He took it tentatively, bewildered.

"I could heal before, but I can do more now. I can restore life. There's hope for change. Someday we can chart a course through the corrupt wilderness to a new world. Or perhaps I could restore Ife-Iyoku and all Afrika to what it was before. In any case, the hope is clearer now than before. I hold the hope in me."

He stared at her in wonderment. She took the leaf from him and let it fall.

"I know it's a little thing. But we can bring back paradise, even if only one leaf at a time." She smiled coyly. "We can now be joined and raise children. Perhaps before they grow to walk, we shall have found a path for the—"

He interrupted her with his mouth on hers, kissing her passionately.

In the gentle breeze that blew, fresh green leaves dropped on them, like the hope they presaged. The breeze which dropped old leaves and overripe fruit, carried new seeds to fresh soil.

A DANCE WITH THE ANCESTORS

by Joshua Uchenna Omenga

CHAPTER ONE

The sound of drumbeats welcomed Kambili to the village square.

He was deliberately late to the festival. He had chosen a time when he would not meet with people on his way. And despite his spirit mask and his raffia hat which cast a shadow on his face, he still feared recognition.

He took his steps cautiously, scanning his environment for familiar faces to avoid. But no one paid him any attention; everyone was absorbed in the gathering frenzy of the festival.

Kambili stood in a less conspicuous corner where his eyes could take the major points of the village square. He sought Lebechi everywhere. His heart skipped at the sight of every maiden of similar build to Lebechi, but he was disappointed each time. And each disappointment made him question the wisdom of his adventure.

This was the only place he hoped to see her without much peril. Several times since his exile, he had tried to sneak into the village to see her, but he had been unable to pass through the watch of the village guards and the villagers themselves. Umueke was a small village where almost everyone knew each other, and he, a warrior of Umueke, had no chance of sneaking in undetected by a familiar face. But today, the road was unguarded and as visitors from other villages also attended the festival, no one cared for the identity of unfamiliar faces and masked attendants.

His search for Lebechi was interrupted by the booming of cannon shots which announced the arrival of prominent persons. The drumbeats ceased, the excited voices faded and, the voice of Unuke, the village head maiden, took over everyone's attention.

Lords and fathers and owners
Your daughters welcome you
Strong men of Umueke
Backs that move the elephants
Voices that speak in silence
Fires that burn the rock
Dry meats that fill the mouth
Lead us where there is path!

And now Kambili saw the addressees, a procession of titled men of Umụeke, led by Omekagu. They wore tiger-engraved robes and chieftaincy caps engraved with the image of the Great Python. Omekagu alone was dressed distinctly in long, flowing leopard skin with white floss on its edges which reflected light and gave it a glittery appearance.

Unuke ushered them into a canopy thatched with palm fronts. One after the other, they took their seats. But Omekagu remained standing, and when the rest were seated, he raised his horsetail to the crowd for calm.

"Umueke kwenu!" His voice conquered the gathering.

"Hem!" the people shouted in reply.

"Umueke kwenu!"

"Hem!"

"Umueke kwezuenu!"

"Hem! Hem! Hem!"

Kambili was filled with bitterness as he watched the people warm to Omekagu's address. He was not surprised at Omekagu's esteem with the people. After the treacherous way in which Omekagu had almost gotten him executed, Kambili knew Omekagu was capable of anything. It was now fifteen moons since the event, but the memory was fresh every time he saw Omekagu.

Kambili had been in the bush checking his trap when he heard a distressed cry and ran to help. The cry was from King Agumba, and he lay in a pool of blood, losing consciousness. As Kambili tried to lift him, Agumba kept muttering, "Agueze, Agueze, Agueze." Then his eyes and lips closed.

As Kambili examined the huge gash on the king's rib cage, he was haunted by the king's parting words. Had Prince Agueze done this to his father? But the wound did not look like spear or sword wound. And then Kambili saw the scratches on the king's body and knew that the king had been attacked by a ferocious animal. As if in confirmation of his suspicion, he heard a scrambling near where the king lay and stood up to inspect. A huge leopard leapt out from the grasses and ran behind adjoining woods. He picked the king's spear and ran after it. But when he thought he had had it cornered and was about to thrust his spear, he saw not a leopard but Mazi Omekagu.

Puzzled but relieved equally, he asked Omekagu if he had seen a leopard pass by. Omekagu shook his head.

"Something terrible has happened," Kambili said.

"What is it?"

"It is the king."

"What about the king?"

"Come and see." Kambili could not pronounce the king's fate with his own mouth.

Omekagu gave an unmanly cry at the sight of Agumba. He shook Agumba and called his name, but no amount of shakes or name calling could revive the king. At last, Kambili carried the king's body into the village.

The royal corpse was swamped with anxious villagers. Other hands took the body from Kambili while he attended to the queries from the elders. It was then that Omekagu appeared and Kambili was relieved to pass the burden of explaining matters to the elders. After all, these were matters to be delivered in riddles of the elderly rather than in the speech of the youth.

And what could he hear Omekagu say, but proclaim before the assemblage of elders and villagers that he, Kambili, had killed the king! Kambili opened his mouth for a long time, unable to utter a word. How did one answer such a monstrous accusation? For even the staunchest denial seemed to lend credence to the accusation rather than refute it.

Kambili was charged before the village judiciary comprising the elders and titled men. Before them, Omekagu swore that he had heard Agumba's cry and ran just in time to hear him calling on Kambili as his murderer. He, Omekagu, had scoured the forest and found Kambili with the king's spear in his hand, dripping with the king's blood.

How did one contradict the evidence of a titled man, the king's brother, on the words of a dying monarch? All Kambili's explanations fell flat against Omekagu's lies. When Kambili tried to explain that it was he, Kambili, who had attended to the king, and that the king's dying words were his son's name, Omekagu twisted Kambili's explanation into another accusation: Kambili had killed Agueze and now sought to lay the king's death on Agueze—for Agueze had been missing since the death of his father. Kambili denied this latest accusation and was told to produce Agueze to prove his truth. All efforts to find Agueze proved in vain.

As Kambili could offer no contradiction beyond his plea of innocence, he was urged to confess and be banished, or be executed with his falsehood. Kambili appealed to the gods for justice, resting his faith in their infallibility. The Chief Priest of Umueke was summoned as the mouthpiece of the gods—and found Kambili guilty!

Kambili was stung not by his condemnation, but by the triumph of falsehood over truth, and most of all by the complicity of the gods in his most unjust condemnation. His blood would have been poured in absolution to the earth god, but for his friend Munachi who conspired with the executioners to release him, on the charge that he should never set foot in Umueke again, for he was henceforth a dead man.

The purpose of Omekagu's treachery had continued to elude Kambili. What wrong had he done Omekagu, except that Omekagu coveted but could not get Lebechi, Kambili's betrothed?

This was the Omekagu who now stood before the people, pouring his sweetened words into their ears and calling for the praise of the equally treasonous gods of Umueke. As the crowd gobbled Omekagu's words, it seemed to Kambili that he alone could see the truth. And the truth was a burden where falsehood sat in high places.

He became aware of the change in the scene when the sound of the maiden drums assailed his ears. Their soft beats brought expectations in the hearts of the menfolk, for the drums heralded the dance of the maidens of Umueke, who had recently undergone their rite of passage into womanhood.

The maidens arrived barefooted, their bare bosoms heaving against copious flaps of beads on their necks. The drumbeats gained tempo, and the dust began to rise as the maidens swayed their hips with increasing vigor toward the center of the village square.

Men watched with drooping jaws. Young men with no women in their huts sought prospective brides among the maidens. Old men with two or more wives sought for maidens to rejuvenate them with new life. But they knew that a number of these maidens had been promised to other men, for they could see the palm fronds on their arms signifying betrothal.

Kambili saw Lebechi among the maidens and his heart fluttered. His bitterness disappeared and light returned to his eyes. As he looked upon her, every other maiden paled in insignificance. Even the drumbeats seemed to have faded into the background, so that he could hear the pattering of Lebechi's feet as she glided in dance. She gyrated in measured grace, titillating him with the movement of her curves. Her firm breasts tugged against their roots as she swayed to the rhythm of the drumbeats. To him she was the most graceful of all the maidens, dousing the beauty of her kindred maidens with her effulgence. Her coy smile charmed him.

Kambili could not believe he had held in his arms that body in which fire radiated from every pore, had crushed those swaying breasts on his chest, had clasped her sinuous waist with his palms. Those legs bristling with sweat had rubbed at his legs, those fine hands had clasped his neck and rubbed his head and caressed the stubbles on his chin. Those eyes white like curdled milk had looked into his eyes with desire, those tremulous lips had kissed his lips in passion. Together they had lain on his bed with nothing between their souls but their skins, whispering unremembered words and secrets sweet because of the tongues that spoke them. Her soft and teasing laughter rang in his ears like the cackle of a mischievous child, daring and yet alluring.

Kambili stretched his hand toward her as though there were only the two of them in the village square. My Lebechi! His soul cried with desire. His hands trembled for possession.

And then he saw her look in his direction, as if she had heard his unspoken call. Their eyes met and everything else ceased to exist. No other sound could he hear but the thumping of his heart. No other thing could he see but the radiance of her eyes. He was frozen with her transcendence. But suddenly, like a spell broken by a strong enchanter, she turned away from him and retreated behind the other dancers. For a long time, while the dance lasted, he had only occasional glimpses of her, until at last he realized, she was deliberately hiding from him.

Darkness descended on his soul. He knew she was no more his Lebechi. For more than a year he had tried unsuccessfully to tell his heart that she was no more for him. For more than a year his heart had rebelled against the facts. He had fed on sparse hope while neglecting the abundance of reality. But now the cruelty of reality broke what fortitude he'd derived from hope, and tears came to his eyes.

He felt empty. He had lost all but his life. And now he was a fugitive who attended his village festivals in disguise. How could such a hollow man like him remain in Lebechi's favor? He imagined how Lebechi must have abjured him when she heard of his accusation and condemnation. Was it not contempt he had seen in her eyes a moment ago?

If he did not know her well, he would have feared that she would betray him to Omekagu. He knew that, though she might condemn him, she would not betray him. But Kambili wanted more than her loyalty. He wanted her to know the truth. He wished he could turn into a wasp, fly into her ear, and tell her all.

He took few steps forward, overtaken by the desire to reach her and have it all sorted out. He no longer cared for exposure; he could die satisfied if executed in her arms.

Lost in thought, he was unaware that the maiden dance had ended until he saw Lebechi approach and kneel before Omekagu. Omekagu raised her up and showed her the seat beside him. Kambili turned away. He could not endure the sight of Lebechi sitting close to Omekagu.

He was gripped by a sudden urge to rush at Omekagu and choke him to death, even if he would be killed in the process. He started forward to execute his impulse, but he was checked by the boom of the Akpara drum. He stopped, like everyone else. A sudden stillness was upon the village square; only the measured beats of the Akpara dominated the air.

A cloud came upon the sun, shading the village square. Wind began to blow sporadically, and the tree branches whistled. The air around the village square was charged; a spirit had entered it, which everyone felt. Goosebumps stood on several skins, though the air was dry and warm. The Akpara continued to boom in rising cadence.

A gigantic man in full ancestral regalia bounded into the center of the village square. It was Odummuo, usher of the ancestral spirits. He waved his yellow wand in the six corners of Umueke, invoking each hamlet in the tongue of the spirits which only the initiates understood. Then he lifted the trumpet hanging on his back and blew it three times. A moment of silence followed. And then the earth began to heave. Lightning flashed and lingered in the clouds. Branches of nearby trees bent and twisted, swayed not by breeze, but by the spirits which pervaded the air.

At last, the ancestral spirits came, surrounded by a column of smoke which gradually dispersed to reveal them in their full panoply. As each of the ancestral spirits were revealed, Odummuo danced from corner to corner, and everywhere he turned, the spectators lay on the earth and greeted in reverence, for one did not stand on one's feet to greet one's ancestors. Although one saw the ancestral spirits from every part of the village square because they were unusually tall, only those who viewed them from close quarters could describe the majesty of their appearance.

The first ancestral spirit had the head of a jackal and carried long swords on both hands which he waved to match his motion. The second ancestral spirit had the head of an eagle, and his feet were of large talons which scattered the earth when he danced. The third ancestral spirit had the head of a goat, with two large and tapering horns, and its feet were of cloven hoof. He bore the sacred calabash of Umueke on his chest, and although he danced as vigorously as the rest, the content of the sacred calabash did not spill.

The fourth ancestral spirit had the head of a leopard, fearsome and aggressive, his dress spotted in red, like the coat of a leopard after a successful hunt. He was the sprightliest of all the ancestral spirits. His movement was like lightning; he was seen here and there almost instantaneously, and one could not quite tell where the leopard spirit was at any moment.

The fifth ancestral spirit had the head of a horse, and his face was mild and noble. His head down to his hips were covered in silver mane, and when he danced it was as if he did not touch the earth. He was called the ancestral spirit of peace.

The sixth ancestral spirit had the head of a dog, and its teeth stood out prominently. It carried a quiver full of arrows, and his iron bow hung on his back. He was the great ancestral hunter of Umueke, reputed to have single-handedly defeated the incarnate lion of a neighboring village pitted against Umueke. He was a restive ancestral spirit and everywhere he turned, spectators made way for him with dispatch.

The seventh, and leader, of the ancestral spirit had the head of a python, an incarnate spirit of Eke Ndamugwu, the Great Python who founded Umueke. He alone of all the ancestral spirits wore an ornament on his head, a semicircular crown cast from pure gold. His cloth glittered as he walked with quiet majesty, taking a step at a time. Everywhere he turned, the people bowed. He did not dance as the other ancestral spirits but took his seat of carved iroko which had been brought to him from the spirit world by Obungada, the incarnate spirit of his faithful servant who had volunteered to be buried with the Great Python to continue in his service in the spirit world.

And now Uremma, the village bard, joined the ancestral drummers with her long flute with which she addressed the Great Python.

Our father Eke Ndamugwu
Ndorimando
Who crossed seven mountains
Ndorimando
To search for black soil and green leaves
Ndorimando
Our father Eke Ndamugwu
Ndorimando
Who rode on the back of an elephant
Ndorimando
Our father Eke Ndamugwu
Ndorimando
Who founded a vast land for his offspring
Ndorimando
And covenanted with the gods
Ndorimando

For the protection of his offspring
Ndorimando
Our father Eke Ndamugwu
Ndorimando
We bow in greetings and appreciation
Ndorimando
Whoever has brought discord to this gathering
Ndorimando
May his peace be taken away
Ndorimando!

After Uremma's eulogy, the Great Python dipped his wand into the ancestral calabash and sprayed its content in the air. The villagers scrambled to be touched by the sprays, the ancestral blessing.

Kambili saw that Omekagu had risen from his seat and was bowing to the Great Python. He could not catch the conversation between Omekagu and the Great Python, but he saw the Great Python dip his wand into the ancestral calabash and sprinkle it on Omekagu before Omekagu rose to his feet.

Then the Great Python addressed the crowd. His voice boomed like thunder and his words were inhuman, interpreted to the people's comprehension by Odummuo.

After the address of the Great Python, two men and a woman came out from the gathering and knelt before the Great Python. Kambili recognized them. They were one of the embattled families of Umueke. Their dispute had been adjudicated several times in the village assembly to no avail. Now they had brought their dispute before the ancestral spirits. The ancestral spirits were the final arbiters; their judgements were infallible. Or so it was held. But Kambili knew better since the complicity of the gods in his unjust condemnation.

At other times, he would have watched the adjudication with interest. But now, he turned his eyes away and shut his ears to the voice of the Great Python as he questioned and pronounced judgement. Instead, his eyes returned to the platform, and he caught Lebechi withdrawing her hand from Omekagu's grasp.

An indefinable rage surged into Kambili's heart. To see Lebechi sitting beside Omekagu was torture enough, but he could not bear to see Omekagu touch her. Omekagu, the notorious woman chaser; everything in wrapper aroused his desire. Although he already had five wives and uncountable concubines, he could not pass by a maiden without casting his lustful eyes at her. Lebechi, like every other maiden in Umueke, had received his advances. But Lebechi, unlike most of them, had turned him down so completely that if he had any dignity, he would have desisted from mere shame. But Omekagu had no dignity and came after Lebechi all the more intensely for being turned down.

And now Omekagu had succeeded in getting Lebechi.

An animated but hushed discussion was going on between Omekagu and Lebechi. Kambili could not hear their words, but Omekagu seemed to be triumphant. Kambili even thought he caught a smile on her face. Oh, fiendish betrayal! He could endure Omekagu's odious hands on her, but not her kind reception of it. And then it dawned on him that he, Kambili, was the fool.

Did he know what had transpired within his period of exile? Although during the maiden dance Lebechi had worn no palm frond on her arm to indicate that she was betrothed to another, Kambili was not sure anymore that she had not been encumbered within the period of his absence. How could he hope? Was he alone in his admiration of Lebechi? How could he expect her to wait for him? And then he recalled that he was a dead man to her and to the rest of Umueke.

I have lost her irredeemably!

The ancestral whistle blew. It was time for the ancestors to sanction the person chosen by the people to the vacant throne of Umueke. Omekagu stepped forward with his wand, deposited it before the Great Python, and knelt on the ground.

The Great Python lifted the wand and beckoned on the other ancestral spirits for consultation. After a while, the Great Python returned the wand to Omekagu and waved him to stand. He had not sanctioned Omekagu as a king!

All eyes watched inquisitively. It was never known in Umueke that a vacant throne was left without a king after the visit of the ancestral spirits. Yet no one in Umueke dared to question the decision of the ancestors.

Kambili alone was happy with this development. It was insignificant to Kambili who was chosen as king over Umueke, but it was much consolation that his rival was not chosen. Omekagu could not have it all, after all!

The visit of the ancestral spirit was over. One by one the titled men deposited gifts of trinkets to the bosom of Odummuo. Omekagu approached, clutching Lebechi's hand. He waited until others had deposited their gifts before he stepped forward, Lebechi following on his heel. Bowing before the Python, Omekagu said some words which Kambili did not catch. Then he gave Lebechi's hand to the Great Python, bowed and walked back to his seat.

Many people saw, but only a few understood the significance of Omekagu's action. Omekagu had given Lebechi as a gift to the ancestors! No one had ever presented a human gift to the ancestors. And when the Great Python started to go, still clutching Lebechi's hand, the people knew the ancestors meant to keep the gift. It was known, although not talked about except in the most secret of fraternal circles, that the ancestral gifts did not follow the ancestors to their world but were kept by Odummuo.

Kambili's hair stood on end. He had thought Omekagu incapable of surprising him further. How could Omekagu not even keep what he had stolen? But most surprising of all was the easy surrender which he saw in Lebechi's face.

Kambili could no longer restrain himself as the ancestral spirits started to go. He broke through the crowd and ran toward the Great Python. But before he could get at him, the leopard-headed ancestral spirit turned upon him. Loud voices broke from the crowd. Kambili slipped out of the spirit's grasp but did not have time enough to see the goat-headed ancestral spirit wielding a five-pronged whip and straddling his way. Kambili received several whips before he had time to turn around. The next one almost caught him in the head, but he managed to dodge it. He turned to escape, but his leg caught the skirt of the eagle-headed ancestral spirit, and he fell. As he tried to rise, he felt a stunning knock on his head and passed out.

CHAPTER TWO

Kambili awoke to the soothing touch of hot-wet clothing on his forehead. It took him a while to make out the face staring down at him. It was Munachi.

Kambili sprang up.

"Keep still," Munachi said, holding Kambili down on the bed.

"Where am I?"

"Don't panic. You're in my house and no one knows you're here." After a pause, Munachi added, "You're lucky your mask was not knocked off, and I dragged you out before anyone else knew it was you."

"What are you talking about?"

As if he had not heard Kambili's question, Munachi continued, "How could you go fighting with the ancestral spirits when you know you're not supposed to be seen in Umueke?"

"Ancestral spirits," Kambili muttered, as if that was the only thing he had heard from all that Munachi had said. And then he remembered. "Lebechi! Where's Lebechi?"

Munachi shook his head. "They took her with them."

"They took her with them?" Kambili brushed away Munachi's hand and stood up. "Where did they take her to?"

"I don't know. But I saw them taking her toward the ancestral forest."

Kambili picked up his dress which Munachi had removed to rub ointment on his body. He put it on and sheathed his sword.

"You should lie down and have a proper rest, Kam. You were badly knocked out."

"I have to find her," Kam said simply, and stepped out of the hut. Munachi followed him.

"You can't be serious, Kam? How do you hope to find someone that has been taken by the ancestors into the ancestral forest?"

Kambili made no answer. He donned his hunting sandals and ran in the direction of the ancestral forest. Munachi called him back, to no avail.

...❖...

Kambili ran without stopping, until the ancestral forest loomed before him. There was no path leading into it. It was a forest unexplored due to the fear of the evils it bred, though just how much evil lurked within the forest no one in Umueke knew for certain. The only man who entered and returned from the forest was Akwudiala, the priest of the forest god, who atoned for the people in the forest every year. And the priest was only a half-human whose spirit half dominated his affairs with other men. This was the forest before which Kambili stood.

He could hear the echoes of his own footsteps. This part of the village was so eerily silent that a sound lingered long after it was made. It was said that sometimes, people with keen ears came here to hear events of long time ago still echoing among the foul grasses and the grisly air which never forgot.

He jumped past the tangled and creeping grasses and slashed at the cobwebs that stood in his way with his sword until he found himself at the entrance of the ancestral forest. He was checked by the thick darkness which emanated from the forest. For a long time, he peered into the forest, unable to make out anything. Then, gradually, his eyes began to adapt to the darkness. Taking a deep breath, he plunged into the forest, his sword thrust forward to forestall preventable surprises.

He cringed at the dampness of the earth inside the forest. The soil was not visible but covered with leaves in various stages of decay. All was unaccountably silent. No breeze blew, no leaves fluttered, nothing stirred beneath his feet. There were no creatures in the forest that he could see. He heard no bird calls or squeaking of rodents or chirping of crickets. He was jittery from the eeriness of the forest. He had expected to be confronted with grisly beasts at every step.

Yet Kambili felt not fear, but curiosity.

The forest had taken on the appearance of the pre-dark dusk of a sunny day after the sun had set and the moon was yet to rise, and households were yet to light their lamps. He halted, and his keen hunter's eyes peered through rows of trees, seeking any movement. Although everything in the forest seemed to be in motion, whenever Kambili looked closely at it, he could not discern any movement at all.

The silence grew oppressive, and he could hear the beating of his heart and the soft crackling of leaves under his feet as his weight pressed down on them. He preferred the crude roars of unfettered beasts to this corporeal silence that tortured him in its inexistence.

Suddenly, smells of fruits wafted into his nose. He looked around and saw what his eyes had failed to see before: pods upon pods of fruits, bunches and bunches, green and yellow; each tree bore its fruit in excess. A few of the fruits seemed familiar, but even with the unfamiliar ones, Kambili could almost tell how they tasted. Every good hunter often relied on his sense of smell to tell an edible fruit from nonedible ones, and from his experience, very few trees were indeed inedible. Nature had a way of keeping poisonous trees barren of fruits.

The abundance reminded him of his hunger. He stretched out his hand to the nearest fruit and then brought his hand down as though someone had ordered him to do so. These were not fruits for human consumption, no matter how edible they might seem. There was a cautionary tale of a man who had eaten the fruits from the ancestral forest to his peril. The man's stomach had distended until he became so big that he was blown away by wind and nothing was heard of him anymore. Kambili could not say how much of the story was true and how much had been added deliberately to keep people away from the forest.

At any rate, Kambili had no intention of finding out.

He continued trudging forward until he came upon footsteps and stopped to examine them. At first, he thought he was back where he had passed, but on closer look, he saw that the steps were not his. They were made with bare feet; he was wearing his hunting sandals. Then it dawned on him that they could be the footsteps of Lebechi. Only she could have made such a print, for the ancestral spirits had neither prints nor shadows. With his hope rekindled, he followed the trail of the footsteps. They meandered with marked purposelessness, and Kambili wondered if the ancestral spirits had missed their way. Or perhaps Lebechi had escaped from them and was looking for her way out?

As he followed the thickening trail, he began to hear a scrambling nearby, and his hope rose. So far, he had not encountered a single animal in the forest, so he did not for a moment imagine it might be an animal. As he drew closer, he heard whistling. He paused and listened; the voice was not Lebechi's. His hope dampened, but his curiosity was aroused. He continued until he saw an erect form, with its back turned on him, plucking fruits into a basket. He moved more cautiously, his sword drawn. The figure turned and saw him, and the basket fell from their hand.

It was a man, Kambili saw in a flash. For a moment, Kambili stared at the man and the man stared at him. Then the man took a few steps forward, and Kambili held out his sword to stay the man's progress.

"Kambili?" the man said.

The voice was familiar, but nothing prepared Kambili for recognition. He sheathed his sword and gazed with puzzlement at the man before him. And then Kambili saw beyond the man's wildness and knew the figure he could not have mistaken anywhere else.

"Agueze?"

The man answered with a smile in which his teeth showed.

"You're not dead?" Kambili asked.

Agueze shook his head vigorously.

"How did you come to be here?"

"It is a long story," Agueze said, lifting the basket and picking some of the fruits. "Let's go to my enclave, and we shall have time to talk about it all."

"I can't come with you now," Kambili said. "I have a duty I must attend."

"I see. What duty brought you here?"

"I'm after the ancestral spirits. Did you see them pass by?"

"The ancestral spirits!" Agueze exclaimed. "Why do you seek them?"

"They have something I must retrieve from them."

"What can that be, that you seek them into this place?"

"I'll explain later. But now I need to find them or the route to the land of the ancestors, if I can't meet them here."

Agueze shook his head. "I wish I could help you, if what you're after is so important you seek it into the land of the ancestors."

"Just show me the way to the land of the ancestors, and I'll do the rest myself."

"How can I show you the way that I don't know? Though in my stay here I've had nights of terror when the spirits of the ancestors wander in this forest, I know nothing about them. I always hear them afar. I've never seen them, or know which route they come from, or return to. I don't wander in this forest beyond my need."

"Ah." Kambili's face fell.

"But there's one who knows the way, if he'll be willing to help."

"Who?"

"He's an ancient creature that lives in a cave not far from here."

Kambili followed impatiently as Agueze led the way, walking slowly through the pathless pile of leaves and interlocking trees. Kambili often stumbled where Agueze passed unfaltering, and Agueze had to warn him at some points what to look out for.

"He's a bit grotesque," Agueze said. "He was once a man, but that was more than a thousand years ago."

"A thousand years ago?"

"That's what he told me. He did something for which he was cursed. What he did he refused to tell me, and if you ever get to talk to him, don't ask because he gets irritated by it. Especially don't say anything about his appearance because he doesn't know how he looks."

Kambili nodded, trying to picture the creature in his head. Of course, he had no business with his appearance, provided he could show him the way to the land of the ancestors.

At last, they came to a small clearing with a circular stone in the middle.

"Azini!" Agueze called.

There was no answer. Agueze did not call again, and Kambili grew impatient. But Agueze motioned him to be calm. After a while, a screeching sound came from the stone and it rolled to one side, revealing an opening. A head peered from the opening, and three eyes like points of a triangle looked out at them.

"It's Agueze. I've come with a friend who needs your help."

The creature stepped out and approached them. It must have been the size of a tall human when it stood upright, but now it had become half the size of a man through its perpetual stoop. It was naked, and its skin looked like dried leather. Not a single hair could be seen on its body. It walked like a dinosaur, with its hands hanging pendulous under its chest. It had two eyes where human eyes should be, and an additional eye on its forehead. The eye on its forehead moved independently of the other eyes and seemed to see things other than what was in the environment.

"He is my friend, Azini. He has come to seek your help."

Azini's two side eyes looked from Agueze to Kambili, while its forehead eye looked straight ahead, seeming lost in some absorbing sight.

Agueze nudged Kambili. Not sure how to appeal to the creature, Kambili tendered his request without any garnishment.

"I need your guidance to the land of the ancestors."

Azini's three eyes darted sharply at Kambili, and he felt a stab from its gaze. Then Azini drew back as if it had seen something repugnant in Kambili.

"Take him away from me!" it yelled. "I do not wish to see anyone who talks about the land of the ancestors."

Kambili had an impulse to kick the creature out of his sight. He had short patience for insult, much less from a creature he could ordinarily not even dignify with his sword cut. But Agueze interposed, though himself not knowing how to plead a cause he was alien to.

"I'm sorry to have brought this matter to you, Azini. But it is a thing that must be done, and he has no one else to guide him but you."

"Insatiate humans, you have the world at your disposal, but you must seek what you are better without. What do you seek in the land of the ancestors that you cannot find in the land of humans?"

Kambili hesitated. Something about the creature other than its grotesqueness repulsed him. However, for Agueze's sake, Kambili replied.

"I seek my betrothed who was taken by the ancestral spirits."

Azini made no reply for a long time. A momentary distress passed over its face, and its forehead eye moved rapidly as if following something. Then it shook its head. "I cannot show any man the way to the land of the ancestors. Whoever seeks what lies beyond this forest should find it out for himself." Then it turned from them and returned to its stone hole.

"I'm sorry he isn't helping," Agueze said as they walked away. "He's sometimes like that. He's not in good spirit today."

Kambili was silent. He regretted coming to seek its aid. Kambili was a man who would rather be deprived than live on charity, even earned charity. The desire to rescue Lebechi had driven him into seeking help from this unlikely quarter, and he had been disgracefully rewarded.

They came to a large, prostrate tree and Agueze stopped.

"This is my enclave," he said, pointing at a groove in the tree. "Please come in."

Kambili followed him inside. It was much larger than it had seemed from outside. Rather than darker, there was more light inside than outside. Kambili looked around for the source of light but found none. He asked no question, for he was not in the mood to satisfy his curiosity.

"Is it true, what you told Azini?"

"What?" Kambili asked, recovering from his mind wanderings.

"You said your betrothed was taken by the ancestral spirits."

"Yes," Kambili said with bitterness. Then he recounted his troubles with Omekagu, and how Omekagu had given Lebechi to the ancestral spirits.

Agueze was deep in thought, pondering over what he had heard. Kambili thought Agueze was unconvinced.

"Omekagu always had eyes on Lebechi," Kambili continued, more to himself than to Agueze. "I know he wanted her, but I don't understand why he gave her to the ancestral spirits. I've always thought he wanted to be rid of me in order to have her. Now I don't understand anymore."

Agueze shook his head vigorously. "He didn't want to kill you because of her. He was covering up. It's clear to me now."

"I don't understand you," Kambili said.

"It was Omekagu who killed my father."

Kambili stared in puzzlement.

"We were hunting together when the leopard attacked. I saw it first and tried to warn my father, but my father thought he could kill it with his spear. He had killed many leopards in his time, and usually no leopard would see his royal dress and attack him. But this leopard was different. It charged at him despite his dress. When I tried to run to call for aid, the leopard came after me. I saw its face. It was Omekagu's leopard.

"I remained in hiding because the leopard kept returning and sniffing around, looking for me. When it could not find me, it transformed to Omekagu, and blew his charm in the air. It entered my nose, and I didn't know anything again until I found myself in this forest where the spell of his charm was broken. For the first few days, I tried to find my way out, but I was only going in circles. I gave up out of weariness and hunger. Azini found me and nursed me back to life. When I recovered and the memory of everything came back to me, I decided to remain here. For even if I could find my way back to Umueke, would it not be to put myself in Omekagu's way, since he now knows I know he killed my father?"

"Ah," Kambili cried. Now he understood the depth of Omekagu's treachery. His own injustice became insignificant. He wished he had seen the bigger picture before. Overwhelmed by the accusation against him, and the injustice of his condemnation, he had been blind to all else.

Agueze went out and returned with a basket of fruits and set it before Kambili.

"Are they not from this forest?" Kambili asked.

Agueze shrugged. "Yes. But they're better than any fruit you could get in Umueke. Here, taste and see for yourself."

Agueze held out a fruit to Kambili. Kambili collected it but did not eat it.

"These fruits are harmless, Kambili. Don't hold it as if it's poisonous."

Kambili smiled and brought the fruit to his lips. His teeth sank into the rind of the fruit and felt its cloying juice splash on his tongue and palate. He tried not to reveal how much he enjoyed the fruit.

"Come with me to my place of exile," Kambili said reflectively. "Omekagu dares not seek you there."

Agueze shook his head. "It's not just the fear of Omekagu that keeps me here. I love this place."

"This place is lovely," Kambili said, "but it is no way to live. You need to mingle in society."

"I don't need society. I get everything I need here."

"What if you are sick? Who will take care of you?"

"I haven't been sick here."

"Well," Kambili pressed on. "You'll need companionship."

"No."

"Female companionship."

Agueze ruminated and then shook his head. "I don't need any companionship."

Kambili threw his hands in the air. "The society needs you."

"Hasn't the society got along without me? Umueke thought I was dead, but did it stop moving?"

Kambili noticed bitterness in Agueze that was beyond the words he said and stopped trying to convince him. After all, had he himself not found comfort in exile? He wanted to tell Kambili about the disappointment of Omekagu by the ancestral spirit. Perhaps there was a sign in that. But just then, a voice called from outside.

"Agueze!"

It was Azini's voice. Kambili recognized it, for it carried a distinctness that only the passage of time could have conferred.

"Has the one who seeks the way to the land of the ancestors departed?"

"No," Agueze answered. "He is here."

"Let him come forth."

Kambili followed Agueze out. Azini stood almost erect, and Kambili saw a defect in the creature which he had not noticed before. It had no sexual organ.

"Do you still wish to be shown the way to the land of the ancestors?" Azini asked.

"Yes," Kambili said, though his desire for it had greatly diminished.

"Come with me then."

Kambili returned to Agueze's groove and brought his sword.

"You cannot go to the land of the ancestors with your sword," Azini said.

Kambili's temper rose, but he shut his eyes until he became calm. Then he returned his sword to Agueze's groove and came back to Azini.

"I'm ready."

"Follow me."

CHAPTER THREE

They walked in silence for a long time. Azini dodged tree branches with a dexterity that marveled Kambili, hunter though he was and used to the ways of the forest. They traversed bend upon bend. In some places the light was brighter; in other places the darkness threatened to shut out what little light entered the forest. But Azini's sight, like his steps, had been trained in this forest, and when Kambili could not see, he merely followed Azini like a lost hunter following the lead of his dog.

Suddenly, Azini paused and Kambili bumped against it. It drew Kambili behind a tree and motioned him to keep still. Then it extended its head and looked out into the vast rows of trees in which Kambili could make out nothing except the outlines of trees. Try as he could, Kambili could see or hear nothing. But prudence prevented him from questioning Azini, even if he needed an answer: the rabbit's instinct in the bush would not serve it in a water pond.

At last, Azini motioned him out of hiding, and they continued walking.

"He is always on the prowl," Azini muttered. "We would have had a hard time escaping him if he had sniffed us."

"What are you talking about?" Kambili asked, seeing that Azini was not talking wholly to himself.

"Did you not see him?"

"See who?"

"That was Uwizi going for his hunt."

"What is there to hunt here?"

"Animals," Azini said matter-of-factly.

"What animals? There are no animals in this forest!"

Azini turned incredulously to Kambili. "This forest teems with animals, fair and foul. But Uwizi hunts only the most dangerous, and that includes humans."

Kambili shut the mouth he had opened to ask questions. For it dawned on him then that there were things in this forest he could not see which Azini could see. It disconcerted him. He felt vulnerable and unsettled that he would have to rely not only on the instinct of this creature, but also on its wisdom to manage a situation as it had done a moment ago.

"What is her name?" Azini asked at length.

Kambili, thinking that Azini was conversing with an unseen being, became wary and waited for its instruction. But Azini was looking at Kambili.

"You do not wish to talk about her?"

"Who?"

"The lady whom you seek."

"Oh." Kambili sighed. "Her name is Lebechi."

Azini was silent as if it had not heard. After a while, it said, "Do you love her so much?"

Kambili was taken aback by the question, and the tenderness with which it was asked. He did not answer. What could he tell this creature about love that it would understand? He almost felt it an insult to talk about Lebechi with this creature.

"Does it give you pain to talk about her?"

"No, it doesn't give me pain," he said. But his soul asked, *Doesn't it?* And he could not honestly answer. "I love her," he muttered, as if defending himself against an accusation of unfaithfulness.

"Would you die for her?"

Kambili paused in his track. It seemed to him that some strange forces had taken over his senses, so that he could now hold discussion with inhuman beings. He had heard stories of those seduced by strange powers into talking with stones and claims that the stones replied to them. Might this not be the case with him? And now he began to doubt not only this creature, but Agueze who had led him to it. Could they all not be entrapment of the forces in this forest to seduce him?

"I do not blame you if you wish to die for her. Sometimes it is wiser to die loving than to live while the loved one is taken away. That is why I have come to take you to the land of the ancestors. If you die trying to find her, your soul will know the peace that you would not know if you live without finding her."

Now Kambili was disturbed, not by these words that even the wisest of men would not deny their wisdom, but by the implicit threat in it. Perhaps this creature had been leading him all along to his doom, and knew of it besides? Kambili wanted Lebechi back, but he had not contemplated sacrificing himself to rescue her. The prospect gave him pause. Lebechi. Her image grew blurry in his mind, and he could not see her face when he tried.

"Far better would it have been for me to have died for mine than to have lived this long without her!" Azini exclaimed suddenly. His voice trembled and Kambili stepped back, at a loss as to what to make of this paroxysm.

"But I was not allowed to die," Azini continued, shaking its head and looking as if Kambili was not there at all. "He took a woman promised to me because he was king. How could I not see her because she was in another man's house? For seeking what was mine, the king had me dismembered and banished from the land of men with curses on my head. O, my Uniwi!" Azini, quite overcome, paused until it recollected itself. "Far better will it be for you to die seeking her than to live knowing someone else has her!"

It said no more words on the subject, and when Kambili asked for further explanation about the lady of its adoration, it turned on him as if it had no idea what he was talking about. Then Kambili recalled Agueze's caution and contented himself with what he had heard. Yes, Azini had been a human. It suddenly occurred to Kambili that for all the incongruities between them, he shared a kindred sorrow with this creature. Does it matter that it might not understand the love he had for Lebechi? Might each creature not be allowed to love in its own way, and the love not be less intense for all that?

Just as Kambili was beginning to wonder if their wandering in this forest would ever come to an end, Azini halted before a very dense part of the forest. There were no trees visible, just darkness. Azini stood staring into the darkness. Kambili stared from Azini to the darkness, wondering what he saw, wondering what he was waiting for.

"This is where I leave you. When that spirit leaves the junction, sneak in and seek your lady. May you have the luck that I did not have." So saying, Azini turned to walk away.

Kambili held it back. "What spirit are you talking about?"

"Can you not see the spirit walking away now?" Azini said somewhat angrily, pointing at the darkness. "Wait until he is far gone. He keeps watch over this entrance, and he can see the living."

"I can't see any spirit or anything!" Kambili said in a panic of confusion.

Azini looked up at Kambili in annoyance. It paced about, then stopped and said, "Wait here for me. I will be back to make you see."

Time passed and Azini did not return. Sometimes it seemed to Kambili that darkness from without was coming upon the forest. But he was no longer sure of anything. Everything might just be a dream from which he would wake up and find himself staring at the thatch of his house.

He looked about impatiently, unwilling to admit to himself how much he had come to rely on his strange companion. Now in its absence, the forest acquired an eeriness that he had not noticed when he entered it alone. Every now and then he seemed to hear some cackling sound from behind, and above, and sometimes below. He would turn sharply but be confronted with only silence. He began to doubt his own sanity.

There came a surge of indefinable power from the darkness in which Azini had directed him to watch. It was like a whirl of wind, and he had felt not a push, but a coldness that manifested in terror rather than in chilliness. His head swelled and became almost too big for his shoulders to carry. His eyes grew dim, the whole forest seemed to whirl around him, and the dense leaves were like claws reaching out to grab him. He swayed but did not fall; it seemed as if the force which tossed him about also held him from falling. He shut his eyes to take refuge in the darkness.

A moment later, he felt a violent shake and opened his eyes with a scream. Azini stood before him, and for a brief moment, Kambili forgot their acquaintance and thought it was a manifestation of the terror in his heart.

"Here," Azini said, holding up kola-sized nut to Kambili. "Swallow it. Do not chew it."

Kambili collected the nut. "What is it?"

"Just swallow it. You shall understand."

Somehow, Kambili did not think this creature could mean to give him something poisonous, when all it need do to torture him was simply abandon him. He swallowed the nut, and instantly his body felt lighter, almost weightless on the ground.

Azini was mashing some leaves in its palm, and when the leaves had been reduced to pulp, it turned to Kambili and said, "Open your eyes."

Kambili did as he was bid. Azini squeezed the liquid from the mashed leaves into Kambili's eyes. For a while, Kambili was sure that his worst fear had been realized: he had become blind through Azini's treachery. He could not see anything even though his eyes were wide open. But suddenly, he saw through the vista of the erstwhile darkness, not the ancestral forest, but a sun-suffused field and trees and grasses and houses in the distances.

"You may go now," Azini said. "May luck attend your quest."

"Will you not come with me?" Kambili pleaded. Although the land upon which he now looked seemed to hold no terror, he could not bear to part from Azini, for it occurred to him that he had no direction in his quest without Azini.

Azini stood hesitantly, looking distressed. "I wish to come with you, but I fear what I will find there."

Kambili noticed the sadness and the desire in its voice and pleaded with it until Azini consented to accompany him. Together they stepped into the land of the ancestors, and the forest behind them disappeared, as if it was never there.

...❖...

In the land of the ancestors, the noon was far spent, but the sun was still somewhat strong. Kambili was enthralled, like a previously sighted man who had just regained his sight from temporary blindness; the sense of familiarity with things previously known came upon him like a sojourner at his homecoming. And then he began to discern that the things he saw now were not entirely different from things he already knew.

"The land of the ancestors is like the land of the living!" Kambili exclaimed.

"Is this how the land of the living now looks?" Azini asked.

"Of course," Kambili said. His heart bounded like a child's, and he did not notice the note of sadness in Azini's voice.

"The land of the living was different in my time," Azini said. "There were more trees and fewer paths." He glanced around and sniffed. "The grasses were less tender than these ones. The air carried more smell of fruits and grasses. The land of the living must have changed a lot, if this is how it now looks."

Kambili had been listening with half attention, for he saw not far from them a spirit with a hoe hanging on his shoulder. With the instinct of a trespasser, Kambili quickly ducked into the nearby brush and beckoned Azini to do the same. But Azini drew him out, shaking its head.

"They cannot see us," Azini said. "Only a few of them can see a living person. When they do see you, they will be the one to run away, because to them you will look like a ghost."

As if in confirmation of Azini's words, the spirit walked past them without as much as looking in their direction. Kambili was puzzled but fascinated.

They came to a small playground where several spirits sat on bamboo benches, displaying their wares of groundnuts and orange on raffia trays. When Kambili's eye fell on the tree in the playground, he recognized the playground. He knew this place!

"This is not the land of the ancestors!" Kambili exclaimed. "This is my grandmother's village!"

Azini shook his head, more in disappointment than in refutation. "Everything you have in the land of the living you also have in the land of the spirits. Only the people are different."

And then Kambili looked past the generality of the people in the playground and saw them individually. He knew some of them—they had all died. Yet they looked no different here than he had known them back in the land of the living. As he saw more and more familiar faces, it occurred to him that if all these spirits were those who had died in the world of the living, he could find his grandmother among them. So he reached out to one of the spirits and asked for his grandmother.

The spirit did not acknowledge him.

"Did I not tell you that they cannot see or hear you?" Azini said. "If you want them to see you, I have something you must swallow and focus your mind to the spirit sense. But I do not counsel that you do it now. Practicing it on the spot can lead to swapping of worlds, and you may get trapped in an evil region that you cannot escape."

Kambili asked no further questions. They walked on. Every now and then spirits of people he had known would walk past him without acknowledging him. He soon got used to the sense of his own incorporeality in their world.

The day lengthened. The sun waned and eventide beckoned. But they had not seen what they sought, and Kambili had no idea where to look. The vastness of the land of the spirits appalled him. He had thought it would be like a hall in which all the ancestors would be gathered as to a feast. But now it occurred to him that he and Azini might wander endlessly, without coming nearer to achieving their aim than they were at their moment of entering here.

He tabled his concern to Azini. Azini made no reply, but he could see it reflecting on his words.

After a while, Azini said, "Let us go to her. Perhaps she can help us."

Kambili did not understand, but he nodded and followed.

Azini stopped and studied the environment, then turned on a path, and they walked for a long time, passing by houses and farmlands and spirits. At last, they came to a large settlement. Azini suddenly halted and stood looking at a tree in the nearby bush.

Kambili followed his eyes, wondering what it saw on the tree. Azini did not stir for a long time. Then Kambili noticed that it was not merely looking at the tree. Tears had begun to trickle from its two eyes while his forehead eye was fixed on the tree. Kambili resisted the urge to rouse it. He stood watching Azini until it regained control of itself.

"They caught us under that tree," Azini said. "Meddlesome guards!"

No sooner had they left the spot than they came within sight of a large, fenced compound with several buildings inside. Here, Azini halted again. But there was no sorrow on its face, just a curiosity that seemed bent on being satisfied. It looked from side to side, sometimes on tiptoe. Sometimes a light came to its eyes on some movement in the compound, but the light would quickly fade when it did not see what it expected. Yet Azini continued watching.

Kambili grew impatient.

"This is the compound of the man who took her from me."

"Who?"

"Uniwi."

Kambili heard the tremor in Azini's voice and understood.

Azini began to sing. Kambili did not understand the words, but its song carried sadness. Kambili looked at the direction in which Azini directed his face and saw a procession of three women. The one in the middle was taller than the other two. Azini was beckoning to her, but she seemed not to see them. Yet her attention was in their direction.

Kambili caught Uniwi in Azini's song and knew her immediately. Each time it mentioned her name, she would dart her eyes about. After a while, she motioned to the two women with her, and they returned to the compound where they had come from. The woman now started coming in their direction, staring left and right as she came. As she approached, Azini retreated behind the tree at which he had been staring a moment ago.

She walked past Kambili without showing any sign that he was there. As she rounded the tree, she yelled out, and Kambili saw Azini holding its fingers to its lips. She did not shout again. A stream of animated discussion passed between them in which Kambili caught only some words. Kambili turned away, knowing he was not supposed to listen. After a long time of not hearing anything from them, he looked again, and saw them locked in an embrace.

Kambili watched with more wonder than admiration. He could not believe that any woman would give her bosom to Azini for an embrace, much less a woman of her class. She was handsome and exuded royalty. Then he recalled that Azini had said she was married to a king. So here was a queen in the arms of Azini, a creature which Kambili would have speared without the least hesitance a moment ago.

Somehow it made him wish for his Lebechi. Not that he envied Azini, but if this woman here could be reconciled with this creature, why should he not be reconciled with his Lebechi?

Presently, Azini came out and beckoned him to join them. Kambili followed. He saw the woman's eyes on him and greeted her, but she made no answer. Then he noticed that she was not looking at him, but at Azini, and felt somewhat ashamed that he had greeted her and been ignored.

"I have asked her to help us find the lady you seek," Azini said to Kambili. "She needs to know everything about the ancestral spirits who took her to help in locating her."

Kambili began to explain, but Azini shushed him. "She cannot hear you." Then Azini brought out a nut from what looked like a pouch on its waist and handed it to Kambili. "Put that in your mouth. Do not chew it. You can talk now, and she will hear you."

Kambili did as he was bid. He explained all he knew about the ancestral spirits who had taken Lebechi, which was not much. She was silent for some time after his explanation. Then she exchanged some words with Azini.

"We shall go with her to where she thinks the one you seek might be held," Azini said. "But we shall wait for her here to bring her chariot."

They waited as she returned to her compound and came back with a chariot, driven by herself. Kambili and Azini mounted on the rear seat, and the chariot galloped away like a bird in flight. Trees and houses flew past them, and Kambili could hardly see things before they had whizzed past them. At last, they came to a walled compound, and Uniwi came down and whispered to Azini, then walked toward the compound.

Evening had come at last. The sun was no longer in the sky, and the daylight had begun to ebb. Several spirits were going and coming on the wide path. Kambili had gotten used to his invisibility, so he often looked right into the eyes of any spirit he fancied. Most of the spirits were old, but every now and then, a young male or female spirit would walk past. Most of these young spirits carried bitter expressions. Kambili was puzzled that these who should be most happy were the saddest. Then he realized that they had been cut off from the world of the living before their time. Perhaps it was not so pleasant to them here after all. But—Kambili thought—who is ever happy with his lot?

Kambili saw his father with his tapping rope and palm-wine gourds, walking with his head bent to the ground, and whistling his usual song. Kambili jumped out and ran toward his father. His father walked past without noticing him. He called after him, but his father continued walking without a change in pace, whistling. Kambili stood like a man whose lover had abandoned him at their site of tryst.

As he stood staring at the diminishing figure of his father, a spirit with a basket on her head approached him and fixed him with her gaze. Kambili saw her, but thinking she was looking at something behind him, ignored her.

She suddenly yelled—"Run! It's a human!" And casting her basket aside, she ran like a hare. A few other spirits ran with her. But some walked boldly forward, looking left and right for what had provoked her yelling, and seeing none—though some nearly stepped on Kambili—they continued on their way.

At last, Kambili spotted Uniwi in the distance, and with her, Lebechi. His heart started. He stood coyly, like a groom awaiting the handing over of his first bride.

Lebechi stopped and stared at Kambili so fixedly that Kambili began to wonder if she had been transformed into a spirit, and whether she could see him at all.

"Have you come to see me now, Kam?" she asked.

Kambili stared at her askance.

"Isn't this you, Kam?" she asked.

"Yes, it is me," he said. Relieved, he closed the remaining distance between them and held out his arm to enfold her. She turned away from his arms.

"What's wrong, Lebem?"

"What's wrong?" she repeated sarcastically. "Do you ask what is wrong after the way you left me in the world?"

"I—I didn't leave you, Lebem."

"You didn't leave me! You made me a widow before I was a bride!"

"I—Lebem."

"You didn't come for me. Night after night I waited for you. You didn't appear to me to console me. Not even in dreams. I sought you through the eyes of oracles, but you refused to appear to me. Other spirits come for those they left on earth, but you didn't come for me until I came for you. And you're asking me what is wrong? No, Kam, I'm the one to ask you what's wrong. What did I do to you, Kambili, that you abandoned me without contact?"

Kambili's confusion grew.

"Anyway, I've come here to look for you. Now that I've seen you, tell me what I did to you that you left me and refused to come to me. Tell me why you never listened to my supplications, and when I laid bread for you, you refused to eat it. When I poured wine for you, you refused to drink it. Tell me, Kam. What did I do to deserve those treatments from you?"

Kambili thought at first that she was not in earnest, but as he saw the passion in her eyes, he had no more doubts that she was determined to be answered. But what answers could he give to these absurd charges?

"Let's talk about these things later, Lebem. I've come to take you back to the world of the living."

"Take me back!" she exclaimed. "You cannot take me back, Kam! Even if you don't want me to be with you here, I'll not let you take me back to the world of the living. I see now that I've sought you here for nothing."

She turned and started walking back to the compound from which she had been brought. Kambili stood like a dried-up tree, unable to think. His eyes followed Lebechi like a caged predator watching its prey romp away to safety. His heart swelled with bitterness, and he turned away from her receding footsteps, wiping the frustration from his forehead.

"Will you not go after her?" Azini asked.

"She hates me now," he said, not turning.

"She does not hate you," Azini said. "But she does not understand you. Go and make her understand."

Kambili shook his head. "She understands me. It is I who don't understand her." Noticing the look of pity on Azini's face, Kambili smiled and said, "Let us go. I have seen her, and she doesn't wish to return with me."

Then Kambili walked to the chariot and stood beside it. But neither Azini nor its lover came. He knew they must be having their own discussion and did not wish to disturb them. He waited until he no longer knew why he was waiting or what he was waiting for.

He was numbed to the flow of sorrow. Denial had not yet thawed his sorrow at her betrayal. Betrayal? He hardly knew what to call it. His head was unfocused. Her words came to him as if she was standing inside his head addressing him, yet he could not understand her.

This is not my Lebechi. This cannot be my Lebechi. What had so turned her against me? Doesn't it matter to her that I sought her here? Would she rather be here than with me? I don't understand her at all.

He heard footsteps behind and thought Azini and its lover were ready for their departure. But when he looked, he saw Uniwi holding Lebechi, and coming toward him. He watched with resignation, knowing that Lebechi had come to say some words she had left unsaid. He was ready for anything. A ram tethered to the shrine has no more fear of the butchering knife.

"You're alive, Kambili?" Lebechi said, examining him with her bristling eyes.

"Yes, I am alive," Kambili said. But his heart doubted the truth of his answer.

"I thought you were dead! Why didn't you tell me?"

She threw herself in his arms and held him tight. Kambili closed his eyes to the familiar feel of her body against his, hoping not to wake up. Questions quavered in his mouth, unasked. He could not afford to upset this moment. It was better for him to wallow in ignorance than to seek any answer that would contradict this moment.

The lovers were still in each other's arm when three spirits emerged from the compound from which Lebechi had been brought and charged in their direction. Azini alerted the lovers and they jumped into the chariot. The chariot sped off as the three spirits and the darkening night pursued after them.

"Who are they?" Kambili asked.

"They are my instructors," Lebechi replied. "The Great Python assigned them to me."

CHAPTER FOUR

At last, they came to the portal into the ancestral forest. The night had closed in. Kambili and Lebechi came down from Uniwi's chariot and waited for Azini to lead the way. But Azini tarried behind, talking with Uniwi.

"I cannot come with you," Uniwi was saying.

"Will you part from me even now?" Azini asked pleadingly.

"I cannot risk his anger."

"What more can he do to you? You were for him while he lived!"

"I am for him even now."

"O, Uniwi, will you be forever his, and not mine at all? Can you not remember those days at the stream and the vows we took and the promises we made?"

"I do not want to remember, Azini."

"It is well for you not to remember. But I cannot forget. How can I not remember those melodies you sang for me? How can I not remember how we danced under the moon? How can I not remember how we played on the farm, and you pelted me with cakes of mud? It is well for you to forget, because you have lived other lives, but for me there has been no life save the one I lived with you. In the thousand and odd years that have passed on me without you, those memories are what kept me from despair. I cannot forget, Uniwi, though eternity passed over my head."

Uniwi made no reply.

"Do you love me no more, Uniwi?"

"Do not talk to me of love, Azini," she said in tremulous voice. "For how long shall I hold on to love?"

"Has your heart finally let go of me, Uniwi? Have you found forgetfulness in his arms?"

"Do not talk to me of forgetfulness, Azini! You do not know how much I have suffered, and still suffer—because I cannot forget or let go! You do not know how lucky you are, that you can live with our memory untainted and unharassed. But alas, not so for me! The last I lived was the day I was in your arms, before the stone eyes of his cruel messengers caught us. Ever since, I dared not think of you while I was in his arms, for in his sorcery he could read the thoughts in my head. Talk to me about forgetfulness, Azini! Yes, I have learnt to forget—and you should be glad you never had to learn that!"

"Forgive me, Uniwi. But how can I know what lies in your breast when you left my messages unanswered? Time after time, my parrots returned to me with silence on their beaks. But now, Uniwi, come with me, and you shall be forever away from the reach of his eyes. I know a place where he cannot come."

"You do not know him, Azini. His curses can go where his feet cannot."

"What matter his curses, Uniwi? Have I not endured his curses for a thousand years? And yet I do not complain, because I have our memories. Can we not live together under his curses?"

There came a flash of light from the portal and an infernal neigh boomed forth. A spirit on a huge, six-legged beast bounded into the land of the ancestors, his hunting dogs beside him, and his games hanging on the rump of the beast he rode. He held a long torch whose flame were blue white, like bellow fire. Azini dashed at Kambili and Lebechi, and led them into hiding.

"It is Uwizi," Azini said. "He has returned from his hunting."

Uwizi glanced briefly at Uniwi's chariot and continued. The beast on which he rode walked slowly, as if it had tired out. The dogs trudged beside it.

"You must go now," Uniwi said. "The portal will soon be locked now that Uwizi has returned."

They hastened to the portal, and Azini gave Kambili and Lebechi nuts to swallow. Then it turned on Uniwi who had been standing watching them. "Will you not come with me?"

"Do not ask the impossible of me, Azini! Do not ask what I cannot give!"

"O, Uniwi—how can our body refuse when our heart has given?"

Uniwi made no reply, and Azini followed Kambili and Lebechi into the yawning forest of the ancestors. The darkness of the forest swallowed them, and the land of the ancestors disappeared as if it was never there.

While they groped in the darkness, Azini said, "Wait for me a while. I shall be back to lead you where you can find your way to the land of the living."

There was a note of sadness in Azini's voice that Kambili had not noticed before. After a moment of its disappearance, Kambili's keen ears picked Azini's soft sobs. He shook his head as if to shake off what he had heard. He could not bear other men's sorrows.

Lebechi, resting on him, asked, "Where have you been all this time that I thought you were dead?"

"I'll tell you when we get home, Lebem."

Kambili was in no mood to discuss the circumstances of his exile. He had wished for a day like this when she would be in his arms, and he would tell her all. But now he wondered what he had to tell her. He wondered what he had tormented himself for. His mind could not unsee those moments she was with Omekagu, and the smile she had given him, and the way she had held Omekagu's hand.

"Tell me, Lebechi. Would you have Omekagu?"

"How can you ask me that, Kam?"

"Answer me, Lebechi. I can bear any truth. Would you have him if I released you from your oath to me?"

"O, Kam! What a ridiculous thing to ask me! You don't know how I pined for you even when I thought you were dead! How can you ask me if I can leave you now that I have you with me?"

Kambili sighed. "I saw you in the village square with Omekagu."

"Yes, I was his chosen maiden."

"You were happy with him?"

"No, Kam. I wasn't happy with him."

"I saw you smiling and holding his hand."

"O, Kam! I was only trying to get him to grant my request."

"What request?"

"I asked him to plead with the ancestral spirits to take me with them to the land of the spirits, so that I could search for you."

"To search for me?"

"Yes."

"He let you come to search for me?"

"He wanted to marry me. You know how he has been pestering me. He somehow got to my parents, so they too wanted me to marry him. But I told him I can't marry him, because I had a covenant with you which I can only break when I meet you, and you have refused to come to me. So I told him to plead with the spirits to take me to you."

"You were there to break your covenant with me so you can marry him?"

"No! How can you think that? I came because sooner or later, I would be forced to marry him. I would rather be with you in the spirit world than with him. And you know I couldn't take my life to be with you, because I would be trapped in the realm of the evil spirits and wouldn't see you. So, I had to trick him into sending me here."

Kambili was stunned into silence. As her words sank into his mind, he could not look her in the face, for he knew she would see into his heart. And what would she find there? He trembled at the inconstancy of his affection.

"Let us go now," Azini said.

Kambili scrambled to his feet, grateful for the interruption.

"Won't you help me up?" Lebechi asked.

He took her hand and felt unworthy to hold it.

...❖...

They marched on in silence and in darkness, Kambili holding Lebechi's hand while they followed Azini's footsteps. Azini seemed to see as well in the darkness as in daylight.

They began to hear voices and the pattering of feet. The voices echoed strangely in the forest, bouncing on the leaves, like words spoken into abandoned tunnels. There followed flashes of light in different parts of the forest.

"Wait for me here," Azini said. "Let me find out what is happening."

Kambili felt naked at Azini's departure. Lebechi clutched at him and pressed her body against him, seeking assurance. But Kambili knew he had none to give. In this forest he could offer no one protection. The most he could do was to surrender himself to be taken before she would be taken. He, a warrior and hunter of Umueke, had become dreadful in a forest.

Suddenly, Azini's voice came at them in startling clarity. "Run! Run! Run!"

Kambili held Lebechi's trembling hand and staggered as he tried to find which way to take. In the darkness, they did not know what they were running from, or which direction to run to. While they groped and stumbled, they were surrounded by torches. The torches converged around them, but Kambili could not make out anything behind the lights.

"Kambili?" a voice asked from among the torchbearers.

Kambili stared more intensely, trying to make out the face of the voice that had spoken to him, for it sounded familiar.

"It's him!" the same voice repeated.

"The gods be praised!" several voices said.

And now the torches drew near and revealed some of the faces. Kambili knew them. They were warriors of Umueke, and among them was Munachi. Warmth surged into his heart.

"Thank the gods we found you before this creature did," one of the warriors said, stepping forward with his sword pointed at Azini, and his dog sniffing at it. Azini kicked and whined, but the hand that held him was strong.

"Let him be!" Kambili shouted. "He's our companion."

The warriors stared incredulously at Kambili. The warrior holding Azini did not let go, but instead thrust his sword on Azini's flesh, and he yelled out.

Almost simultaneous with Azini's yell, there came a gust of wind which shook the branches of the trees overhead and blew out some of the torches. An instant coldness came upon Kambili, and he noticed it was the same with Lebechi, for she shivered and clutched tighter to him. A whizzing sound swept around them, bouncing from leaf to leaf. And while the warriors scoured the branches with their eyes and held out their swords and arrows to shoot at whatever was coming for them, there arose as from the earth a soft arc of light.

The dog ran toward the light, barking. The advancing light stopped. The dog caught up with the light. A scuffle ensued between the dog and the light until the light lifted from the ground like flame ascending to the sky, then transformed into a woman, and returned to the earth. It was Uniwi. She was radiant, and Kambili almost did not recognize her.

She snapped her fingers at the dog, and it dashed away, barking furiously. She advanced toward them. All eyes were on her: Kambili and Lebechi out of familiarity; the warriors in curiosity and hidden dread.

Azini, taking advantage of the warrior's petrifaction, made to run towards Uniwi, but its captor interposed with his sword.

"I know you're in consort with the spirits, but if you move a step, I'll cut you in pieces!"

Uniwi held out her hands as if to shield Azini, and some of the warriors surrounded her.

"Don't hurt her," Kambili said. "She is my companion as well."

The warriors did not heed Kambili. They thought he was under her enchantment and saying whatever she had put in his head. They raised their swords to strike, but Uniwi raised her hand and suspended theirs in midair.

"I have not come for you," Uniwi said. "I have only come for him." She pointed at Azini. "Release him to me, and it shall be as if we have not encountered each other."

Azini's captor very reluctantly let go of Azini, and it ran to Uniwi and clutched tightly at her. She circled him in her arms. The warriors watched with wonderment. Kambili knew they would not understand. As Azini and Uniwi walked deeper into the forest, Kambili waved his goodbye. But the lovers did not notice it.

The warriors picked their way forward.

Munachi walked by Kambili's right, while Lebechi clutched his left hand.

"How did you find her?" Munachi asked in a whisper, as if he did not want Lebechi to hear.

Kambili pretended he had not heard Munachi. He did not wish to speak of his sojourn into the land of the ancestors. Instead, he yearned for an answer to the question that had troubled him since the appearance of the warriors.

"Have you brought them to arrest me?"

"No! Why would you think that, Kam? I brought them to find you."

"To find me, and return me to Omekagu?"

Munachi cackled and Kambili was annoyed at his frivolity over such a serious matter, for it seemed to Kambili that he was in for another treachery.

Munachi patted Kambili on the shoulder. "Something extraordinary has happened in Umueke. Omekagu is no more."

Kambili and Lebechi stopped simultaneously.

"What happened to him?" Kambili asked, unbelief in his voice.

Munachi sighed before he answered. "After the ancestral spirits departed, Omekagu claimed that the Great Python validated his election upon accepting his gift, and it was time for him to be crowned. Everyone saw him rejected, but the titled men did not question his claim, some because he had bought them over, and others because they were afraid of him. He summoned the Chief Priest to crown him. But as soon as the Chief Priest placed the crown on Omekagu's head, lightning struck the Chief Priest and he died there and then. Omekagu fell on the ground and started pleading with the gods not to torment him, that he would make his confession.

"You won't believe the things he confessed to, Kambili. Omekagu confessed to killing Agumba, his own brother! He drove Agueze out of Umueke so that the throne would come to him. When the ancestors refused to acknowledge him, he bought over the Chief Priest to crown him. The flood of twenty moons ago which carried Odibe's farm was Omekagu's doing. He confessed to a lot of other things, after which he fell foaming at the mouth until he passed away."

Kambili felt neither happy nor sad at this development. Somehow, he felt like a man who had been ignorant by design, for had he not seen some signs of these things?

"After his confession had exonerated you," Munachi continued, "I told the elders how you have been in exile, and they ordered that you should be brought home. Since I didn't know how you have fared in your search for Lebechi, I had to seek the aid of these warriors in finding you."

Kambili did not say a word for a long time after Munachi had finished speaking. He was not stunned by Omekagu's confession; the missing gaps to Omekagu's confession, Agueze had filled in. Kambili had known all along that Omekagu's heart reeked of evil, and that for such a heart, no evil deed was a surprise. But he was stunned that Omekagu had not only bought over humans to his atrocity, but also the mouthpiece of the gods. And now the gods had been stirred to justice.

The gods had not betrayed him after all; he had held his bitterness against them from sheer ignorance.

Kambili no longer believed in his own sense of right and wrong, justice and injustice. As he contemplated his actions, he could not say how much of a victim he had been, and how much of a perpetrator of injustices. And what did it matter? The one who could do injustice in his mind could do injustice with his hands when the power was granted him. Had he the power to chastise the gods, could he not have done so before he knew the truth? Was it not his justice which condemned Lebechi unheard? Was it not his justice which presumed the worst of all around him and condemned them accordingly?

"Only time reveals our errors in their odiousness," Kambili muttered to himself.

Suddenly he remembered and called on the warriors to halt.

"There is someone here we must visit," he said.

The warriors turned to him with puzzlement. They had believed the enchantment on him had been broken with the departure of his grotesque companions, but now he was talking again of someone else in this forest. Nonetheless they followed him warily. With the light of the torches, he sought Agueze's enclave. They wandered for a long time before Kambili came upon familiar trees and traced the way to Agueze's enclave. He bade the rest halt, then approached it alone, and called.

Agueze recognized his voice and answered from inside.

"Have you returned, Kam?" Agueze asked in a sleepy voice.

"Yes, I've returned."

"You didn't find her, did you?"

"I found her. Come out and see."

There was a momentary silence before Agueze came out. He stopped short when he saw the warriors with their torches.

"Who are these?" Agueze asked.

Before Kambili could answer, the warriors drew closer, for they too sought to know the identity of the person whom Kambili had summoned out of the groove. Agueze recognized the warriors before they recognized him. He looked betrayed.

"Why have you brought them here, Kambili? Didn't I tell you that I don't wish to return to Umueke?"

"You'll understand in due time. Then you'll decide whether you wish to return to Umueke or not." Turning to the warriors, he said, "This is Prince Agueze, the son of Agumba."

The warriors shined more light on Agueze's face and loud murmuring broke among them as they recognized him. They scrambled to touch and hold him. Warrior after warrior embraced him. Agueze smiled through the whole confusion, and when it was over, he called Kambili aside.

"I appreciate your bringing these people to see me. But you must tell me what is going on."

Kambili narrated to him what had transpired in Umueke and how Omekagu had been forced by higher powers out of the way. "I urge you to return to Umueke with us," Kambili ended.

Agueze shook his head reflectively. "I'll return, but not immediately."

"You don't understand why I want you to return with us, Agueze. I haven't brought these warriors here to bring you back, but if you don't return with us, they'll come back for you, now that they know you're here. I want you to return of your own will. That's a more dignified way for you to return."

"What if I don't wish to return?"

"Can't you see, Agueze? The ancestors refused to sanction Omekagu because the throne is for you! Do you think the ancestors will let the throne of Umueke remain vacant at your pleasure?"

Agueze sighed. "I can't thank you enough, Kambili, for—"

"You've nothing to thank me for," Kambili interrupted. "I'm the one beholden to you for directing me to Azini, but about that later. Go get yourself ready, and I'll tell them to wait. And remember to bring my sword along."

The party set out when Agueze emerged. Kambili trudged along in exhaustion, Lebechi leaning on him. But he was never happier to be so burdened.

The half-moon outside provided faint illumination, and as they stepped out of the ancestral forest, its silence gave way to the sound of pestles pounding on mortars, and the distant moon songs of children.

A DIFFERENT KIND OF SHOW, NOT TELL (ESSAY)

by Oghenechovwe Donald Ekpeki

It is difficult for a writer not to have heard of the ubiquitous writing advice: "Show, not tell." The aim is to use language to portray events unfolding in action rather than mere narration which inevitably results in "info-dumping."

Grand as this advice seems, it is not always practicable, and one may sometimes wisely resort to simple narration to avoid bloated writing. There is, however, a different and more dangerous kind of show, not tell in the publishing industry. It demands of the writer not simply to have good work, but to show that the writing will be accepted. Like the show, not tell of writing, this too is sometimes unworkable in publishing.

When you pitch a project to a press, you are usually asked for similar works to gauge the market viability of the work. The industry does not want to take your work solely for its merit; it wants a certain level of assurance, to see the action of how that success has been affected before in other similar works. It wants you to show, in effect, that your work can succeed by showing others like it have before.

When similar works don't exist, you will find it harder to sell the project. This show, not tell of publishing is something that disproportionately affects marginalized creators as there are fewer projects by people like them to show the viability of the current project being pitched. It then becomes a self-fulfilling prophecy. Their pitches aren't accepted when there's no precedent that they can work. And there's no precedence that the stories can work because they are never accepted.

The vicious part of this kind of technique is that it goes beyond just the work itself to the creator. So you have to not just show that the story can work, but that it can work for and from someone like you. An older writer recently regaled me with the tale of how Octavia Butler tried to put together a Black speculative fiction anthology with one of the big five, but it fell through. Whereas there were writers at the time doing just that and you could find stories about Africa, but only from white, male writers. This is but one example of how show, not tell in publishing is particularly disadvantaging to marginalized writers.

Often when the work of a marginalized writer has no heralds, it falls on the would-be creator to convince their investors to take on such a project, an immense and laborious task, but far less gruesome than the alternative, should they fail to get that.

The alternative is what is faced by many indie creators who cannot successfully get their works "greenlit" by major publishers and studios. They then have to create that work, fund it themselves, and make it a success, without the publishing apparatus and machinery or funds available to the bigger players in the industry.

Oftentimes, this will involve scaling the work down immense levels, to be something that can be managed with their limited resources. While doing this, they face the two-fold danger of succeeding with the scaled-down version, but in a way that's so far from the original concept, it seems they failed even in their success.

The second is failing altogether, and in either case, proving to the initially unwilling bodies the rightness of their prior decision in not taking the project in the first place. It is often a brutal experience that leaves marginalized creators low down, and the industry itself poorer for it.

It is a testament to how difficult being a pioneer and creating a first is, and why such pioneers are more celebrated by marginalized creators. The effort that goes into ensuring such a project lives, and not only lives, but also succeeds, is humongous because it charts a course, creates a path, and the success and chances of other preceding works getting greenlit may depend on the outcome of that one. New works are sold off the back of successful works by marginalized creators and indie creators who have to go through a vicious, uphill climb to success.

It may seem like tokenization, but this is why firsts are, and should be, even more celebrated in a world that enforces higher standards and takes fewer chances on marginalized creators. They chart the course, pave the way, and fulfill the show, not tell that exists in publishing.

The first ever *Year's Best African Speculative Fiction* anthology was published only recently, even though Year's Best anthologies have been a staple of the industry for decades. It was met with vicious opposition from troll farms, and even titans of the self-publishing industry, like Amazon KDP, Smashwords, and Draft2Digital. It had to be pulled down from those platforms, and will eventually be given out for free, after a successful GoFundMe to recoup the monies invested in it.

The system and publishing machinery is deeply inaccessible for indie and marginalized creators, especially those residing outside the West. But it is not entirely bleak. *The Africa Risen* anthology will be published this 2022 by TorDotCom, following the success of the *Dominion* anthology by two of the creators, Oghenechovwe Donald Ekpeki and Zelda Knight, in conjunction with Sheree Renee Thomas, the editor of the groundbreaking *Dark Matter* anthologies.

Not to forget the various other, to varying degrees, successful indie anthologies like the *Africanfuturism* anthology, *AfroSF*, and more. On the long fiction end, new works by marginalized writers are being picked up as well. Recently, Tordotcom Publishing announced a three-novella deal with debut author Moses Ose Utomi, the first of which will be *The Lies of the Ajungo*. Suyi Davies Okungbowa also just released *Son of the Storm*, the first book in his fantasy trilogy The Nameless Republic.

May we endeavor to support both marginalized, indie creators, and those debuting to major presses, as their important works contribute richly to creating and growing a genre tradition that allows marginalized writers to thrive. Until a time, hopefully soon, we abandon the unwieldy, unworkable show, not tell requirement in publishing, as we are starting to do in writing.

MOTHER'S LOVE, FATHER'S PLACE

by Oghenechovwe Donald Ekpeki

Bassey walked bare chested into his wife's hut, where she was being attended by the midwife and her two younger apprentices. His sweaty, gleaming muscles reflected the faint light cast by the candles in the hut. He exchanged a look with his wife then turned to the midwife.

"May I have a moment with my wife?"

"Her time is done, and she may begin to push any moment from now."

"I'll be brief," he said with suppressed impatience.

The midwife glanced at Ofonime, who every now and then mopped the sweat on her brow with the edge of her wrapper. Ofonime nodded at the midwife, who motioned to her apprentices, and the trio left the hut for husband and wife.

Bassey grumbled at the departing women. "Warriors get less and less respect these days. See what regard I get as a Captain! These missionaries of a foreign god and their acolytes are doing a great harm to our people with their gospel of peace and equality ..."

"The same missionaries advocate for the lives of twins, something that you may be interested in," she said with a pointed look.

He hesitated, then said, "Just because they seek what may"—there was heavy emphasis on the word may—"be to my advantage, doesn't make them my friends. One thing I have learnt as a warrior, is that the enemy of my enemy will not leave you surviving a long campaign. It will soon leave our entire way of life eroded, and our land sacked and looted."

"But it will get you through a long night of battle, will it not?"

He huffed at this. "And what would you know of battles and long nights?" He mused, amusement heavy in his tone.

"Am I not about to face one now, my husband? A battle *and* a long night?"

He stopped as his eyes rested on the frightened and anxious look on his wife's face. He stared at her askance. But in place of an answer, she raised two fingers at him.

"Are you sure?" he asked, hoping to be contradicted.

"I have no doubts," she said. "I have suspected it since. Now I am certain."

He was silent a moment, then he started, "That means we have to—to—"

"Eliminate one of them," she interrupted him with a choked sob.

He nodded and laid a hand on her shoulder. "We may yet cut our losses," he said. "I shall pour some money into the midwife's pocket to dispose of one but leave us with the other. That way we can circumvent the abomination and attendant consequences."

"No, no, no," Ofonime protested, shaking her head vigorously. "I shall not live to see any of them eliminated."

"The second of the twin is a child of a spirit union. It will bring nothing but destruction to us. Would you rather we are disgraced and destroyed than eliminate the abomination?"

She brought her distraught eyes to his face, looking deeply hurt. "You do believe it then, that I was unfaithful to you with a spirit? I who cannot have another man apart from you—took a spirit to my bed?"

"I don't doubt you," Bassey said. "But even then, you know the customs. Having a twin is a taboo in this land. Had we left for the Ekoi when you told me—but as a warrior and captain and member of the Ekpe fraternity, my place is here, a place of honor, with my children and family. We have everything to lose by leaving.

"No, my husband," Eso said sadly. "You have everything to lose. Your children, your family, your place." She spat that last one out. "None of it mine, at least that I would keep by allowing the killing of my child. I have given you my body. But I will not allow you to bribe the midwife to deliver and dispose of one of my children as you and your other fraternity members do."

Bassey stared at his wife.

"Do you think that we women don't talk amongst ourselves? We know this is what you do. But you'll not succeed. I will deliver both my babies."

Bassey shook his head. "The children will be taken from us, put in a pot and left in the evil forest to die. You will be exiled, at best, or killed."

"I will not sanction the killing of one of my children to escape the fate decreed by men of old Calabar. I will be exiled or die with my children if I have to."

He was quiet a moment. His next words carried more admiration than censure.

"Your love for your children is great, even if it will doom us all. Will you hold off delivery for as long as you can? I want to consult with Archibong and see what the spirits have to say."

"I will hold off delivery as much as I can. I love you, but once my children come, I owe them the duty of protection. I'll not sanction the death of any of them, even for you. If you do not value their lives do not return to us."

Bassey turned to leave. As he stepped out of the hut, the head midwife confronted him.

"Has the arrangement been made, Captain?"

"I haven't decided."

"Decide fast, for the hour is almost upon us." She spat. "It is bad enough for me to be part of bringing your cursed offspring to life, but I won't do it for free."

Bassey glared at her but kept his cool. "Do nothing foolish until I return."

...❖...

Bassey walked into the house of Archibong, the priest of Ekpe fraternity.

"My friend," Bassey saluted. "I need your services."

Archibong smiled and led him to a special alcove in his house, dropping the curtains behind them. He sat on the floor, cross-legged. Bassey sat facing him. The room was accoutred like a shrine. Lanterns and candles dotted the place, but their light only served to deepen the shadows it could not touch. The darkness clung to the walls and the sacred objects in the room. Behind them was a bowl of water from which rose steam, though there was no fire lit under it. The ghoulish features of masks and the regalia of masquerades hanging on the walls leered at them. Archibong himself had one of his eyes rounded with white chalk, and his neck and hands were loaded with cowry necklaces and hand beads.

"You were expecting me?" Bassey asked.

Archibong smiled. "Far is the sight that needs no eye to see, my friend. I see things before they manifest, be they inside a man's vestments or a woman's belly. But I suspect your affairs are far from hidden even to mundane eyes."

"They are not?" Bassey asked with glittering eyes.

"Of course. Being favored by the king makes you interesting to watch. And anyone with eyes knows the right omens to seek if he must know a woman who will bear twins."

Bassey snorted. "They may speculate and pander rumors, but they have no proof."

"And how long before the proof is born, and their rumors justified? You will do well to be swift in dispatching the cursed one. Eyes are on you. Your brother warrior and rival, Offiong, has been spying on you, and his blood is hot to displace you as the Obong Ebong title holder."

Bassey dismissed the threat with a wave of the hand. "Longer may he wait for the office. He is a toothless dog and lacks the ambition that moves men to proper action. He lacks the mettle to carry out his schemes. I do not worry about him. I worry about the fate and destiny of both my unborn children. That is why I'm here."

Archibong sighed with raised eyebrows. He hadn't missed Bassey's claiming of the children. "I hope you know what you are doing, old friend. And I hope you are right about your old rival."

The priest pulled at one of the necklaces on his neck, and it cut, spilling its beads on the floor. Archibong's eyes watched the spiritual ordering of the beads as they danced and became still. He read the cowries on the floor quietly for a moment. Bassey opened his mouth, about to demand what tidings the spirits bore for him, but Archibong's raised finger forestalled him.

"They wish to speak to you."

"Who?" Bassey said in alarm.

"Your children wish to speak to you."

Bassey was about to query the priest when the lights went out, and the room was plunged into pitch blackness. Then a faint light intruded. Bassey squinted at what appeared to be a misty dawn.

He was in a clearing. He turned about and saw a figure walking toward him. It was a sturdy young man, with a firm jaw and broad shoulders. Bassey was struck by the familiarity of the figure: it was a reflection of his younger self.

"Father," the younger man said, walking toward Bassey with a smile. "I bear the tidings of the spirits."

Bassey opened his mouth to speak, but the words stuck to his throat.

"I am our spokesperson. My sister waits in the beyond, in the waters before birth. In the forward flow of time, you accepted us both, though you yet have not decided. I come as the one you have accepted for the present."

Bassey stared solemnly at this apparition which looked so much like himself.

"What must I do, my son? What do the spirits bid me do? Do I give up the soul of the many for the one I have not chosen?"

"You have chosen, my father," the apparition said. "Just as you have been chosen. In choosing us both, you chose the many unborn twins that will be cast away in misguided sacrifice. In saving one, you will save the many. This is what the spirits bid deliver to you."

The apparition came forward and laid his hand on Bassey's chest as he tried to speak.

"Go now, my father. Save us and raise us, that we may raise you."

Bassey raised his arms to embrace his son, but his form faded into him, enveloping him in darkness. His eyes opened to the yellow flames of Archibong's room.

"Welcome back, my friend. Have you received your message?"

Bassey nodded. "I know what I must do."

Archibong nodded in understanding. Both men stood up and hugged. Archibong held Bassey at arm's length, silently taking him in. They both knew this was farewell.

...❖...

In the birthing house, the head midwife placed the second twin on Ofonime's breast, having cut the umbilical cord and cleaned it. Her disgust was evident on her face. She had held the baby at arm's length while handling it. The new mother of the twins had a glowing and relieved look on her face, despite the impending doom she anticipated. She held the babies protectively, announcing without words her willingness to die for them if need be, in defiance of the custom that declared them taboo.

She saw the disgust on the midwife's face and asked, "If you hate my children so, why did you deliver them?"

The midwife's eyes bulged, unwilling to believe that she was being questioned by one consigned to a fate less than human's.

"Your children might be spawn of evil, but I do my duty as a midwife. I leave the men to purge the evils you have brought to the land. I shall send for them immediately." So saying, she beckoned on one of her apprentices.

Ofonime pleaded with the midwife. "Please, Uwemedimoh." Ofonime called her by name, hoping to invoke mercy through familiarity. "You know us. You came for my sister's marriage ceremony and delivered her three children. We are not strangers, for you to wish to be so heartless to me. At least let their father see them first."

The midwife's brows were full of scorn. "Because I brought your cursed offspring into life does not mean I shall not do my duty of alerting the land to the curse you have brought out of your belly." She spat on the bed at Ofonime, her spittle just narrowly missing her.

Ofonime looked at her, her eyes hardening. "You didn't deliver them out of duty. You delivered them because you are too cowardly to actualize your hate. You delivered them out of greed." Ofonime held her babies closer.

The midwife's eyes fluttered in her skull, glittering doorways of evil that offered a glimpse to a dark realm beyond. Her fingers were curled like an eagle's talons, and she glared at Ofonime and her babies as if contemplating strangling them in her grip; a grip slick with wickedness. She even took a step forward but snapped out of it at the sudden wailing of one of the babies.

The midwife turned to the apprentice she had summoned. "Run to the guards and the council and inform them of the atrocity that has happened here."

But the girl had hardly left the room when she stumbled back in, shoved back by Bassey. The midwife shouted at the girl to go get the guards. She took one look at Bassey's imposing, bulky figure dwarfing the door, and stepped further back. The midwife stepped forward in anger, and Bassey's fist caught her by the throat, lifting her easily off the ground. She struggled and gasped for breath, her face turning purple as she asphyxiated. The midwife's frightened apprentices stumbled to and fro. But for Ofonime's voice calling repeatedly to Bassey, he might have killed the midwife.

There was no anger in Bassey's face, only curiosity. It seemed as if he was pondering what would happen after he had drained all the air from her body. But he let go of her and she crumpled to the floor in an unceremonious heap.

Ofonime laid the babies down and struggled to stand. Bassey rushed to assist her but was frozen in place at the sight of the babies.

"You would have killed her," Ofonime said.

"She would have killed my children and wife."

"She is not the problem. Our ways are. Killing her won't kill the problem."

"She is part of the problem and killing her will kill a part of the problem."

Ofonime shook her head. "You are a great warrior, but you are not famous for cleverness."

Ofonime bent and pulled a bunch of wrappers from under the bed, throwing them at the girls helping the midwife massage her throat. "Tie her up," she instructed them.

The girls sat staring, motionless. "Now!" Bassey barked. And they rushed to comply with his order.

Bassey turned to Ofonime. The babies were quiet, asleep. He cupped her cheeks. "I have decided. Both my children must live. They have a great destiny."

Ofonime held his hand on her cheek, breathing deeply.

Bassey continued, "But we must leave, now."

Ofonime glanced at the sleeping babies in concern.

"They will be fine," he said.

She moved to wrap them more securely.

Bassey turned to the girls, who had tied up the midwife securely. "You will stay here and guard her. You will not leave this hut till the light of dawn dots the horizon. If you do, I will find you and kill you. Do you understand me?"

They nodded in fright. Bassey and his wife and newborns slipped out of the hut.

As they stepped out, they were confronted by the figure of Ukeme, Bassey's second wife. The trio froze, staring at each other without speaking. Bassey gripped his slipping spear tighter, as his palm was slick with sweat.

Ukeme spoke first, her eyes narrowing. "I knew what you were up to. I just wanted to see with my own eyes, you abandoning us to abscond with her," she said this with a glare at Ofonime, who dropped her eyes. "We were always nice to you, I and Mama Nkeme. Now you repay us by stealing our husband."

Bassey sighed, taking her hand and pulling her aside. "I am a warrior, not an object. She's not stealing me. She's trying to live, with her children. And she can't without me."

Ukeme folded her arms, not placated. "You have been a good father thus far. A good father and husband. Now you abandon your other wives and children and place here."

Bassey sighed. Ukeme whistled, and a young lad came forward from the shadows where he had been standing. A boy of about five years. The boy walked up to Bassey, then seeing, rushed toward and embraced him. Bassey bent to hug him. "Your youngest. He dotes on you. Wants to be a warrior like you when he grows. You would leave him without even a goodbye?"

Bassey held the boy back at arm's length. "My son, part of being a warrior is knowing the right and most needed battles to fight. Someday when you grow up, if I have done my job half as well as your mother says, you will understand this. Okay?"

The boy nodded solemnly, trusting in his father's wisdom, and he went to his mother who beckoned.

Bassey looked at his second wife and formerly youngest son. "You will both be fine. He has his mother. And you have the rest of the town."

Ukeme was silent for a while, then she nodded. "Go be a good father, my husband." She nodded at Ofonime too, who smiled gratefully. "Farewell, my husband. I never saw you tonight." Having said that, she took her son's hand and faded into the night. Bassey and Ofonime, with their twin babies, did the same.

...❖...

They made their way out of town with Ofonime carrying the two children, swaddled safely in blankets, and shuffling after Bassey, who led the way with a spear clutched in his hand. He peered in every direction.

"Perhaps you could let go of the spear and hold one of your children," she said.

"We are not past the danger yet," he sneered. "My enemies shadow me, and I must be on the alert. I told you my rival Offiong will seek me and try to disgrace me for my place of honor with the king and in the Ekpe confraternity. It is not enough for me to just leave."

"Men and their rivalry. If only you left me and my children out of it," she grumbled.

"Be quiet, woman. Haven't I given up enough? My place, for you and your children, and chosen a life of exile?"

"How gracious of you," she muttered, ensuring he did not hear her.

Bassey continued talking. "A boat is waiting for us by the river to take us to the Ekoi, where twins are celebrated."

Ofonime was silent. Her husband seemed to have it all worked out, except that he had not considered the plight of carrying newborns just hours after a rigorous labor.

Bassey stopped suddenly. She looked askance at him, distraught.

"Keep going," he said. "When you get to the river, you will find someone to paddle the boat and bear you away, if I don't join you on time." He forestalled her protests with a kiss. "You have done your part. Let me do mine." He shoved her gently.

She trotted away, looking back at him as she went. He didn't look back. He stood facing the other direction as the sound of footsteps became clearer. A group of men emerged from the night, spat out of the shadows by the envy of Offiong. He and about a dozen men approached. They stopped when they saw Bassey waiting with his spear extended in a stance of ready combat.

They approached cautiously. Bassey motioned toward the direction they just came from, and they looked up at the sky to see a plume of smoke rising from the direction of the palace.

Offiong stepped forward. "What have you done, traitor?"

"You didn't think I wouldn't cover my escape, did you? I started a fire at the palace before I left. And I have people waiting to ambush and kill the king in the chaos. He will die, along with your hopes and wishes for power. Perhaps the new king won't be so disposed to favor the warriors that failed the prior one."

Offiong spluttered in anger. "You're mad, you traitor!" He motioned to his men. "Rush to the palace to warn the king of an ambush. I will kill this traitor myself and drag his wife back to burn with his cursed evil spawn."

The men started to rush back the way they came as Offiong unslung his cutlass.

"I might have merely maimed you and let you leave if you had left my wife and children out of it."

Bassey's eyes glittered as Offiong came for him. Offiong rushed forward with a snarl and slashed at Bassey, who sidestepped his swing smoothly, and swept Offiong off his feet with the haft of the spear. In one smooth motion, he planted the sharp end into Offiong's gut as he fell, pinning him to the earth. Offiong groaned and struggled.

Bassey plunged the spear further through Offiong and into the soft earth. "Stay on the ground where you belong, vile serpent. You will be a long time dying."

Offiong was grinning even in his pain. Blood burbled from his lips as he struggled to talk. "I have sent men to the boats. Your escape is cut off. I win …"

Bassey turned back in shock. He pulled the spear from Offiong's gut and ran after his wife. Offiong's wheezing laughter combined with his blubbering and tears of pain. The sound chased Bassey onward.

…❖…

Bassey and Ofonime walked on in the night. He had discarded his spear now and carried one of the twins while his wife carried the other.

"Offiong might as well have killed us rather than simply cut off our escape," Ofonime said. "We are doomed to be inevitably found and worse would befall us."

"We shall triumph," Bassey said simply.

"How? Where do we go now?"

"The forest," he answered.

"What?" she exclaimed. "The evil forest? The same forest where monsters and evil spirits devour twins doomed by the people of the land?"

"May I have peace, woman," Bassey said wearily. "There is a path through the forest. Through it we can make our way to the Ekoi."

"If we don't all die there," Ofonime grumbled.

"I did not leave Old Calabar only to come and die here."

As they plunged into the forest, she trembled at the thought of the numerous twins who had been brought here to die and whose souls were left here to languish.

…❖…

King Eyo stood in front of the smoking ruins of his palace.

"We will find the traitor, your majesty," the king's adviser said.

"No!" the king barked. "Haven't you shed blood enough? Let him be. What has happened was bound to happen. Unless we change our way, I foresee more woes to come."

"But it is our custom," protested the adviser. "Twins have always been taboo. It is the law that they be put to death and Bassey committed—"

The king raised his finger, and his adviser stopped talking.

"Send for the chiefs," King Eyo said. "I have some strong words to pass to all and sundry under my domain. A culture which has outlived its use is dispatched with a bad year."

…❖…

Bassey's hand found Ofonime's free hand as they plunged into the darkness of the forest. He nodded to her reassuringly. The darkness swallowed them. As they were sucked into the darkness, it opened suddenly to a vista of light. They found themselves in a glade filled with light and laughter and running water. Children of varying ages played in the glade.

"Are we dead and have come to the land of our ancestors?" Bassey asked.

"You have been unborn," a voice said to them. They followed the voice, and Bassey realized that it was the young man he had encountered in the vision at Archibong's. His son. Ofonime looked askance. She peered at the young man curiously. It was as though she was looking at a younger copy of her husband.

"Welcome, mother," he said, smiling.

She gasped. "How?" she started to ask, at the same time feeling the burden on her hand. Bassey felt this too. Husband and wife held empty cloth bundles where they had each held a child.

Another figure walked forward, a girl identical to the boy, the same height and age.

"Welcome, father and mother," she said. She looked shyly at her father. "I could not show myself till now."

The parents stared at them, surprised.

"Follow us," the twins said in chorus.

"I will take you to the great spirit who rules this place," the young man said. "It is a place of unbirth where the souls of unborn children dwell before they are born. It was created to save the souls of rejected twins and return them to their unborn state before they find worthy parents. We were chosen to be guardians. That is why the flow of time is different for us. The Great Spirit will decide if we can keep you here with us as it seems you have been exiled from your people on our account."

Bassey finally found his voice. "What qualifies us to stay?"

"Mother is already qualified by her love. Mothers are allowed to see the spirits of their children before they pass. It is the privilege for their great sacrifice of love. As for you, father, we shall need to convince the great spirit of your place here."

They walked into the Great Spirit's den, and the light swallowed them.

O_2 ARENA

by Oghenechovwe Donald Ekpeki

"Where there is no inner freedom, there is no life."

—RADHANATH SWAMI

My sweat ran in rivulets, caught between my skin and the Lycra bodysuit. It slid down my spine and chest as I regarded my enemy with detached exhaustion. Though my vision was hazy, my focus was sharp. My intention: to do murder, even a murder sanctioned and abetted by the same system that was slowly killing us all.

The man in front of me paced, fatigue showing plainly in his bearing. My body was depleted of the energy needed to carry it, and my breathing came in short, gulping gasps as I inhaled the bittersweet air. Bitter because it reeked of my own possible—no, likely—death, and sweet because of its purpose: winning a life for another, one far more deserving of it than I was. I breathed in that sweetness as if it was a promise, a sustenance of a selfish love, which, to me, was everything.

I knew my opponent was not my enemy, although he might be the instrument of my death, or I the instrument of his. The one I truly needed to defeat, our collective enemy, was unflagging: the society that broke us and engineered our existence as an inexorable journey toward death. Quick or slow, the system forced us into a profound lifelessness just so we could breathe one more day, then yet another.

I was at the arena for the second time, of my own accord, but in a trap by the society to which I had been born.

My opponent shuffled forward, all the humor bleached out of the desperate grin he wore plastered on his frozen features. A snarl spread across my own face, and I rushed at him to take life if I could, that I may cherish and gift it to another.

A small part of me whimpered and briefly wondered at the monster I had become.

...❖...

A few months earlier ...

The chattering in the hall faded as the speaker mounted the podium. Four thousand of us fell silent as he removed his O_2 mask and began our induction into the Academy of Laws. The Head of the Department (HoD) of Property Law proceeded to tell us why we were here.

I shook my head ruefully. In the Nigeria of 2030, people still insisted on telling others their purpose, as though we did not know or could not decide for ourselves. Cursed was the one with their own will and individuality, and woe unto them if they aspired to more than the O_2 credits needed to keep them breathing.

What was our daily reality? You had to pay to breathe. Since the global warming crisis had affected phytoplankton and hampered the production of breathable air, our lives were our own to maintain at the requisite cost.

Plodding along, the HoD explained to us that we were amongst the chosen few privileged to earn the Bachelor of Laws (LL.B) degree. Having studied for five years to obtain an LL.B degree, and having passed a very difficult entrance exam to be admitted to the Academy of Laws, one wondered where the "privilege" came from. Here we had to survive a rigorous, nearly militaristic regimen of study and indoctrination, and only then would we be allowed to take the almighty Bar exam.

I couldn't help thinking that if I had wanted to show off superhuman stamina, I would have joined the army. Then I reminded myself that I wasn't here by choice. It was the Bar that would usher me into my position in the corrupt system where I could earn the kind of O_2 allowances that would quash my CO_2s. It would be a herculean journey, not helped by these pompous men making it seem like a grand privilege.

The HoD's talk prompted several students, naïve in my opinion, to ask about our rights. He informed them, almost scathingly, that they had no rights.

I inwardly shrugged. I would sort it out the way I sorted everything. Succeeding was all that was required. It didn't matter how.

The HoD introduced a second lecturer, a professor of the Commercial Law Department. Without removing his mask—which he didn't need here, where O_2 generators regulated the air—he outlined the curriculum. A program that should ordinarily take three years was crammed into eight intensive months, giving room for periodic admission of new students. The more students admitted, the greater the fortune of O_2 units the school made. He concluded with a reiteration of our privilege as law students. I shook my head and, slipping on my O_2 mask, left the hall.

...❖...

Outside, I saw that Ovoke had taken a break from the rhetoric too. She smirked when she saw me and came over to give me a hug. She felt the way she looked: delicate, as if she would crumble if I squeezed her too tightly. What was it about her fragile look that all the boys found irresistible? I held her at arm's length to inspect her as if trying to find her appeal.

She smiled at the confused look on my face, raising an eyebrow.

I never missed an opportunity to tease her, and I couldn't resist it now. "I would say I missed you, but I don't want to lie."

She laughed. "And yet you hold me like you care."

I struggled with a response, and she filled in for me. "Is it because I'm dying?"

"Of course," I agreed, hoping my off-handedness would hide the double bluff. "Why else would I care?"

She smiled again, and I soaked in her presence as we leaned against the parapet in companionable silence.

"Do you want to feel it?" she asked blandly after a moment.

"Feel what?"

"My tumor. The death inside me. I can feel it, you know."

I looked away, over the railing. When we had first met during registration for the program, she'd told me she suffered from ovarian cancer. She'd told no one else, not one of her close friends from our university days when I had been just a course mate she hardly noticed. She hadn't told her new friends here, either. Just me, who didn't fawn over her like everyone else. Me, who teased her like a brother, and never let her take anything too seriously.

The way I was around her was also her preference. Not like everyone else, who were always in puppy-mode around her, even when she wasn't ill. They didn't see what I saw: a strong, intelligent, frighteningly competent woman with teeth and claws and a mind all her own. When I saw her fight, I called her fearsome, horrifying, a raging animal in a world too delicate to cage her. When others saw her fight, they called her "brave."

It was easy then to see why she told just me.

"I told only you," she had said, "for the same reason I left home for this rigorous, unhealthy program. I don't want to be treated like I'm a sick, broken thing. I want to live before I die." And then she'd added, "If not caring is your normal, then that's what I want."

But I had always cared, even when it felt hopeless to do so, even when I didn't want to.

I realized I'd not answered her about touching her tumor. I didn't want to respond. Teasing her about death made it seem less real, but really talking about it was too hard. I had to keep pretending that I didn't care.

"Hey, mumu," I teased her, rather than humor her macabre mood on this, a day to acknowledge the new challenges ahead of us at the Academy of Laws. "We had better go in before the patrollers come looking for us."

She chuckled. "Okay, big head."

We slipped off our oxygen-filtering masks as we returned to the hall. We only needed them in the harsh, oppressive, and barely breathable air of the outside.

The lecturer, while deep in a section on campus rules, had found his good humor. I preferred him without it.

"You are not allowed to eat when classes are on. Not even to chew gum. Unless you are pregnant and carrying a kid, then you can chew like a goat. Hahahaha."

He continued on, outlining all the lack of privileges we had at our privileged school, with the interspersing of jokes, often classist. I grimaced, but some students chuckled. You knew the ones who would succeed early by ass-kissing.

Next up was Dr. Umez of property law. A man in his early forties, he rasped on about his religious, conservative principles and rules that I am sure weren't sanctioned by the institution, as strict as it already was. His last edict was that phones wouldn't be allowed when his lectures were on, and any found would be confiscated, permanently.

"Well, that's not extreme," I quipped sarcastically. "He's trying to go into phone retailing?"

Ovoke leaned closer and whispered conspiratorially, "He trades them back for favors."

I looked at her blankly, not getting her point, so she continued, "He's famous with the ladies."

My eyebrows climbed in realization, then furrowed in confusion again. "But why? For a phone?"

"He promises an easier time for them here, and better chances of passing."

I scoffed. "I have actually looked into bribing people to pass and to game the system. 'Phone Seizer' here can't guarantee anyone will pass. The scripts are marked by external examiners and people in HQ, Abuja. That's where it all happens."

"Well, the average student doesn't know that. Between deceiving the gullible and promising to make their lives hell, Umez has quite a tutoring program."

"How do you even know all this?" I asked.

"I'm a woman. It's our business, our survival, to know about people like this."

I was quiet for a bit. Ovoke touched my angry face.

"If he ever bothers you," I told her softly. "I'll kill him."

"Awww," she said. "You're every girl's dream: a psycho best friend who would kill for her. However, start with my cancer."

"I'm afraid that's beyond the reach of my goons," I said apologetically.

"Are you useful for anything?" she asked with a playful push. We both laughed under our breath.

Mrs. Oduwole was at the podium now. The Head of Hostels began by stating that the generators would be on until midnight for reading and for the making of breathable air. After midnight, we would revert to our O_2 cylinders, which we must keep by our bedsides throughout the night.

The tuition was expensive but was only meant to cover the central hall's oxygen generation when lectures were on. O_2 masks filtered the bad air temporarily, for the brief periods when moving between places. O_2 cylinders were for longer periods when there were no O_2 generators.

We weren't allowed to be in the hostels during the day when lectures were on, for any reason. She didn't care if you were a girl on your flow, no matter how heavy. And this was apparently the only example she felt obligated to give.

Another lecturer talked about modest and decent dressing, and one unfortunate girl was singled out as an example of what not to do.

The female lecturer, gesturing at the girl's long and painted nails, said, "Such is not allowed here. They are an unnecessary distraction to both ladies and gentlemen. The ladies might feel pressured to compete and focus on their looks, and the men might want to ... well, we all know what men want from women."

There was a low chuckle from the students, and not for the first time I wondered at the unhealthy focus of this school to use sexist mores to try to keep everyone in their place.

"Well, we know some women also want the same from women," she continued, and the chuckle rang louder. She leaned forward now and whispered, even though she knew the microphone would carry the whisper. "So, with your nails, how do you wash your ..."

The laughter rang long and unrestrained now. The girl being queried wilted in shame, and the woman moved on, having achieved her objective.

"Well, that's professional," I whispered sarcastically to Ovoke.

But she wasn't fazed by any of this. Of course, she had more immediate worries on her mind.

I had to wonder why our society still looks down on women so much. Was gasping your lungs out in between toiling to purchase filters and breathable air in an atmosphere ruined by global warming not enough? Or was the audacity of being here, daring to compete with men in the most lucrative and influential profession in the Republic, simply too bold?

At the end of the induction, students remained seated while the lecturers left. There were electronic fingerprint scanners embedded at our desks and, in order to be counted as having attended, we would have to use the scanners to sign in and out. If there wasn't eighty-five percent attendance over the entire program, you couldn't take the Bar exams. That also ensured that students were holding each other accountable.

Once the teachers were gone, the students rushed out through their exits.

Exit A was left for the Bar 1 students, the elite gang in their expensive-as-hell O_2 regulator masks. They had all schooled in China and America for their LL.B. Foreign schools were attended by only the extremely wealthy and took less time—three years instead of the five in domestic schools. These elite students were generally regarded as "better" and were treated accordingly. They didn't mingle with the students from Nigerian universities. It didn't help that the Chinese government, in partnership with the CAT—Chinese American Tobacco—had donated a stash of high-quality masks for them and took care of O_2 regulation in most of our institutions, in exchange for certain economic and political concessions.

The British American Tobacco (BAT) was consumed by the CAT after the Chinese had bought all the interests, infrastructure, and institutions that had been left over in Nigeria after the Weather Crises. They effectively split the country down the middle to share with American investors in an uneasy alliance. Both former tobacco companies quickly caught on and began to produce air-filtration systems, air regulators, masks, and other paraphernalia needed by all for survival.

Before the Crises, they had sold death in the form of cigarettes, when life was in abundance to those who didn't care about life. But after the thinning of the air and the severe climate changes that had made the earth near uninhabitable, the industrial conglomerate had switched. Now the merchants of death sold life and oxygen because death was in abundance, and life was the commodity in demand. You had to pay to breathe. O_2 credit was life. And your deficits, your debits, were in CO_2. They sold to the highest bidders: the government who purchased and subsidized it for their workers, and for the rich. So there was short supply for the rest.

I made a move to follow as the peacocks trooped through their exit, but Ovoke's hand tugged my arm.

"Not that way, trouble-lover."

I smiled, and we went out through one of the other doors, heading for the hostels. I looked at Ovoke. She had taken the induction far less seriously than me, rolling her eyes through all the nonsense. She was well attuned to my moods and temperament.

"Want to take a walk?" she asked.

"Yes," I replied. "I need a break since there are no more induction classes today."

She clasped my hand as we strolled out.

A security guard was patrolling outside, and I passed him an O2O card, to forestall his inquiries. He pocketed it smartly and moved on. I bribed the security men at the gate too, and we left campus to walk illegally into the sunset of a quiet afternoon, away from the toxic Law Academy.

...❖...

Weeks in, we had adjusted to the toxic institution; to the assignments and group work that ran on into late nights and had to be presented in class the next day; to the frantic, extra reading after classes to avoid being embarrassed in the randomly administered, rapid-fire quizzes; to the shaming and disgrace that followed failure to get an answer right; to hoarding our oxygen cylinders in the hostels for when the power generators switched off in the night.

We had a plethora of assignments and projects that kept us buried to our eyebrows, even on weekends. But assignments were rarely my concern on weekdays, much less weekends. And on this weekend, Ovoke was gone.

She had taken a trip home to Ikeja, where her family lived, for chemo sessions scheduled into the middle of next week.

I missed her. Taking care of her at school—buying her food, drawing her water, and keeping her company with jokes and sallies, both of which made her happy—was the one thing that kept me anchored and from snapping at the horrid attitude of everyone here.

Without her here, there was no life to be experienced. I felt acutely every pull of the thin and corrupted air. The mechanically purified and generated atmosphere wasn't much better. We hadn't had good air in a decade.

It's no surprise that Ovoke was my breath of fresh air, my reason for being able to withstand this place—for not exploding at all the verbal abuse and stupidity from lecturers, students, and other staff. I needed to stay here to stay with her.

And it was this realization that sent me on my own little detour. I needed to visit the mainland. Not that the air there was any better there. It was much worse, in fact. The people there were poor. The island that held the school campus was the part of Lagos kept for the elite, with regulated air, as seen to by Governor MC Oluwole.

You see, only the rich deserved to breathe.

Still, the mainland was home. Usually, I would take my Temperature Regulating Suit. I needed the TRS when going to the mainland so as not to suffer heat stress from the ever-rising temperatures, another effect of the warming crises of a decade ago.

But I had given Ovoke my suit, so I stood sweating, waiting for transport until one of the government-regulated Bus Rapid Transit (BRT) vehicles arrived. It would take me to the outskirts of the mainland and was fitted with its own temperature-regulation systems. Inside, I leaned back and let the cold-yet-polluted air fan my anxieties away.

I was fine until I got into the Danfo bus, the first of many on this transfer line that would convey me the last distance to my home. They were usually faulty and broke down a lot, exposing the occupants to serious dangers of heat stress.

I paid the Danfo driver $O_2$17. His bus, at least, had a marginally working air-filtration system, so we could have breathable air. I baked in the heat, but I could tell that the other passengers were not as affected. They were hardy, sturdy folks who looked like they were used to this. People who lived on the mainland but worked on the island made the trip to the high-rise and office complexes they toiled in daily, so they were used to the extremes. The island housed most of the companies and corporations that thrived in this troubled world, along with CAT, the company that owned the breath in our lungs.

I stopped at Oyingbo and took a bus going toward the University of Lagos, my alma mater. I wasn't going to my old school, though. I stopped at the university gate and took another bus to Bariga, the student community that housed most of the 100,000 student population, teachers, and other mostly junior staff that ran the institution. You only got accommodation inside the school if you were senior staff.

The hostels were for foreign students who paid top O_2 credits. I was heading downtown, to the most dangerous parts of Bariga, the parts I knew were occupied by the Eiye and Buccaneer cultists.

I paid the keke driver $O_2$4. My mask was already on. I took the Ikoro, the side streets that led to the house of the friends and fellow cultists I came to see, members of the vanilla Buccaneer cult I had belonged to during my years as a University of Lagos student.

It was not as dangerous as it sounded. The Buccaneer was a cult made up of better-off kids who wanted to be dissidents. We paid the Eiye guys to handle the few infractions we got into. The Eiye was a more impoverished fraternity with their members nicknamed "bird," or "winch," for the rough and dirty crowd it attracted. They were always eager to do any jobs for the right pay, which was any pay.

I passed a few people carrying old, crude oxygen cylinders. People on the mainland here, aside those in high-profile jobs, could rarely afford filtration masks sold by CAT, so they made do with old oxygen cylinders they had to refill. The agencies that should have handled filtration and regulation systems here were moribund from having their initially insufficient funding further looted by officials who went on to buy high-rise apartments on the Island.

The passing folks glared at me, taking in my fine and obviously expensive air-filtration mask. To them I was a "butty," a rich kid who had lost his way—and I knew some would try to rob me, then severely wound me if I tried to resist. I looked back to see them already preparing to come at me. I flashed one of them the Buccaneer hand sign. He hesitated. I flashed the Eiye hand sign too, thus identifying myself as "brother to pikin of last two years, egede number one." The guy at the head of the company nodded in respect and waved me on as "master."

My destination was the house of one of my old Buccaneer friends yet to graduate. It was crowded with a number of students and indigenes of the Bariga community who hung out with them. Loud music blared from speakers somewhere in the two-bedroom apartment. It was old and decrepit, like most of the houses here.

The generator, running outside for electricity, powered an old air regulator which coughed out good air, marginally improving what we had. Ironically, it was ruining the good air outside, to provide for us inside. Talk about robbing Peter to pay Paul. Not to even mention the noise.

But, anything to breathe better. I could smell igbo, which had become dirt cheap when everyone moved on to drugs and synthetic substances for highs to compensate for an otherwise shitty life. Well, almost everyone. It didn't make sense to me to smoke and damage your lungs and the most precious commodity you had: air that was in such short supply. But then, no one ever accused cultists of wisdom.

I went to my friend's room, where the smell of weed was coming from. Jaiyesimi and some friends were smoking and playing cards while another group was gambling with dice. Some had passed out on a rickety-rackety bed in the corner.

Jaiyesimi nodded at me. He had to finish his game before we could speak.

I greeted the occupants of the room in confralangua, to show I belonged. I had taken off my air-filtration mask when I got into the house, seeing as they had a regulator. But the smell of weed soon overpowered me and it was either choke or put on my mask, neither of which was a good option here; both would make me look weak. So, I signaled to my friend that I would be outside when he was done. I choked down a small cough as I stepped out. I could see them chuckle and one of them say slyly, "Ju man."

Outside, I slipped my mask back on and inhaled deeply. Air was life. For this, I was content to be a "Ju man," a slur for people who didn't belong to cults in the university. Or for those who, like me, belonged merely as honorary members for protection, social and other nonviolent reasons, paying dues and not engaging in any of the requisite violent activities that gained one respect and prestige as a cultist. I had joined to be left alone. There was no middle ground in a community like this: you were either the oppressed or the oppressor.

I opted to join the latter, even as an honorary member.

Jaiyesimi soon joined me. Chuckling at something someone inside had said, he took a pull of his blunt. Looking at my disapproving glance, he put it out and deposited it in a pocket.

We both stood in silence for a while, then he asked, "How the academy be na?"

"It's fine. By that I mean everyone there isn't."

"As it should be." He chuckled. "You know, we hear gist from folks there. It sounds like the university all over again."

"Basically," I agreed. "Just more studying, more nonsense. Less time though."

"Mmm," he nodded knowingly. "More of the bad things, less of the good."

"Yeah," I agreed. "The academics are really the worst. But I will sort myself out. You know I know how."

He nodded.

We were quiet again and then he said, "I heard about this guy in your academy, Dr. Umez. Has he been bothering you?"

"How do you mean?"

"You know how I mean," he said, leaning closer. "I heard he pressures folks for sex. Has he—"

"Wait," I stopped him, confused. "Why would you think this would be a problem for me? He pressures g— Oh! You think I'm gay, and Dr. Umez is into boys?"

Silence.

"Dr. Umez does boys?" I asked. "But he's so married, with kids, and religious, and being queer is a …"

"… Crime with a fourteen-year jail term here and a death sentence in the North?" He rolled his eyes. "That's for the little people. Not an academy lecturer."

"But he's married, to a woman!"

"That never stopped anybody either. He's either bi or he does girls as a feint. In any case, he does both, so I've heard."

I thought back to what I had learnt about the lecturer. "Isn't he religious and a deacon at church?"

"Definitely a smokescreen."

"First of all, it's a wonder how you know so much about what's going on in the academy from here. Yes, I know gist filters down. But you know so much about the sexual lives of people there. Me, him. I am curious."

"Well, I like to check up on mine and know what's going on in the community."

"Since when was the academy part of the community?" I asked. At his raised eyebrow, I paused. "Wait, are you gay?"

I think he knew I didn't care about a person's sexual orientation. Straight or gay, bi or otherwise, as long as the relationship was healthy, who was I to judge?

He sidled closer. "Well, I could show you," he said softly, winking. "Show, not tell. Right?"

I laughed, knowing he was being playful, but also wondering if he was partly serious. It was so hard to tell in a society that didn't talk about such things openly, for fear of condemnation. "Don't ask, don't tell," I rejoinder. "This is flattering, but I prefer a partner who is cerebral."

"Are you mad?" He laughed too. "Last I checked, your grades weren't all that, so how will you be wanting a cerebral partner? And didn't you graduate with a third class?"

"I said cerebral, not academic. Also, you managed to not graduate at all."

"True," he conceded.

"Also, I'm not …"

"Right," he said.

We were both quiet after this, till I punctured the silence.

"So, Dr. Umez harasses and rapes both boys and girls, huh?"

"Yup," he said without looking at me.

"Dude sounds like he needs killing."

Jaiyesimi now looked at me. "Can you kill someone?"

"I'm not sure. We're going to find out, I guess."

He looked at me askance. Silent.

I hesitated. "You get my text na, didn't you? O_2 Arena."

His eyebrows raised in genuine surprise. "You were serious?"

"Yes na," I confirmed, irritated by the notion I would joke about something like that.

"Wetin you need money for so bad?" But he barely paused to breathe before answering his own question. "Ah … Law Academy."

It wasn't hard for him to figure out. I was a decent student when I tried. But I rarely did. School was a necessary evil for me. Something I did but had no choice.

I preferred art and writing, which I couldn't get parental approval to pursue. The only thing they endorsed or cared to entertain was a career that allowed one to get a job in the government administration as a civil servant and be entitled to O_2 credits and an allocation of oxygen.

What use was a life where all you did was merely exist? So, I cheated when I could, and bribed my way through when I couldn't cheat or wing it. My dad had died in my third year at the university, and his monetary support had dried up.

Now I required five times the amount of money I had needed in the past to pay my way through the university. And I would need it all at once. So O_2 Arena it was.

Jaiyesimi met my eyes sternly, and I realized he also, on some level, only thought of me as a Ju Man—faking it until I make it. Never completely all in. "You sure?"

I nodded.

"Well, na, your life, sha." He shrugged. "Make I call Papilo to carry us go."

...❖...

We made our way to the underground square, led by one of the Eiye boys and my friend Jaiyesimi, to the place they called O_2 Arena. It was a fighting pit, a solid Plexiglass cage, its transparent walls harder than steel. Two combatants in skin-tight black bodysuits were inside, cameras focused from every angle.

This was what had replaced selling your kidneys and internet fraud: the only get-rich-quick scheme, regulated secretly by government and top CAT officials, illegally and discreetly. The cage fights were streamed and sponsored by equally rich and highly placed folks who had an appetite for this kind of entertainment.

Thugs and all sorts of desperate people who were ready to risk it all for a huge payoff came here. Cult members came to settle squabbles. Instead of wasting a death, they came here to fight it out and at least know that one of them stood the chance to make what equaled near three decades of standard wages. Fifty thousand O_2 credits, a lifetime supply of air. You fought and died to keep breathing. And this was how I planned to make money enough to sort my exams.

Jaiyesimi looked at me strangely, trying to figure out my sudden need to make such a huge gamble with my life. I ignored him.

They announced the fighters who got into the arena, glass doors sealed behind them. Pure, breathable air was provided inside so combatants could breathe well, could draw lungsful of the air they fought, and maybe died, for. The irony was not lost on the online spectators.

The fighters in the arena squared and faced off. The mic man and moderator atop the cage commentated, move-by-move, on the entire match, which turned out to be dirty, long, and ugly. I watched as the two men pummeled each other till they were almost too exhausted to stand. I didn't know them, or why they had come here to murder or be murdered, but I understood them. They were both me. I was both of them. Cultist, thug, desperate son, brother, or father—this was as fair a fight for oxygen as any of us would ever have.

One of them slipped, perhaps on the sweat on the floor. The other set to stomping the fallen, on and on. When his target stopped moving, he took him into a chokehold. The other struggled, but not for long. When he finally lay still, the victor stood up, screaming to the rafters.

Then he fell to his knees in exhaustion.

Canned cheering and applause answered him; there were no spectators live here—just the technical staff working the equipment, and thugs and cultists screening fighters or helping victors to process their payment.

The Eiye boy with Jaiyesimi looked at us both. "You don see am abi?"

I nodded. They brought trusted, wannabe participants here for a viewing, to see the action before they committed to their fate.

Jaiyesimi looked at me with disbelief. "Why you wan do this kind thing? For school? You fit read na. You fit pass on your own. And if you fail, e no matter."

I shook my head. He didn't understand. I couldn't risk it. It was not that I could not do it on my own, but if I failed, my mom and family at home, who needed the status of having a graduate from the academy of letters, would miss the income I could contribute to keeping them breathing. Not to mention the stigma of my failing. I would rather die.

The thug who brought us to the arena rapped Jaiyesimi on the shoulder. "He no get the mind." Meaning that I didn't have the guts to do this.

They were right, as I realized on the bus the next day. It's all well and good to think you can do it until you actually have to.

...❖...

I had only been in school for barely a week when Ovoke called me. A week after my first trip back from the mainland. I had left after she left, because in her absence, there was not enough presences to keep me occupied. The campus was filled with students, but while she was gone, it was empty of companionship in her absence.

I had been lazing through the school activities with disinterest when she called me one evening, her voice such a tiny, scratchy whisper, I had to strain to hear her. "Ode, I'm back."

"Oh, really?" I said, feigning disinterest. "Why is your voice so tiny? I could come see you in your room. Or should I wait for you to come downstairs?" I was eager not to seem too eager. She chuckled, no doubt aware of my ruse.

"I'm not in school yet," she said. "I'm outside. Chemo was rough and those hostels are not the best place to recover. That's why my voice was, is, tiny, by the way."

I swallowed a lecture about how she should have stayed at home to rest, something she sensed. Instead, I said, "Well, you were no Beyonce to begin with, so it's not like your voice is a great loss."

She chuckled and answered my unspoken question.

"My parents agreed I could lodge in one of the more affordable hotels around, for a day or two, to get over chemo before moving back to the hostel. So, will you come and see me there?"

My phone chimed immediately after, and I received the address in my WhatsApp. Golden Tulip Hotel. I knew the place. No wonder it was affordable. It was a not-too-terrible place, but in the more run-down part of the Island.

"Okay, girl. I'll see you in a bit. Though I have important things to do, so it won't be for a while."

"Of course, busy man," she said mockingly.

"Bye." I hung up, a little annoyed that I was worried, and she would know I was. I would have to deliberately delay now. Wait for a whole day before going to see her, so I could be fashionably late, not show how much I cared, and make it seem like I wasn't even going to show up.

...❖...

It was 8 p.m. when I knocked on the door of her room. She opened the door, looked me up and down, then let me hug her. I held on a bit, then she pushed me away. I sat on the bed, she sat at the table, and in her scratchy voice, told me how her trip went. After a while of listening and punctuating her recollections with sarcastic quips that had her chuckling all throughout, she got up and pulled something from a drawer.

"What's that?"

"Neulasta."

"What's that? Are you doing drugs in addition to your cancer?" I asked, almost impressed.

She sighed.

"It's a follow-up for my chemo, to wake me up."

"Wake you up?"

She sighed and beckoned to me.

I pulled closer saying, "Oooh, the sex talk."

She shook her head. "Do you know how chemo works?"

"I know what goes in where and how to use a condom."

She punched me. "Be serious." I affected seriousness and she continued. "What chemo is supposed to do is kill you."

I raised an eyebrow.

"Along with your cancer cells," she added. "It kills you and the cancer, almost. It stops before you are dead. But the cancer is weak, the chemo has made you even weaker, so then you take this after." She held up what she had called Neulasta. "It's for my vitality. Wakes me back up, brings me back from the edge. Almost kill me and the cancer, then slip out of Death's grasp with this, leaving it the cancer, to die a little more each chemo session. Rinse and repeat, till it's eventually dead. A little game of cat and mouse."

She stopped talking. There was a lingering silence in the room. I didn't say anything, but the unspoken question hung between us: What if you lose in this little game of cat and mouse?

I asked, "Does it kill your brain cells then? Cuz that would explain—"

She punched me and we both laughed.

"I'm supposed to take this by 9:30 p.m.," she continued. "And I must take it before two hours elapse after the last chemo."

I nodded solemnly. "What happens if you don't take it within that time?"

"It's supposed to keep me alive, so . . . ." She shrugged. "Your guess is as good as mine."

I swallowed.

"Come here, scaredy cat," she said, pulling more stuff from her drawer. "I had a cannula in my hand from chemo, which I would have simply taken it with. All you would have needed to do was inject it into my cannula. But it fell off you see . . ."

"Of course it did," I muttered.

"So I'll need you to ..."

I looked at what she was holding closely now. It was a syringe.

"I'll need you to fix this new one for me."

I felt blank and empty.

"I can't break my skin myself," she continued. "I'm scared of needles."

I looked at her face now, my disbelief plainly etched in it. She smiled a little, what she must have imagined was an encouraging smile.

"You know I'm not a doctor, or even a nurse," I said. "But I'm supposed to, let me get this straight, pierce your skin, fix a cannula—which I've never done before—and correctly administer this drug. Which if I don't, you might die?"

She didn't nod; she just made the encouraging face. I groaned and she proceeded to convince me that it wouldn't be that difficult.

...❖...

It was difficult as hell. Her veins had collapsed from the many needles and her general condition. She had what she called "vein trauma," which made it more difficult. And I just couldn't believe how difficult it was slipping a needle into a human vein, especially for someone with no professional training. Her skin was soft under my touch, and she tried to hide the tremble, then the tears, as I missed the vein over and over and over again. Then before I knew it, I flung the needle away.

"This is supposed to be a normal visit. You just called me to come hang as a friend. Why didn't you warn me? Why didn't you tell me? How am I supposed to do this, which I haven't done before and it means so much, maybe even your life? How can you put this on me?"

I realized I was yelling.

She was quiet. I already knew the answers to my questions. She wanted to leave home to make her own choices, not stay home with her stifling family and get proper care and miss out on life and all that. Especially if she was already on borrowed time.

I swallowed the rest of what I was going to say about this being irresponsible and unsafe. She handed me another needle nonchalantly.

Yeah, I realize she must be used to these kinds of outbursts. I was one of those worrying people that didn't understand the situation.

So I took a fresh syringe and tried again, and again, and again. This time, I didn't snap; I just tried. But if she took my yelling stoically, she didn't take my failure the same way. She had already been too weak—and time was running out. She was crying. And then I was crying, too. She hugged me and rubbed the back of my head, saying she was sorry.

I snapped out of it. She shouldn't be the strong one, comforting me. I was not the one at risk of dying.

I pulled back and looked at her.

It was an hour before the maximum time limit for when she should take the drug, and she was starting to show signs of damage. Her eyes were dripping an odd, slimy liquid, and she was drooling too. She looked a little distant, not quite herself. Then the realization came to me, and I said aloud, "I can't do this. I'm going to get help."

She nodded weakly as if absent-minded and not present. I looked at the time. One hour more, going by the time she said she was supposed to take it. While the chemo might not take her this time, the Neulasta would give her the chance to fight another day.

I was conflicted when I left. Should she lock the door? What if she was in no condition to open it when I got back? Should she leave it open? What if someone came in to do something to her while I was away? Should I lock it and take the key? What if she needed help while I was gone and couldn't get out?

The area where we were was just rife with criminal opportunists.

I slipped on my O_2 mask and left. One hour to go. I stumbled through the streets, asking directions to a chemist, any chemist. It was dark, past 10 p.m., and I got suspicious looks as I strolled along. I stumbled from closed chemist to closed chemist, frantic, semi-insane with the urgency of the help I needed. Then someone told me about a lady—not a chemist, but a nurse. She sold drugs at home.

I rushed to the location I was given and found the nurse. She was in her backyard smoking weed. She said she'd had a long day and just wanted to chill, maybe noting the desperation in my bearing. She offered me a blunt. I looked at her incredulously and almost started to cry. But there was no time for that.

I walked over to her and said as emphatically as I could: "PLEASE HELP ME."

She simply grunted, wearily dragging herself out of her fold-up chair. She followed me to the hotel. On the way, I explained in more detail that we only needed her to administer the injection. She was high and sang all the way. But her hand was rock steady.

She asked no questions; apparently, she was used to strange, odd-hour jobs. I was glad of that. I was in a random hotel with a very sick, near comatose girl and a strange, high nurse injecting something I didn't understand into her at my behest. I briefly wondered what would happen if Ovoke were to die. What kind of narrative would come out of this, and what kind of explanation would I give?

Then I violently shoved the thought from my mind. Ovoke ISN'T DYING.

...❖...

The nurse finished her job. I gave her a bunch of O_2 credits; all the cards I could lay my hands on. She thanked me, lingered long enough to look back at me and Ovoke. She opened her mouth as if to say something, then decided against it, and left.

I watched Ovoke for the next 30 minutes, paranoid the injection wouldn't work after all. The color came back to her. Her eyes had stopped dripping, and she was not drooling anymore. I crawled into the bed and fell into a dead, dreamless sleep.

When I awoke in the morning, someone was holding me gently, cradling my head to their chest. I extricated myself and she woke.

I got up, frowning at her, trying to brush off the intimacy—to not show her how much I cared. Platonically, anyway.

She smiled.

I pointed at the bed.

"We're not like that. Also, did you get my consent before cuddling me?"

"Morning, grumpy."

I shook my head.

"Oh, and your breathing is really bad," she said sympathetically. "You slept so badly, I was worried all night."

"Worry about yourself, punk." I said in mock annoyance.

She smiled and got up, pulling a toothbrush from her bag. "You should call a cab now while we get ready for class. You know they usually take forever to get here."

"Why are we going to class again? After last night?" I asked. And then I answered the question it myself. "Live before you die, right?"

She beamed at me. Grumbling, I pulled out my phone to call a cab.

...❖...

The moment I had dreaded happened a week after her second trip back home for her chemo sessions. I had been restive, expecting her call, thinking it was about the time she should return. I knew something was wrong. I could sense it. And I was right, I realized in dread when the call came. My breath was loud in my ears. The filter did what it was meant to, and the air that reached me was clean, but it couldn't stop my labored breathing. My heart was thumping so hard.

My friend, Ovoke, was dying.

…❖…

Ovoke's brother, Efeturi, had been the one to call; she was asking to see me.

I greeted him at the University of Lagos Teaching Hospital (LUTH) then rushed to where she lay on a stretcher outside the building. She'd always been so full of life, but now she looked smaller, diminished.

How she had shrunk in such a short while, I couldn't understand. I held her bony hand in mine, rubbing it on my cheek, desperate to feel something of her as I'd known before. Her fingers were warm, and I felt a faint throbbing as she breathed laboriously from a cylinder by the side of the bed. Over the edges of the mask, her panicked eyelids fluttered, and I couldn't tell if she knew I was there.

Her dad sat fanning her, and, while I held her and told her it would be all right, I met his stricken eyes.

She was outside, he said, because a year of cancer treatment, of chemo, had exhausted their money. They couldn't afford a ward. A bed would come at the daily cost of $O_2$200. Getting her into the ICU and hooked up on proper machines would be even more.

So here we were. The chemotherapy treatment had been meant to kill her cancer, but it was killing her instead. Now those precious, delicate lungs had stopped coping.

"So what now?" I asked.

He couldn't meet my eyes. "If we could raise the money for the ICU and a proper bed, she would be allowed time to heal her lungs. Then the cancer treatment could proceed. If not …"

I stepped out to talk to Efeturi, leaving her parents and other brother with her.

When we came back, Ovoke was near hysterical from breathlessness and desperately thirsty. With the breathing mask briefly removed, we dribbled water into her mouth, letting her lay back. Everyone could see that it was taking all her energy just to suck what little air was given her by the mask, which we replaced after every paltry drink.

Too tired to talk, she communicated only with her eyes, and I gave her my best reassuring smile as I squeezed that fragile, tiny, bony hand.

"You'll be all right. Your dad says that you're considering surgery now."

She nodded.

I sighed, trying not to let my surprise and heartache at that news show in my eyes.

Back in school, before her chemo, we'd had a discussion about her treatment method. Chemo had burnt her out and she had lost her voice, her hair, her weight, energy, and vitality. And now she had also lost her air, the most precious commodity she, and any of us, had.

But back then, there had been an alternative: surgery. I had suggested she have her ovaries removed, removing the cancer with them. But she had refused because that would also mean losing her chance at future children.

"And what kind of life would that be?" she had asked. She was convinced that she'd be left a broken woman—a woman who wasn't a woman.

I had tried to tell her that her ability to give birth was not what made her a woman or gave her value. But even as I said it, I knew how false it would ring in her ears, as it might in mine, if I had been subjected to the other side of our patriarchal society.

She thought she would be nothing in a patriarchal society that valued men for their ability to provide and women for reproduction. I had never told her that even in such a society, she was everything to me. How could I, when she needed me to tease her, to treat her the same as I always had? When she demanded nothing could change, and I had to pretend I still cared for nothing.

"A freak," she'd insisted, "wanted by no one."

And so she had given up her air for future, unborn children. She'd risked it all. And only now could she see that her ovaries were not her, not worth her life. She was ready to let them go, if it wasn't too late.

Her labored breathing kept me fully focused on our painful reality. I held her hands as air flowed raggedly through her damaged lungs, while she cried in between gasps, calling for her mom, and then pushing the distraught woman away when she came.

Ovoke's dad, gone for a good while during the afternoon, eventually came back. He had gotten the funds, probably by selling something, if they still had anything to sell. Whatever it had been, I could tell from his hushed conversation with his wife, and the stricken and defeated look on her face, that it wasn't good.

But it must have been enough. They would move Ovoke to the ICU. Her lungs would get the chance to stabilize while we looked for the funds to remove the offending cancer.

The surgery was a fortune, one beyond any resource the family could tap. Without it, she would die. At that moment I knew what I had to do.

I told her she would be all right. I held her hand, stroking it again lightly over my cheek. I told her I had to go get something and would be back. She gestured weakly that I should come closer. I leaned over her until I could feel each labored, precious breath against my skin.

"I love you," she whispered in my ear.

I screwed my eyes tightly closed until the flood of tears no longer threatened. Then I smiled as bravely as I could and kissed her on the forehead. I left without telling her I loved her. There would be time later when the fire was back in her eyes and light gleamed from her smile. I would tell her I loved her then because she would know then that my love was not pity, or hopelessness, or humor.

I would tell her. But now, I had to focus on what I had to do.

...❖...

Life for Life. #SaveVoke

The hashtag had spread throughout the interwebs, leading up to the fight, prompting an increased online viewership for the arena, their corrupt owners resharing the tweet, watching their bank account balance rise with glee.

Jaiyesimi was incredulous, disbelieving; his Eiye friend, our guide in this terrible place, was surprised but impressed.

And my opponent looked eager. His eyes glittered; all he saw in my place was a bag of O_2 units. What I saw was life. A chance at life for the friend I loved, and I was willing to pay the ultimate price: to kill or to die.

My love and desire didn't automatically hand me the fight. I had done a little karate, up to green belt, so I took the stance and threw a flurry of punches. He took the blows, grabbing my hands and then delivering a headbutt that broke my nose and drew first blood, sending me sprawling to the floor.

There was no skill to it, no sparring strategy or technique, only experience and power.

He let me get up, perhaps disappointed by how little excitement such a victory would bring our audience. A mistake, as our next encounter had me rubbing the blood in his eyes and knocking him almost senseless.

Now we had both done damage.

I tried to take advantage of his confusion at his newfound blindness, but then it was me in a chokehold that would have ended things then and there, if I hadn't discovered a last-minute taste for human flesh. I sank my teeth into his arm, and he let me go with a brutal scream. A reverb-heavy roar from the remote spectators filled the air around us, and the announcer's words bounced off the Plexiglass walls, feverish with renewed excitement.

This would not be an orderly fight; it was a meaningless grapple for survival, for air—and drowning men didn't struggle prettily.

But I wasn't a fighter like these street thugs were; like he was. They had the crucial advantage of killing before and were ready to kill again. I had paid for protection. I had always taken the easy way out. Cheated, lied, stolen. I'd never cared about anything except survival. And here I was, willing to die for something.

Someone.

I had no experience with the instinct to kill, and yet clearly this man had lived that way his entire life.

He pummeled me thoroughly, always darting back after each blow, wary of the bite of my teeth and determined to finish me without getting into close-quarters combat.

It was my reason for being here that kept me from giving up, from dying. I saw then his confusion at not having an easy kill, confusion that turned this thug's eyes into desperate rage. He caught me again in a clumsy chokehold. He was tired, but he was also eager to finish the job, to earn his fortune, to earn air—my air, my life, and Ovoke's right to life as well.

Outside the cage, I could see the Eiye cultist nod at me. I was brave, but I was done. My friend Jaiyesimi turned away. He wasn't ready to see me go.

Covered as I was in blood and sweat and tears, it was easy to slip out of my opponent's grasp. Clearly, he expected me to run then, to retreat in a futile attempt escape with my life. Instead, I went for him. His stunned response at my small rebellion was only a small advantage. With me a spent and beaten animal, there was little I could do once I had him in my grasp.

But even a wounded wolf is a dangerous thing. I still had my teeth, and his neck was bare inches away, so I went for his throat, biting through his skin into salty, coppery flesh.

He choked and slammed his fists into me repeatedly, but I held on tight, for life, for air. His blood filled my mouth and though I wanted to retch, I tightened my jaw with grim determination and felt skin and tendon cords between my teeth and lifeblood pump against my tongue.

With one final thump, he lifted me off the ground. Ovoke, I thought. I tried …

He slammed me back down.

The lights went out.

…❖…

I woke days later, surprised to be alive.

Jaiyesimi had stayed by my side and now recounted to me what had happened. My opponent had bled to death after he knocked me out … and I had won. The fortune in O_2 units was already sitting in my account. I was in some kind of recovery unit for the victors, but there was no time to celebrate my survival. I stumbled out of the bed, found my clothes, and rushed back to the student hospital.

I was met with numb looks and reddened eyes. Ovoke's brother's' faces were filled with restrained pain. Her mother sat weeping, and her dad's defeat was evident in his hunched posture. He straightened when he saw me, letting go of his wife's hand and coming to hold me, to gently break the news.

In my absence, Ovoke had passed. Her oxygen-starved organs had finally given in. The substandard breathing apparatus that was all her family could afford couldn't sustain her through the three cardiac arrests she'd suffered in the night.

She was gone, her delicate, wild spirit, flown, borne away by the wayward winds we dealt so recklessly with. Winds which had paid us in disgruntled O_2 coin, exacted in fulfillment of poetic justice, its pound of flesh.

I had fought and killed so she could breathe. Had taken a life so savagely, so pointlessly—all for her. I had the fortune in O_2 units and now had access to the purest of air. But there were no longer lungs for me to put it in.

I crumbled to the floor and wept.

…❖…

I walked into one of the admin offices at the Academy of Laws. The man I handed my form to was old, graying, and a bit stooped—old enough to have retired. Probably one of those who falsified their age so they could work longer.

Why anyone wanted more time in this place, I couldn't fathom. His shrewd eyes regarded my narrowed ones. His kindly smile answered the question I hadn't voiced: survival. That was why he stayed. Of course, he worked to keep breathing, for air, for a continued meager flow of O_2 units for him and for his loved ones.

Survival was overrated. I knew that now. You would live long enough to see your loved ones die.

"Son." His voice stopped me as I went to leave. "Why fill this? Why defer?" He asked, waving the paper at me.

Of course, I thought. The nosy old man wants to make sure I am utilizing my life well, not wasting my "potential."

I could try to explain the futility of it all, the fact that they were trapped here living a life that wasn't worth the O_2 units it took to buy the oxygen to sustain it, but he wouldn't understand. It would shock him, my directness and honesty, my lack of respect, and brazenness.

"This isn't the place for me anymore," I told him.

His brows furrowed. "Why?"

It wouldn't be worth the O_2 units it would take to explain. I had a fortune in oxygen, true, but still, every breath was precious. Instead, I raised my hand toward him, my voice raspy, Darth Vader-like, as if I had smoked a lifetime's worth of cigarettes.

"This world needs a wake-up call that might only be found in an arena of our own making."

I stepped out. The commotion was just starting.

I could hear the siren of the Reddington ambulance driving in as I stepped outside the school and into the world. After Dr. Umez didn't show up for his lecture, and they found his door locked, his calls not being answered, they would have broken in to find him slumped and unmoving, his oxygen air-filtration system in the office mysteriously disabled.

I drew in a loud, raspy breath through my own portable air system. Air that I had earned—air that was now a means to an end.

Most of us had been hiding behind these masks, telling ourselves it was because they let us breathe. It was time for the world to see the true face of things. I placed the call to Efeturi, my second in command, and, in the same raspy quality, breathed out my orders to my men.

"This world, *our* O_2 arena, is now open."

...❖...

This story is dedicated to Voke Omawunmi Stephen, Emeka Walter Dinjos, and all those struggling with cancer and other similar ailments. Especially to beautiful young Nigerians who had to and are still laboring under the yoke of disability and various health maladies in a broken system with poor-to-no healthcare. One that's failed thoroughly and forced them into a death match in the hopeless arena of life, leaving them to struggle viciously and alone for the very air in their lungs. And lastly to all those living where there is no freedom. For without inner freedom, there can be no life.

THE DEIFICATION OF IGODO

by Joshua Uchenna Omenga

One night, Oba Igodo awoke to a voice that seemed to come from the stones of the wall.

"Why remain a king, when you can be a god?"

The voice spoke only once, but it echoed ever after in his head. The sleep fled his eyes. Silence took over the night as he pondered over the words and wondered at the daringness of the voice. And in his mind came memories of how he had delivered Igodomigodo from peril.

Before he was born into Igodomigodo, it was a troubled land without a name. It was a land ravaged by famine as brigands pillaged farmlands and carted away crops. There was sadness in every face, and people died before their time. Laughter was scant in the land. Mothers despaired with each birth, for the children they brought forth were ravaged by hunger or carried away by marauders to unreturning lands. No help came to the land from men or from the gods, for the chieftains of the land were weak, and her gods had forsaken her.

Igodo's father was a poor man, but renowned for charm-making. At his death, he had nothing to bequeath his son except the power of his charms. Igodo was raised by his uncle and apprenticed to a hunter under whom he became distinguished in hunting. He dwelt chiefly in the forest and knew the ways of wild animals more than the ways of men.

One day, while Igodo was in the village to fetch supplies, the marauders came on their usual plundering. People fled before them, but not Igodo. He hunted after the marauders unaided and overtook them and took from them all they had plundered from the people.

The people rejoiced in his triumph and detained him in the village. In days that followed, they sought his aid against the assaults of the marauders. And each time he came, he triumphed over the marauders and recovered their loot. Stories began to circulate that the land was no longer undefended. Attacks on the land lessened, until enemies turned to friends, and strangers no longer entered freely into the land as in the days of its vulnerability. Farms became secure and crops flourished undisturbed. And smiles crept onto the faces of the people.

The people began to call the land Igodomigodo, for the land was delivered by the might of Igodo. They persuaded Igodo to forsake his dwelling in the forest and live in the village. They cleared a large and choice land for his compound and erected for him a magnificent building and fenced his compound with bricks of mud. When at last he consented to dwell in the house they had built for him, they flocked in his compound with tributes of yams and goats and palm wines.

With peace and abundance, Igodomigodo grew and expanded. The people perceived the need for a king, as in the kingdoms in their tales. They thronged into Igodo's compound and in a united voice, begged him to be king over them. Igodo accepted their proposal with secret joy, for the praises of the people had entered his head and he had begun to glory in his own excellence. At his coronation, he took the title of Oba, king of the people. And for a time, the love of the people for Oba Igodo bloomed.

But in proportion as he was loved and revered, Igodo's heart began to grow haughty within him. He looked upon the prosperity of Igodomigodo, listened to the laughter of children, perceived the peace and freedom of the people, and recalled that none of these would be but for him. Had he not saved the people of Igodomigodo when no man or deity could save them? And Oba Igodo began to demand more from the people of Igodomigodo than they were willing to offer. His utterances became laws which the people must obey or be chastized.

The people of Igodomigodo could no longer see in their king the benevolent man who had brought them peace and security. Oba Igodo frequently descended on his subjects, and for errors that tongue would have righted, he addressed with sword. Many disapproved in their hearts, but none dared to condemn aloud. Igodo mistook the silence of the people for approval and sought continually more than the people could give.

Still, he was not content to be merely a king. Had he not done for the people more than a king? And then had come the voice whose echoes continued in his head long after the words were spoken:

"Why remain a king, when you can be a god?"

The words of the strange voice validated what he had been brooding upon. After days of pondering, Oba Igodo made up his mind to be more than a king. He declared Babura, festival of deification.

Babura was celebrated only when the people desired to create a new god by elevating an ancestor into godhood. No living man had memory of the most recent Babura, for the people had lost touch with their gods. Much of what was known about Babura came from the mythmakers. It was said that during Babura, the incarnation of the deified ancestor appeared to the people before ascending to join other gods at Orun, the abode of the gods.

The day was come for the Babura. The compound of Oba Igodo started to fill as soon as the sun was high in the sky and people stood on their shadows. No one in Igodomigodo was allowed to work that day, except the palm-wine tappers whose palm wines were for the entertainment of the people at the Babura.

The night before, the best cooks selected from the wives of the men of Igodomigodo had stayed up preparing the meats brought by the hunters. There had been a whole week of collective hunting in which all the hunters of Igodomigodo participated and the game was pooled for the Babura. Young maidens were recruited to fetch water from the purest stream in Igodomigodo, which was very far from the compound of Igodo. Young men accompanied the maidens, ostensibly to protect them, but really to find their way into the hearts of the maidens. Children hung about without parental scolding.

Meanwhile, Oba Igodo remained in his charm house where his spirit was being fortified. Not trusting solely in the power of his own charms, he had summoned the best of Babalawo from the remotest corner of the known lands. For almost two weeks, they labored in fortifying him, rubbing and infusing him with different charms and adding layers upon layers of power on him.

At last Oba Igodo was satisfied with his powers.

Oba Igodo sent words to the elders that the new god was ready to be revealed to the people of Igodomigodo. The elders sent messengers to alert everyone who had a part to play in the unveiling of the new god. A moment later, the sound of flutes and drums blared in harmony, and the dancers broke the tension of waiting. The air was charged with anticipation, for though no one yet knew which ancestor was to be deified, everyone was eager for the unveiling of the new god.

Then Oba Igodo revealed himself, radiant and fearsome to behold. His face was fierce, his arms bulged and rippled, and his raiment glistened in the sun. On his neck were beads of power; across his shoulder, protective shells; girded on his hips were corals potent with charms. He carried no sword or spear, and yet as he stood before the people and fixed his blazing eyes on them, they had no more doubt that they stood in the presence of a god.

But the elders of Igodomigodo were uneasy. They knew many gods who had been men before, according to the lore of the land. But none had heard tell of a god deified from among the living, for the privilege of deification was reserved only for the deceased who had passed into the land of the ancestors, and whose intercession in the affairs of the living had earned them the right to be elevated among the deities of the land. And least of all, none had heard of a man who had declared himself a god. It was the people who created their gods and destroyed their gods when they deemed fit. But how could it be with this self-created god?

The new god addressed the people of Igodomigodo, and his voice was loud in the silence of the gathering. He recounted to the people how the gods had forsaken them when they needed help, because the gods lounged in the distant Orun. But he, Oba Igodo, had been sent from the sky to be a god among them, to be at their beck, to listen to their supplications directly, unhindered by distance. Henceforth, he was no longer to be addressed as Oba but as Ogiso, ruler from the sky.

His voice ceased and he looked upon the people of Igodomigodo with challenge in his eyes, but every man his eyes came upon lowered his gaze. Deep silence fell on the people, and many longed to be away from the sight of their new god, for his eyes tormented them. Yet none dared to leave when the command had not been given, and all waited for release from the spell of his presence.

But in the midst of the quiet, there came a shuffling from the crowd, and a smallish man in a tattered red garment approached the new god. All eyes were turned to the stranger, for his appearance would have induced laughter in a less solemn time. His steps were wobbly, like a man who had had his fill of palm wine.

Ogiso Igodo regarded the stranger with stern and astonished eyes, for the stranger had passed the bounds of his charms unharmed. The stranger stopped a few paces before Ogiso Igodo and began to laugh.

"Igodo, son of Ivbiotu," the stranger said amidst laughter. "I have come to participate in your godhood."

The people of Igodomigodo looked with pity upon the stranger. It was clear to them that the stranger did not know whom he addressed. Ogiso Igodo had killed for far less insubordination when his power had not yet grown to its fullness.

"Who are you that seek death so willingly?" Igodo asked, his curiosity overtaking his annoyance.

"I am the air in fire. I am the water in coconut. I am the pepper in soup pot. I am the oil in eyeball. I am the stone cast in the day of peace for destruction in the day of war."

"Tell me who you are, stranger; not the riddle of your land."

"I am whom you know but cannot call. I am what you see but cannot know."

"You are insolent of tongue, and yet you speak with assurance. Temerity such as yours could serve a god, but your dressing is most unbefitting."

"If my dress is the hindrance, then I shall change into something more befitting."

The stranger bowed and rose, and his attire was a replica of the Ogiso's. The crowd cried out in astonishment.

But Ogiso Igodo was furious that of all the dresses to imitate, the stranger had imitated his, for he had arrayed himself to be distinguished above all. Ogiso Igodo retired to his hall and clad himself in another raiment as magnificent as the former. But the stranger, sighting the Ogiso in his new raiment, bowed again and rose clad in the same raiment as the Ogiso. Infuriated, but still containing his anger, Ogiso Igodo retired again and returned with different raiment. The stranger again imitated the Ogiso's raiment.

Ogiso Igodo, unable to contain his fury anymore, decided to humiliate the stranger. He twisted his fingers and whispered words of summons into the air. There was a slight howling in the wind from the distance. Soon it drew nearer until a single point of wind leapt into the gathering, settled upon the stranger, and shredded his raiment about him. The crowd cheered as the stranger struggled with the wind for the shreds of his raiment.

In a moment, however, the stranger was draped in the Ogiso's raiment while the Ogiso was in the shredded raiment of the stranger. The people of Igodomigodo turned their eyes away from the humiliation of their king, their god.

The Ogiso retired for the fourth time and clad himself in different raiment and returned before the people. But his eyes regarded the stranger warily, for he perceived a power in the stranger that he could not understand. Not desiring to humiliate himself any further, Ogiso Igodo summoned three of his guards and whispered in their ears to dispatch the stranger from the compound. But, turning to the stranger, Ogiso Igodo said, "They shall take you to your place of service."

"I am grateful," the stranger said. "May your godship prosper."

There was something familiar in the stranger's voice at his parting words, and Ogiso Igodo thought of recalling his command. But just then, the stranger began to laugh loudly. This the Ogiso could not endure. He could endure the stranger's challenges, but not his contemptuous laughter. The Ogiso's wrath was kindled, and he commanded the guards to dispatch the stranger from life as well. Then he turned to the people of Igodomigodo, as if nothing had disturbed his deification.

But no sooner had Ogiso Igodo regained the audience of the people than the stranger returned, leading three dogs on leashes. The Ogiso was astounded, not the least at his order not having been carried out, but in the stranger's bringing dogs before him. The stranger, laughing, unleashed the dogs at Ogiso Igodo. The dogs circled but did not attack the Ogiso.

Ogiso Igodo, more than insulted at the daring, shut his eyes and conjured his favorite form in its darkest nature. His nails grew to claws, his beards turned to mane, his bust enlarged, and hair grew wild on his legs and hands. His figure began to stoop until he was fully transformed into a tiger. He released a mighty roar into the air. The dogs cringed and stepped back. The tiger lunged and caught one of them in the neck. The rest took to their heels.

The tiger tore the head off the dog and cast it at the stranger. The stranger kicked the head back to the Ogiso, and as the head fell before the Ogiso, it turned into a human head. It was one of the warriors which Ogiso Igodo had sent to dispatch the stranger.

"Eat your dog, Ogiso son of Ivbiotu," the stranger said. "Next time, send something worthier to annoy me."

Ogiso Igodo stood hesitant as the anger in him boiled. Then he lunged at the stranger with his claws, his teeth bared. But the stranger was swifter and dodged the tiger, and his laughter, louder than before, was full of mockery. And more fury went into the tiger's claws and muscles as it lunged again.

The stranger stood his ground, and before the tiger was upon him, he transformed into an elephant and the tiger hit against its bulk and fell hard on the ground. The elephant raised its leg to bear on the tiger, but the tiger wriggled out of its way and dug its claws into the elephant's foot. The elephant's trumpet shook the compound. It charged at the tiger and caught it in its trunk and lifted it high in the air. The tiger transformed back into Ogiso Igodo, wriggled out of the elephant's trunk, and landed on the ground.

Ogiso Igodo ran into his armory for his bow and quiver and his long sword which had lain idle since he left forest life for the tranquil life in Igodomigodo. The last he had used the sword was for the slaughter of an enchanted wolf conjured by the wizard of Idomina against Igodo. The wolf's blood had turned the sword black, and black it remained thereafter, for no amount of cleaning could remove the foul blood that the wolf had spilled on the blade. This sword Ogiso Igodo now hefted, and his hand recalled the familiar feel of its hilt.

Although this sword had cut into the thickest hides and bones, Ogiso Igodo did not feel confident in the ability of the sword to deal with the stranger unaided. So he went into his charm room and greased the edges of the sword and tips of his arrows with poison. Then he stepped out to confront the elephant.

The elephant's back was turned to him. He strung his bow and aimed his target shot. It was swift and landed at the elephant's armpit. The elephant gave a loud trumpet and stamped its hind legs on the earth. Ogiso Igodo shot more arrows at the elephant, targeting its joints.

The earth shook as the elephant foundered. Ogiso Igodo ran swiftly to the elephant's swaying trunk, and in one clean cut, slashed it at the base. The elephant lifted its forelegs and swayed, then fell with a heavy thud. Ogiso Igodo plunged his sword into the elephant's neck. It dived deep into the elephant until its hilt touched the neck of the elephant. The elephant's struggle became weaker until it ceased. Ogiso Igodo pulled his sword from the elephant, but there was no blood on it.

He turned with triumph toward the people of Igodomigodo, expecting their cheering. But instead, it was the laughter of the stranger that came to him. He turned and saw that the elephant had transformed back into the stranger, and his taunting laughter was louder than before. Ogiso Igodo stepped back and watched the stranger warily, for now he knew the stranger and his laughter were not ordinary.

Still, Ogiso Igodo was unwilling to admit the power of the stranger. He bided his time and watched the stranger until his back was turned. Then, in a motion as swift as lightning, Ogiso Igodo slashed at the stranger's neck. The sword bounced from his grip and fell to the earth. The stranger turned at Ogiso Igodo and laughed still in derision.

Ogiso Igodo was kindled to more wrath, and he was determined to eliminate the stranger. He now knew that neither sword nor arrows had power over the stranger. He knew few men who had charms potent enough to stay swords, but no man he knew had the power to withstand fire. So Ogiso Igodo purposed to eliminate the stranger by fire but fearing that the stranger would be difficult to subject to fire without adequate force, he conjured enchanted ropes to bind the stranger. The stranger did not resist the binding as Ogiso Igodo had feared, but laughing, surrendered himself as the ropes curled around him until he was tightly bound.

Ogiso Igodo sent for fuel to be piled on the stranger, and when this was done, he ordered that oil be poured on the fuel. Then, deeming that ordinary flame might not prevail on the stranger, Ogiso Igodo invoked fire with his charm. The fire caught on the fuel and kindled into great flames whose smoke rose high into the cloud. Not a struggle was heard from the flame, or a shriek of pain, only the crackling of wood as the fire consumed it. The people cheered Ogiso Igodo for his triumph over the stranger. But Ogiso Igodo watched still, waiting to scatter the ashes of the stranger before he rejoiced over him.

At last the fire died down. Ogiso Igodo stirred the embers for the bones of the stranger, but there were none to see. And while the fire was still smouldering, there came laughter from the crowd, and Ogiso Igodo turned to see the stranger emerging from the crowd, unscorched. The stranger once more approached Ogiso Igodo and stood as on invitation.

"Who are you?" Ogiso Igodo asked, taking care to show neither fear nor admiration in his voice.

"Have you not learnt, Igodo, son of Ivbiotu? Who I am is of no import to you. My mission is all you need to know."

"And what is your mission, stranger?"

"My mission is to put your godhood to the test or strip you of it."

These words Ogiso Igodo would not hear, and his determination to eliminate the stranger grew stronger. But seeing as he could not accomplish this on his own, he retired to consult his divination calabash. The answer took a while in coming, but it was simple when it came: the stranger could only be decapitated with a blade of grass. Ogiso Igodo was surprised, yet he dared not question his calabash, for it had never uttered a word that did not come to pass.

Ogiso Igodo had a blade of grass fetched for him. Concealing the grass behind him, he walked up to the stranger, and while the laughter was in the stranger's mouth, Ogiso Igodo slashed the stranger's neck with the blade of grass. The grass cut through both flesh and bone to the other side. For a moment, it seemed as if Ogiso Igodo had merely cut the air. And then the stranger's head detached from his neck and fell. The Ogiso held out his hands impulsively, caught the head, and clutched it to his bosom before he was aware of his action. He then tried to throw the head away, but the head would not go. He pried it with both hands; still the head would not go. The stranger's head taunted and laughed at the Ogiso. And fear came into Ogiso Igodo for the first time; erstwhile, he had only wondered at the power of the stranger.

Seeing that his hands could not pry the head off, he tried his charms, but the head remained fixed to his bosom, ever laughing at him. At last he despaired of his own efforts and summoned his Babalawo to his aid. They arrived disembodied and took their forms before the Ogiso.

As soon as the first Babalawo took his form and approached Ogiso Igodo with his charm bag and his invocation staff, the stranger's head laughed and called out to the Babalawo.

"Obite, son of Obuta from the land of Ipetu, you have come in an auspicious time. But do you think your charms from Ikiru River will avail you before me?"

The charm maker was astonished at being identified without revealing himself, and still more by the talking decapitated head of the stranger. Still, the Babalawo cast his spell and commanded the decapitated head to release itself from the bosom of Ogiso Igodo. His efforts were in vain, and he got only laughter from the stranger's head. He tried to use his hands to disengage the head, but as his hands came upon the head, his hands withered and flapped down against his rib cage like shrivelled flax. The Babalawo departed in sorrow and humiliation.

Ogiso Igodo summoned another Babalawo. At his materialization, the head began to laugh and address the Babalawo.

"Dabo, son of Ekusi. Are you come from the land of Eduri to try me with your charms from the forest of Udonri?"

The Babalawo ignored the taunt and proceeded with his mission. But he too got no better result than the laughter from the stranger's head. Still, his fate was better, for he was prudent and refused to touch the stranger's head when bid to use his whole resources to free the Ogiso from the stranger's head. The Babalawo left with only the humiliation of failure.

Ogiso Igodo summoned still more Babalawo. But none proved to be of any help. The head had grown more daring and taunted not only Ogiso Igodo but also his Babalawo and their powers. Ogiso Igodo bore the insults, but his desperation increased.

The day had grown thin and had the Babura gone as expected, Ogiso Igodo should now be a god, and the people of Igodomigodo would be carousing to his godhood. Now they watched his humiliation in silence. But Ogiso Igodo was no longer bothered by what the people of Igodomigodo thought of him. He was more concerned with the hunger which had now added to his woes.

He called for food, and it was swiftly set before him. But as he took a morsel and tried to put it in his mouth, the head snatched the food and swallowed it. Ogiso Igodo tried another morsel, and the head wrenched and swallowed it as well. Morsel after morsel the head swallowed and kept growing bigger. Ogiso Igodo saw the extent of his peril, for not only would the head not allow him to eat, but as it fed, it grew and increased his burden.

Ogiso Igodo was at last compelled to summon Baluwa of Iwo land, the most revered of Babalawo, but also the most difficult to summon.

Many a time Igodo had summoned him, but his spirit refused to answer to Igodo's summons. Today, the spirit of Baluwa refused to answer to Igodo's summons until he learnt fully of the Ogiso's plight. He answered the summons, not for love of the Ogiso, but to demonstrate his power where others had failed. He appeared from the air in the most gorgeous panoply of charms. Every part of his body bore an item of charm and they jangled as his feet touched the earth.

The head did not laugh at Baluwa as it was wont, but called out to him, and named the order of his charms. Baluwa, looking upon the stranger's head, prostrated to the earth and began to sing fervently.

Esu,
Esu Odara,
Esu lan lu ogiri oko.
Okunrin ori ita,
A jo langa langa lalu.
A rin lanja lanja lalu.
Ode ibi ija de mole.
Ijani otaru ba d'ele ife.
To fi de omo won.
Oro Esu to to to akoni.
Ao fi ida re lale.
Esu ma se mi o.
Esu ma se mi o.
Esu ma se mi o.
Omo elomiran ni ko lo se.
Pa ado asubi da.
No ado asure si wa.
Ase.

[Translation:
Eshu Elegbara,
Divine Messenger of Transformation,
Speak with power
Man of the crossroads
Dance to the drum.
Tickle the toe of the drum.
Move beyond strife.

Strife is contrary to the spirit of Orun.
Unite the unsteady feet of weaning children.
The word of the Divine Messenger is always respected.
I shall use your sword to touch the Earth.
Divine Messenger, do not confuse me.
Divine Messenger, do not confuse me.
Divine Messenger, do not confuse me.
Confuse someone else.
Turn my suffering around;
Give me the blessing of the calabash.
May it be so.]

Baluwa rose from the ground and approached the head with suppliant palms.

"I bow before you, Eshu Elegbara. One who finds a mansion too small to sleep in yet sleeps in comfort inside a coconut shell. One who throws a stone today and kills a bird yesterday. One who turns right into wrong and wrong into right. Pardon my intrusion; I have not come to annoy you. But one who is summoned is duty bound to answer, though he may refuse the reason of his summons. I have come to behold you, not to command you."

The stranger's head smiled, and when it spoke again, its voice was transcendent and held no mockery.

"Rise Baluwa, son of Obatokun. Respect does not depart from the house of the man whose mouth is full of respect. It is with soft tongue that the snail rides on thorns and blade points. The eye which sees far is not for the restive head. The water does not run deep which chooses a path in the mountain. Baluwa, son of Obatokun: because you have seen where your peers have failed to see, and spoken with tongue of wisdom, I shall crown your mission with success."

So saying, the stranger's head disengaged itself from the bosom of Ogiso Igodo and joined its body, and the stranger once more stood before the Ogiso. But the stranger was now taller and was clad with red raiment of royal design. He turned his face at Ogiso Igodo and it no longer held laughter but rebuke and Ogiso Igodo trembled.

"Igodo, son of Ivbiotu, know me and know wisdom," the stranger's voice boomed, and Ogiso Igodo recognized it as the voice which had spoken to him in the secret of the night, urging him to godhood. "I am Eshu Elegbara, maker of gods. In me is the godhood which you seek, and yet you treated me with disdain. For that, you shall never be granted the powers of a god."

So saying, the stranger turned his face away from Ogiso Igodo and held out his palm to the sky. He called out to the cloud, and his voice echoed. Three times he invoked the cloud; three times his voice released ripples of power into the air, and terror crept into the bones of the people of Igodomigodo.

Suddenly the cloud rumbled overhead, and a blast came from it like a thunder attempting human speech. The response of the cloud was brief, but it seemed to have answered the stranger's purpose, for his laughter once again pealed in the air.

The cloud directly overhead the compound roiled and swirled in rapid commotion toward the earth, until it stood above the stranger's head as if it would engulf him. But instead, streaks of flame began to form from the cloud. The flame enlarged and took the shape of a throne. And the throne descended until it hung suspended beside the stranger. The stranger climbed the flaming throne and from the midst of the flame, his voice thundered.

"Igodo, son of Ivbiotu; wretched shall be the rest of your days and no son of yours shall sit on the throne which you have glutted upon."

Then the fiery throne was subsumed in the cloud as the cloud returned to the sky.

Ogiso Igodo returned to his hall and was never seen again in the land of Igodomigodo.

It was rumored by the wise of Igodomigodo that Ogiso Igodo did not die, but bearing hard the humiliation of Elegbara, he had gone into Igbo Eda, the sacred forest of Olodumare, wherein the powers of the earth were buried. It was said that as he could not be admitted into the abode of the gods, he besought Olodumare for the power of dominion over the earth. But Olodumare, mistaking his request, turned Ogiso Igodo into a tree whose root went deep into the earth's core. Nurtured by the earth's magma, the tree bore no fruits, and its leaves were red like flame, and bitter and poisonous, like the soul of Ogiso Igodo.

And to this day, men who seek the powers of the earth bow to the tree and tap from its pitch and drain the bitterness of Igodo into their soul, and the powers they wield are cruel and merciless.

THE MAGAZINE OF HORROR

by Oghenechovwe Donald Ekpeki

[Cover letter]

February 19, 2020

Dear Editor,

I am a Nigerian writer and slush reader who is studying law in the University of Lagos, Nigeria.

Please find attached, my 6,732-word horror short story. I thank you for your time and consideration and look forward to hearing from you.

Sincerely,
Oghenechovwe Donald Ekpeki

P.S. As an aside, I was wondering, and didn't want to add something so silly to the main body of my cover letter. It's silly really. The worries of a newbie writer. I heard that your magazine is the greatest horror magazine, and they will only publish the greatest horror story at a time; and in the lifetime of the published writer, will publish no other story until the accepted writer expires. Also, that should a story be accepted, the current story is deleted, and the displaced writer dies.

What is worse, I heard that all those rejected by your magazine also die. This is of course all just silly rumors. I notice that your magazine only has one story on it, despite its ridiculously high pay rate of a hundred thousand dollars per story. These are just the silly worries of a newbie writer, and your standards are probably just high. I figure you can't pay many writers with the pay rate what it is. Feel free to ignore my ridiculous query. Unless of course you want to respond to clarify that they are, indeed, just rumors.

...❖...

[Inbox]

February 20, 2020

Dear Oghenechovwe,

Good morning. I would like to allay your fears that what you have heard are rumors, but I cannot. We do take what we do here very seriously, as storytelling is a life-and-death matter. You saw our pay rates. We are recommitted to paying handsomely for the best horror story existing in the world at any moment. And should we fail to pay the funds, we pay in other ways.

Sincerely,
The Editors
The Magazine of Horror

...❖...

[Outbox]

March 19, 2020

Dear Editors,

It's been exactly one month, and I am now wondering what the status of my submission is. Do let me know if it's being seriously considered and when I may hear back from you.

P.S. The tone of your last message, your response to my questions, was really spooky. But I appreciate the humor of it from a horror magazine such as yourself.

Sincerely,
Oghenechovwe

...❖...

[Inbox]

March 21, 2020

Dear Oghenechovwe,

Good morning. I would like to inform you that your story is indeed under consideration. But we lost two members of our staff to untimely death, and our slush reader and submissions editor just passed, immediately after sending your story on to me. We have logged your story into the "under consideration" pile. Funny I use the word pile, as it's the only one there. You'll be hearing from us soon, in one way or another.

Regards,
The Editor
The Magazine of Horror

...❖...

[Outbox]

April 26, 2020

Dear Editor,

Good afternoon. My condolences on the loss and untimely death of your slush reader and your submissions editor. Meanwhile about your aside, what did you mean you want to know if I am willing to consider withdrawing my story? I just want to say that I am comfortable and okay doing whatever it takes to get an acceptance in your magazine. Do let me know if the corrections I have made are sufficient. I look forward to hearing from you.

Sincerely,
Oghenechovwe

…❖…

[Inbox]

July 19, 2020

Dear Oghenechovwe,

Good morning. Sorry for the late response. I am the new Editor-in-Chief. The old one passed away shortly after logging in your story as an acceptance and before notifying you. Congrats.

I had to dig around a bit for the fine print of what to do. It says here that the contract will be delivered to you personally by, "the rider and his pale horse." I chuckled at that. They do love dramatics here. Still, personal delivery, that's odd. It says that no place is beyond the reach of the pale rider, not even the beyond.

I suppose that's it. I have followed all other instructions on how to activate a dispatch, unorthodox as they were. So, I suppose you shall be hearing from this pale rider. Oh, and they spoke of some final test. Assessment by the rider to ascertain if the writer is as worthy as his story. An old tradition. The rider will bear both the "prize and price" and deliver both, depending on the worthiness of the writer.

Not sure what that means, but it's probably an old-fashioned way of checking your personal info, and story, for plagiarism, or just more dramatics. Do let me know if you are contacted and we can move on to fixing a publication date.

Sincerely,
The Editor
The Magazine of Horror

…❖…

A young writer sat in front of his PC in his self-contained apartment in Abule-Oja, the student community of the University of Lagos. A very electric thrill ran through him, a feeling of unquantifiable euphoria. For he had just finished reading an acceptance letter. Not just any acceptance, not even just one from a pro magazine, but one from the greatest horror magazine, and certifying him the greatest horror writer alive, along with a monetary prize of a hundred thousand dollars. The grand lottery of short stories. The unusual terms and requirements did not dim his joy, but added to it. His excitement, though not dimmed, was mixed. Euphoria, and trepidation. A rider, delivering the contract and payment, a final test …

His breathing increased with the sound of hooves outside his door, a slow canter. No way was a horse in Abule-Oja. But he heard the unmistakable whinny of one. The scrape of something sharp, like a scythe on the cement as the rider dismounted. His eyes widened in terror as the door swung open to reveal his dispatch. He could never have imagined …

DESTINY DELAYED

by Oghenechovwe Donald Ekpeki

Mr. Mukoro was sitting at the front of his veranda at about 5:30 a.m. The faint glint of early dawn revealed the figure passing his frontage. It was Chinedu Okah, and he stopped to greet.

"Bros, how you dey? You're up early oh."

"No," Mr. Mukoro replied. "I'm down late."

"Working on your research?"

"No. Working on an old project, approaching a breakthrough. I need funds to finish it, but I'm trying to find a way to finish it without the funds."

"It would be a real breakthrough if you can finish your project without funds .... Finish your project, abolish capitalism, and change the world to make life good for us all!"

Mukoro was amused in spite of himself.

"I have to be off early to escape traffic," Chinedu said. "I'm going to head office on the Island."

"Have you been transferred?"

"I hope so. Or at least, it should be promotion."

"That's some news," Mukoro said, standing up to give Chinedu a handshake.

"When you return, we'll drink to it."

"Of course. That's if you aren't too busy with your project."

Mukoro laughed gently. "Go come, brother."

"Greet Madam and Nyerhovwo for me," Chinedo said as he departed.

A moment later, a slim, dark Itsekiri woman stepped out with a seven-year-old girl, still groggy with sleep. The girl saw Mukoro and ran to hug him. "Daddy miguo."

"Vrendo, my child."

The woman curtsied "Miguo papa Nyerhovwo."

"Vrendo mama Nyerhovwo," he said with a smile.

She smiled back, smacking the child's butt playfully, and pulling her from playing with her father's beard, which she held on to. He screamed in mock pain, and she giggled as she was pulled away. The child slipped out of her mother's grip and ran back to him.

"Oghenenyerhovwo," her mom called sternly. "Come and bathe now, or you will be late for school, and they will flog you when you get there."

The little girl looked at her father askance. He nodded. She kissed the cheek he turned for her and returned grudgingly to her mother who dragged her to the corner of the house.

Mukoro sighed and closed his eyes, and the numbers and equations came unbidden to him as they usually did.

…❖…

Chinedu Okah alighted from the Keke Napep that dropped him at a side street and walked a few steps to the head office of AUB, the Africa United Bank. He blended in with the top bankers and persons in the finance sector, his crisp blue suit and starched white shirt making him look as sharp as the drawn blade of a Mushin gangster intent on robbing someone at two in the morning.

He was glad to be here. He was glad to have left the position of cashier, handling the grubby notes of traders and students at the Yaba branch of AUB, and marketer briefly thereafter.

He approached the nearest help desk and presented his ID, informing the attendant that he had an appointment with Mr. Abiola Yusuf of Human Resources. She placed a call before signaling him to wait, for Mr. Yusuf was in a meeting. This early? Chinedu wondered. Well, he would wait. He had been waiting a long while after all: three years as a contract staff, and six years at the Yaba AUB branch. He was led to the waiting room to do what it was named after.

Finally, Mr. Yusuf walked in and shook his hand.

"Good morning, sir," Chinedu said, surprised to see Mr. Yusuf sporting a blue Kaftan on a Monday morning. In Yaba branch, even the branch manager didn't wear native dress unless it was Friday. But this was head office. He guessed when one was this close to the top, one did what one wanted.

"Mr. Chinedu Okah, is it?" Mr. Yusuf asked in a Hausa accent.

"Yes, sir."

"Walk with me."

Chinedu followed him out of the waiting room to an elevator. Mr. Yusuf punched in the thirteenth floor and spoke to him as the elevator rose.

"You read the e-brochure, right? So you know what we do here."

"Yes, sir."

"Well, I want to give you a few pointers and show you around, so you see and understand a bit more of what we do in this department."

They came out of the elevator and walked down a hallway.

"You were the most active marketer in the Yaba branch," Mr. Yusuf continued. "Only the best get recommended here. Your record is stellar. They say you pulled in six billion naira in six months, a billion per month." Mr. Yusuf stared at Chinedu and nodded. He seemed to like what he saw in Chinedu's eyes. "Well, now you will be helping us with something more than money."

They stopped in front of a large department marked UBD at the top of the entranceway. United Bank of Destiny.

Chinedu could hardly believe himself when he was ushered into the UBD. Although he had read the brochure, he wasn't sure if he was being pranked.

"This is the measurement and extraction room," Mr. Yusuf explained. "This is where a destiny is mapped, measured, and extracted."

A procedure was in progress. A young man was standing in front of a machine that looked like an X-ray machine. Mr. Yusuf waved to the technicians in lab coats, gloves, coveralls, and goggles.

The technicians switched on the Destiny machine, and it emitted a whirring noise. There were a number of wires connected to the machine, which in turn were connected to screens around the room. The machine's whirring turned louder, and the air rippled in front of and behind the young man. The air took on a dark gray hue. The hue turned from dark gray to purple and then to gray again. Then the air stopped whirling, and one of the technicians switched off the Destiny machine.

"The screens do the soul reading, and the vibrancy of the colors displays the intensity of the destiny," Mr. Yusuf said, turning to Chinedu, who still stared at the operation and the operators. "The process measures the capacity of a man's destiny. The destiny is then extracted by the machine and stored in a soul cube."

As the young man was led away to put on his clothes, Chinedu noticed that his eyes looked dead, and his face was bleached of color.

Mr. Yusuf led Chinedu to another room marked Acquisitions and Mortgages.

"This will be your office. The destinies you determine and measure will be extracted and kept as collateral for their loans. Your job will be much like the old one as a marketer at the Yaba branch. But this time, you'll market young people who want loans but who have no property for collateral. You'll convince them to use their destinies as collateral. It's a way for us to be of service to the needy. Think of it as an empowerment scheme, to help those who would otherwise not be able to get the funds they need. It's like student loans in America. This is, of course, a very sensitive department. You will see our lawyers to sign a nondisclosure agreement. That's fine with you, of course?"

"Yes, sir," Chinedu smiled knowingly. The monthly salary here was more than he earned in a year at Yaba Branch. In no time he could clear all his loans, even get a car. And moving to the Island would be possible.

Mr. Abiola's voice snapped Chinedu out of his reverie. "I read your dossier and knew that an overachiever like yourself would definitely be up for the job. Otherwise, we would have had you sign the nondisclosure even before you came in here. But I like to think I am a good judge of people. Or I wouldn't be head of HR."

Mr. Yusuf chuckled, and Chinedu chuckled politely in return. Mr. Yusuf kept walking and talking.

"Discretion is very important to what we do here. Not that it's illegal. The young men and women who come for loans all consent to have their destinies extracted and kept as collateral. Not that there is anything in the law about this, nor can the law make sense of it. We just don't want the uproar it would cause if uninformed ears got to know of what we do here. You know Nigerians are superstitious. They won't understand that we just want to help people."

Mr. Yusuf led Chinedu to an office in the Mortgages and Acquisitions department. It was well furnished with a sofa for visitors, and a Surface Book on an expensive-looking mahogany desk. "This will be your office," Mr. Yusuf said, gesticulating.

Chinedu was breathtaken by the office. It was three times larger than his branch manager's office at Yaba. Mr. Yusuf chuckled at his incredulity. Just then, a man in a purple suit walked in carrying a briefcase. Mr. Yusuf touched Chinedu on the shoulder.

"The lawyer is here. I'll leave you both so you can get started in earnest. It's a new week, and you already have your quota." Chinedu nodded.

"I stuck my neck out for you," Mr. Yusuf said as he stepped out. "There were dozens recommended for this post. All with stellar records. But I picked you. Like I said, I have a head for people. Don't disappoint me."

Chinedu assured Mr. Yusuf he wouldn't be a disappointment. "I'll have my first catch for you this week," he said. "I know just the person."

Mr. Yusuf nodded. "I knew you were the man for us."

He patted Chinedu, who bowed before returning to the lawyer. Mr. Yusuf whistled as he left.

...❖...

Mukoro and Chinedu sat drinking at a beer parlor at Montgomery, Yaba. Bottles of Alomo, Guilder, and small stout littered their table. Hunched over, they discussed dreams and ambitions, as fermented as the leftover alcohol in their bottles. They were seeking ways to escape the penury that clung to them, like paint on the wall, ever fading, but never quite gone. It clutched them with the tenacity of a wounded soldier behind Boko Haram lines, far from home, but unwilling to leave this world without a goodbye to his family.

"So, I let them extract her destiny as collateral for a loan of any amount I want?" Mukoro was asking.

"Not 'any' amount, but an amount not exceeding eight figures in naira. And that's after reading her destiny to ascertain its worth."

Mukoro rubbed his beard. "I see," he said thoughtfully.

Chinedu looked at him with shrewd eyes that retained their sharpness despite the numerous bottles of alcohol they had consumed. "You don't seem overly surprised by any of this?"

Mukoro shook his head. "I studied systems engineering, and my PhD was in soul mapping and interaction with spirit particles." He glanced at Chinedu before adding, "What do you think my research and projects are all about? You could say destiny led us here."

Mukoro leaned forward and continued. "My grandfather was a great Jazzman in his time. He was blind but could see more clearly than those with two eyes. He could uncannily put together pieces of the unformed future. You know, that is what they do when they map the soul and read a person's destiny. The device they call a soultrifier can map what we now call spirit particles, or what the rest of the world knows of as dark matter. The soultrifier is built to calculate the propensity of the soul, like a sort of advanced probability. If you want to simplify it, you can say it's a combination of very advanced possibility tied to your DNA structure and other things we don't yet understand. Kind of like how we know a fit person might go into sports, or a lonely person into arts or literature. The soultractor is the real breakthrough. It finds a way to extract the unique strands of each person's propensity and store it in a soul cube."

Mr. Mukoro stopped talking to take a pull of his beer. Chinedu called for a waiter.

"Two more bottles of big stout." When the waiter departed, Chinedu turned to Mukoro and asked, "So what does all this have to do with your grandfather?"

"Oh yes. I got caught up in explaining about the process and my work. I love to talk about my work with those who can listen. Anyway. My grandfather prophesied that I would give my child a great destiny. This was before my first degree, when I didn't know anything about this. He used the word 'destiny,' in English. Even though he wasn't educated or spoke any language other than Urhobo."

Mukoro's eyes became distant, as if he could stare across time to the event of the prophecy's utterance. "My grandfather had never been wrong in such utterances before. I don't think this one will be wrong, either. That is why I'm so focused on my research. I want to leave a legacy for my child. I want to ensure she gets that promised destiny. This is for her, you understand? It's my destiny to grant her a great destiny.

I must bequeath her more than was bequeathed on me. But I cannot do much as it is. It seems destiny cannot be realized without funds. I can't even get a reasonable job with my PhD, much less funding for my research. I can't apply for foreign grants with a project like this. It has only made headway here because of our combination of science and spirituality. It took the work of the council of Dibias, Babalawos, and scientists to discern how to interact with the spirit particles. So I can't get funds from outside, as they would not think much of a project like this. But if I can get the loan from your bank to finish my research, I can leave something for Nyerhovwo, and fulfill my destiny to gift her a great destiny."

"I see," Chinedu said. "Not that I wish to make you question this, since it's my job to get people to take loans. But you are also my friend. Isn't the loan unnecessary? The breakthrough has been done already and monetized. Of what use is your research?"

Mukoro laughed until tears trickled from his eyes, and he wiped them. "You should know that no research is ever finished. All the technology we have is still being improved on. And this is a new area. There's still a lot more to discover."

Chinedu smiled. "So I'll see you at the office tomorrow, then?"

"Yes. You said extracting the destiny doesn't hurt?"

"Yes, it doesn't hurt. It's just a net weight of probabilities and the person's propensity to achieve a thing. In the same way that being paralyzed doesn't kill."

"I know. I just want to confirm. And the destiny will be kept intact, returned and reintegrated with the source?"

"Of course, it will be returned and reintegrated once the loan is fully paid, along with interest."

"And it's legal for parents to take a loan with the destiny of a child, a minor?"

"Yes, although it's a legal gray area, as the law doesn't recognize the procedure yet. But the law is still catching up, so you have nothing to worry about. You cannot sin where there is no law. Parents and legal guardians can consent on behalf of their children. It's like taking your child for a bone marrow transplant."

"I'll talk to my wife about it tonight," Mukoro said, and frowned as if he hadn't been reassured by the idea that what he was doing wasn't a sin, even if he wouldn't be held responsible.

Chinedu noticed the look on his face. "Remember you are doing this for her. And to fulfill your grandfather's prophecy."

"I know." Mukoro nodded.

Chinedu poured his remaining drink from the bottle and ordered three more bottles for Mukoro.

Mukoro thanked him, took another long pull, then asked, "Nothing more for you?"

"Naaah, I'm all right for now," Chinedu said. "I have to rise early for work tomorrow. I have to wake up by four and leave before five to beat Island traffic."

Mukoro rose to shake Chinedu's hand and see him off. "All right, good night."

"Don't forget to talk to madam about it this night," Chinedu called as he left.

Mukoro returned to his drink, his somber thoughts rising vampire-like, despite his efforts to bury them in ethanol.

...❖...

That night, Mukoro cuddled his wife, Bianca. She snuggled into his arm.

"Was she asleep before you left her?" she asked.

"Yes. Her love for that story never stops her from falling asleep before the end." He chuckled, remembering his daughter's droopy eyelids closing as he read to her.

Bianca shook her head. "She'll only ever fall asleep when it's you reading. When I read to her, she stares at me with glittering eyes till the story is done. She trusts you."

Mukoro was silent, knowing where the talk was headed.

"I heard all you said before. I need to know that I can trust you to do right by her."

Mukoro sighed. "She's my daughter, too. And I love her. You know that."

"I know. You have been a good father to her." She paused a moment, then asked. "You say this mortgage of destiny won't hurt her?"

"No, it won't hurt her," he said. "The process doesn't hurt, it only dulls one's chances. It is a destiny, after all. I can't use mine because I need to be sharp to use the funds. And it can't be you either," he added, forestalling the question he knew she wanted to ask. "They won't take a middle-aged housewife's destiny. I know, sexist, but that's how it is. It has to be hers. As it is, what future does she have here?"

He waved at the dilapidated structure in which they lived. "Things aren't like in my time when education was government subsidized. Since the monetization of schooling, the university is beyond our reach. They say education is the future. And we can't afford to pay for a college degree. So what's a destiny without a future? This is for her." Then he whispered, "And for them." He looked at his wife's stomach.

She turned to face him. "What do you mean by 'them,' papa Nyerhovwo?"

"Do you think I don't know you're pregnant?" He cupped her cheek gently. "I have known since you stopped asking for money for pads two months ago."

"I should have known that would give it away," she said. "I was just relieved to save you the expense."

"Well, there will be other expenses. And my on-and-off consulting job can't help us. I need to do this for them." He held her hands. "Let me save this family with this loan. With her help, I'll secure a future for her and her brother. But once I finish my project and have a bit of stability, I'll repay the loan. Then we can ensure a great destiny for them."

Bianca was quiet for a while, then said "Or sister."

He smiled and kissed her. "But we already have a girl."

"Well, boys are trouble."

"Good trouble."

"Like you, huh?" She jabbed him in the ribs.

He laughed. "I have to leave with her early in the morning to beat traffic. And you have to take permission for her absence to her school. So should we sleep now?" he asked with a slanted eyebrow.

"Did you also learn how to be so subtle at your PhD program?" she asked, pulling her shirt off, mounting him and kissing him deeply.

"I mean, it's not like you can get pregnant again," he said.

She leaned back, letting the sounds of joy that flittered from her and bounced off the walls, bring a little blue to the cold yellow of the room.

...❖...

3 years and 8 months later ...

A Black Range Rover and a white 4matic Benz parked in front of a Chinese restaurant in Awolowo Road, Ikoyi. Mukoro climbed out of the Range Rover while Chinedu climbed out of the 4matic.

They shook hands and were about to go into the eatery when Chinedu tapped Mukoro and said, "Let's talk in the car first. I have some sensitive information."

Mukoro nodded and opened the door of the Range Rover, and they both stepped in and closed the door. The AC was running.

Mr. Mukoro spoke first. "There's something wrong. The loan defaults in seven months, isn't it?"

Chinedu nodded.

"I don't understand why I'm unable to clear the interest, try as I might? There's always something left, and the loan itself never goes down."

Chinedu shrugged and said, "But you seem to be doing well."

"Which isn't the point," Mukoro cut in harshly. "You know I want to clear the loan and recover something else more than money. Nyerhovwo is in secondary school and just wrote her Junior WAEC examination. In another three years, she will be looking at attending the university."

"You have the funds for that, don't you? And enough for Oghenemudia too, for that matter. How is he, by the way? And Madam?"

"They are fine," Mukoro said perfunctorily, dismissing the question. "I'm not talking about any of that. I'm talking about Nyerhovwo. Her teachers report that she lacks interest in everything, even though her grades are middling and fine. And her eyes are always dead."

Chinedu's brows creased momentarily. Mukoro would not have noticed if he had not been watching for it.

"You know something of this, don't you? And why my businesses seem to be doing well but never well enough to clear the loan?" "I don't ..." Chinedu began.

Mukoro cut him off. "No, no, don't do that, please."

Chinedu sighed and looked Mukoro in the eyes before he began. "I turned a blind eye to a lot of things when I started, because I needed the money and the upgrade. But the truth is, I always knew something was off. The way I was chosen, the department, my handler. But I was hungry, and they knew it. Too hungry to ask questions, too hungry to think, or choose to do the right thing. Head of HR truly was a good judge of people. I think I'm basically a devil in a suit, sent to tempt the vulnerable for their destinies. I get the low and the desperate like myself and yourself."

"The destinies," Mukoro said, returning to the subject he desperately needed to discuss.

"They were never going to be given back," Chinedu said. "Your businesses are monitored and sabotaged. Not enough for you to notice, but enough so you can't repay the loan on time, and the destinies become theirs. They are sold at ungodly amounts to powerful men who take them for themselves to enhance their chances at success, or gift them to their families. That's why the rich and powerful in Nigeria are becoming richer and more powerful."

Mukoro listened in silence. Chinedu said, "You knew this, didn't you?"

"I began to piece it together recently. I suppose, like you, I always knew. But my poverty prevented me from thinking straight. The obfuscating green of the naira tempted my gaze away from the truth."

"Your research?" Chinedu asked.

"I've finished it. The machine I built can map souls and extract destinies, just like the one at the bank. But mine is more energy efficient, as it runs on solar power. I tried to get investors, or talk to people in government, but I met roadblocks at every turn. I couldn't even register a company for it. I was blocked from Corporate Affairs Commission up."

"This is a government-enabled monopoly," Chinedu said. "They don't want competition. That's why the rest of the world doesn't know about it." Chinedu lowered his voice and added, "If you push too closely, try to go to the press, or talk to too many people about this, you might wind up in a shallow grave somewhere."

"Or an accident," Mukoro said calmly. He lit a cigarette and handed one to Chinedu who took it and lit it. Both men smoked in silence for a while.

"I can't let it go," Mukoro said. "It's my daughter's destiny."

"Don't be stupid," Chinedu said. "The powers that be …"

"I made a promise to my wife. I told her she could trust me. She did."

"You have a family now. Your son …"

"So what? I should sacrifice my daughter's destiny for the family? For my son?" Mukoro looked at Chinedu with wild, angry eyes. Chinedu sighed and resumed smoking. After a while they both finished.

"I am not nobody now, you know," Mukoro continued. "I know things. And I have power."

Chinedu shook his head. "Not compared to the people who control the bank. They are the same people who control Nigeria. The governors, senators, the cabals behind the president."

Chinedu opened the door but did not get out. "I've been looking for a way to quit. Being a headhunter for destinies is taking its toll on me. I just haven't found a way to do so safely. I'll be heading home to my fiancée now. See that you return to your family, okay? Don't do anything rash."

Mukoro said nothing in response. Chinedu closed the door with a sigh, got into his car, and drove off.

...❖...

Eight months later ...

Mukoro walked into the AUB head office and was led to the Department of Soul measurement and extraction. He had an appointment. It was the appointed time ... for him ... for Nyerhovwo. He had a debt to pay. Or not pay, rather. Some debts you paid by not paying. He had dined with the devil. And it didn't matter how long the spoon. Silver bullets kill werewolves, it is said. But Nigerian devils ate silver and chewed their way up the spoon to your fingertips, then down your hands, till they licked your brains off their own fingers.

He looked at his Audemar. It was such an expensive timepiece, but despite the costliness, the glowing jewels, his time was up, and he couldn't buy more. It was eleven o'clock. Fittingly the eleventh hour.

He walked into Chinedu's office. The lawyer—the devil's advocate—was there, along with another man, probably Chinedu's handler. They were there to oversee the handover.

Chinedu said some words to Mukoro, but he couldn't hear them. The words flittered past him. He caught some words. "Defaulted on the loan ... destiny is forfeit ... sign here ... Mr. Mukoro. Sign?" There was a paper in front of him. They handed him a pen.

He looked at them and smiled. He would sign for them in blood. He stood up and tore his jacket open. "When you sell your soul, or another's, you should always sign in blood. I'll sign with my blood, since I made the trade."

The occupants of the room gawked at him. Lining his jacket were a number of wires running into a device sewed into his coat. He pulled out a detonator. The occupants of the room all backed away.

"Bomb?" Chinedu's handler queried.

"No, it's not a bomb," Mukoro said, spitting. "Not the type that takes lives, anyway. Just the type that takes destinies."

The handler raised an eyebrow. "What do you want? More money? You can relax. We have money."

"I don't want money. I want my daughter's destiny. I knew you would never give back what you stole. So once I confirmed, eight months ago, I started reworking my prototype. It will rip the destiny from everyone within a ten-mile radius and integrate them with the operator of the device."

He turned to Chinedu. "I told you it is my destiny to gift my child a great destiny.

And I will not be denied by thieves and saboteurs." He screamed at them. The lawyer backed off.

"Yes," Mukoro continued. "When I activate my device, it will rip the destinies off everyone in this den of thieves and integrate them in me. Including my child's. I can ask for just hers, but you all don't deserve what you have. Thieves!"

The handler rushed at Mukoro, and he pushed the button on his detonator. The air came alive, crackling with electricity. Thunder boomed outside, and it began to rain. A blast tore through the room, mini blasts occurring around everyone, as their destinies were ripped from them and drawn to Mukoro. His eyes blazed with each destiny he integrated, while those whose destinies he took, fell with dead eyes. A dozen—two, three, four—dozen destinies, and Mukoro's eyes glowed. Then his device overheated and burst into flames. He ripped it off and tossed it away.

Chinedu, the lawyer, and the handler stood before him with dead eyes. Mukoro turned to them.

"I know you pressed the security button, and the police will be here soon," he said, pulling a gun. They all backed off.

"Have you heard the saying that destiny can be delayed, but not denied? A seemingly nonsensical phrase, but true nonetheless. Destiny is like energy; it can be transferred, but not destroyed. And it can't be transferred permanently. Its unique code is tied to the original owner's DNA. So when it's not gifted to anyone and the current holder dies, it goes back to its original source if they are still alive. When I die, all the destinies I have taken will go back to their owners if I don't gift them to anyone else. You will have your sordid destinies back." He paused. "And my daughter, too. That's all I wanted. I am after what is mine."

"What is yours?" the handler asked. "We gave you the loan. You defaulted. You have no right."

Mukoro pointed the gun at the handler, and he backed away.

Just then, the police—three men and a woman—burst into the room. Time slowed. Mukoro smiled at the handler, who was waving at the SARS unit not to shoot. But Mukoro knew. The Nigerian police would not refrain from shooting an armed man pointing a gun at a senior bank manager. You could trust the police to do their jobs the one time they shouldn't.

Mukoro heard the shots of multiple guns going off. His body hit the ground. The bullets had hit him faster than it had taken the sound to travel to his ears, breaking him, along with the sound barrier. His vision dimmed. The handler was screaming for an ambulance and for a destiny extraction machine before he died. Mukoro willed himself to die, his destiny. He closed his eyes permanently and fulfilled it.

...❖...

2 weeks later ...

Chinedu sat with Nyerhovwo and her mother. The relatives had all traveled back to the village after the funeral, and they were alone in their apartment in Lekki.

"The bank reached out," Chinedu said. "I am no longer with them. But I agreed to liaison with the family on their behalf." He did not say that he had negotiated his release by promising to smooth things over and ensure the Mukoro family's silence. "They are offering to discharge the debt of Nyerhovwo's destiny and also pay a huge compensation for the accident of Mr. Mukoro's death."

"I still don't understand how they can mistake a respectable businessman like Mukoro for a robber," Mama Nyerhovwo lamented.

"You know how stupid Nigerian police can be …"

As Chinedu glibly droned on, Nyerhovwo got up and left them to it. Her brother Oghenemudia was asleep, and the adults were happy to see her go, not wanting to have such difficult conversations around her.

She went upstairs to her father's room, then to his private study. She riffled through the papers scattered on his desk, pulled out one, and scanned it briefly. It read "Destiny extraction and replication." She knew this already. Her father's last work was not just about extracting destinies forcefully, it was also about replicating energy signatures and mimicking them. When he died and the originals went back to their sources, the copies stayed or came to her, his closest DNA match. So now she had the destiny of a couple of hundred people. Her father had gifted her a great destiny, as he had always wanted.

She closed her eyes, letting the thoughts and desires wash through her. She opened her eyes, and they glowed fiercely. Some things pushed her from within. She had to finish her father's work. She let the thoughts and visions drive her as she began to look over his research.

As she read, her eyes closed, but her reading did not stop. Voices whispered the words to her. The voices were the physical manifestation of possibilities that had torn a path through other realities to find their way to her. She already knew the words. Other voices whispered to her, increasing in tempo and numbers: "We are legion. We bring you your great destiny."

She dropped the book and held her head in agony. A great destiny did not mean a good one for the holder, or a sane one for that matter. She willed the voices away. They grew silent for a moment, then issued from her as colors: violet, violet-gray, then purple—dark manifestations of all that was in her. The colors gathered in the room above her, then merged together, changing and expanding into a black, torrential darkness that gathered around her. She looked at it with eyes wide, and through this open doorway to her soul, the colors rushed furiously into her.

She closed her eyes. When she opened them, they did not seem like the eyes of a twelve-year-old. They were deep and mysterious, shining with a dark, speckled light of unspoken things; of a great and powerful force waiting to be unleashed on a greedy, wicked, and unsuspecting world. But her look contained something even more wicked. This destiny would not be denied.

TOO DYSTOPIAN FOR WHOM? A CONTINENTAL NIGERIAN WRITER'S PERSPECTIVE (ESSAY)

by Oghenechovwe Donald Ekpeki

It is a common conception that people come to fiction, especially the speculative, to escape reality. And that is indeed one of the purposes it can serve. Another is that conversely to escaping, people come to fiction to encounter or experience reality. A paradox? After all, we already live in reality, one that is ubiquitous. We have it all around us, painfully so sometimes. Hence the need for an escape. But you see, reality has different facets, different windows, like eyes, that reveal different vistas.

This is why the consumption of fiction and Science Fiction/Fantasy based on other cultures and by people of other demographics is a necessity. Doing so helps us diversify our understanding and encounter all these different realities that lie beyond our immediate purview. What we are often steeped in is our own immediate reality, which is, while occasionally painful, also painfully limited.

It has often been surmised, most especially around discussions of war, climate change, natural disasters, and more recently the outbreak of COVID-19, in articles like this in *Wired* and on The Apeiron Blog, that we are living in a dystopia. This realization has weaned many of the need for apocalyptic, postapocalyptic, and dystopian fiction, and has them preferring instead to immerse themselves in lighter, more upbeat and positive work. This is of course valid, as we all must do what we feel right. But beyond personal preferences of individuals for lighter, "happier" works in this period of gloom, there is a wider and more general assertion that dystopias, apocalypses, grimdark, dark fantasy, and the like are now unnecessary because we live in and have it all around us. A *Publishers Weekly* piece talks about dystopian fiction losing its lustre due to the pandemic and spells doom for the subgenre of doom. But is this really so? In a viral tweet, the account tweets its disagreement, which I quite agree with, saying that: "Dystopian fiction is when you take things that happen in real life to marginalized populations and apply them to people with privilege." The dystopian reality is not new and has been with us for a while. Its fictionalizing continues to date, despite those debates regarding its relevance or necessity.

My Otherwise and Nommo award-winning novella, "Ife-Iyoku, Tale of Imadeyunuagbon," also a finalist in the Nebula and Sturgeon award, is a dystopian tale. Prior to its publication, I submitted its draft to a beta reader for assessment, because I feared it was too dark and the reactions and experiences of some of the characters were extreme to an unreasonable and unbelievable degree. My beta reader confirmed my fears. There was no gainsaying that part of my intended market and audience in the West, where I intended to publish it, would find it so. But—he said—the story was deficient in yet another dimension: certain events and happenings in our society mirrored the ones in the book almost exactly. And the reactions, conclusions, and climaxes of those in the real world and our immediate environs were far worse than I painted in my work of fiction. My softer depiction of reality would be less believable to a certain audience base of readers, editors, and publishers than what life here threw at us, with no care at all for their willingness to believe or disbelieve it. It was too "strong," and at the same time, not strong "enough." The paradoxical difference lying in the gap between our realities.

Nigeria, where I live, became the poverty capital of the world in 2018 and maintained it for the next three years, having more poor people than India, the former poverty capital, with more than five times Nigeria's population. We were surpassing them in sheer numbers, not just percentages. A population of 200 million, managing to have more poor people than one of over a billion with the closest poverty numbers in sight, illustrates just how steep and staggering those numbers are.

It is also number one in open defecation, with the fourth-lowest life expectancy on earth, lower even than war-torn countries like Syria, Afghanistan, and Palestine, that have had conflict on and off for nearly seventy years. All this is understandable in a continent plagued by centuries of slavery—colonialism and continuing neo-colonialism—that has had its resources, both human and material, plundered. So, this is not to be unreasonably critical of Nigeria's woes. It is also plagued by a plethora of issues that follow these levels of poverty, lack of power, access, security, healthcare, and more.

In 2017 alone, there were about 150 attacks mounted by Boko Haram. Ninety of them were armed assaults, and 59 suicide attacks. If you divided the number of attacks by the 365 days of the year, it would mean there was one attack every two days or so. Little more than two days, less than three. The residents of that region, and it was one concentrated region in Northern Nigeria, had to deal with deadly, fatal attacks every other day. No time to recover, to heal, to mourn their losses. That's almost as many workdays as an average civil servant in a white-collar job somewhere sane had. Especially if you threw in leave time and public holidays. Meanwhile, these people had no leave periods, no holidays. If anything, the terrorists struck almost unfailingly on holidays. The one advantage holidays then offered was one could count on an attack and move to protect themselves or plan for it on those days. It's almost mind boggling that this is possible. At 150 attacks, one every two days, one wonders the level of organization the terrorists dedicated to killing innocent people. No respite for them as well, time to recover, rest, plan the logistics of it. Every. Other. Day.

I casually consider the sheer resources and willpower it would take to pull off something like this, in case I wanted to create a force of evil that dedicated, in my fiction works. Then I abandoned the thought for being a touch too much. But real people were this much relentless in committing evil as any villain or Dark Lord ever was. They displayed a thoroughness in inflicting pain and damage that would be unbelievable from almost any force but a zombie army, if written in fiction. The zombie army being believable for their mindlessness. Yet these were living, breathing human beings who planned and affected this consistently, for a whole year. Too dystopian? Perhaps. But you'd have a hard time convincing the people it happened to. But then again, you might not, there being a chance they want to disbelieve it just as much as you do. They may indeed blur some of the details. But the trauma of it will be etched in each of them, burned and branded into their brains, seared into their souls even as their bodies crumble, passing pain on to their progeny through DNA. And that's the lucky ones, the survivors who live to tell this deeply tragic, dastardly, and "too dystopian" tale.

Recently, the US Supreme Court overturned *Roe v. Wade*, ending 50 years of federal abortion rights, and paving the way for the rolling back of LGBTQIA+ rights, which conservative politicians have hinted is coming. This led to widespread panic and outrage by people who value life, bodily autonomy, and freedom both in the United States and around the world.

After *Roe v. Wade* was overturned, many parallels were drawn between the society of today and the one in Margaret Atwood's *The Handmaid's Tale*. Meanwhile *those* events are akin to those that have happened to Black and Indigenous women in the past, and people of color. Forced sterilizations, abuse, and violation of bodily rights are currently happening to people in ICE custody, to date. Margaret Atwood herself admitted that when she wrote *The Handmaid's Tale*, "Nothing went into it that had not happened in real life somewhere at some time." Yet people want to, and hold the view, that these are new or recent events.

In Nigeria, abortions have always been illegal, and as deadly as the onslaught of Boko Haram mentioned earlier has been, more people die from unsafe abortions in a year than from direct Boko Haram attacks in nearly a decade. Meanwhile, being gay is also criminalized, with a death penalty, carried out by stoning in Northern Nigeria, and a fourteen-year jail term in Southern Nigeria.

Some other dystopic facts about Nigeria, it has the largest number of out-of-school children on earth, and blasphemy is a crime with the capital punishment to be carried out by stoning in Northern Nigeria. Suicide, or rather its attempt, is also a crime. Since if you succeed, you are beyond the arm of the law. Long as it claims to be, it's thankfully not that long. This is ironic though when taken with everything else. You see, you cannot live. But you must not deny the government the pleasure of killing you. The dystopia is here, has always been. It's just not evenly distributed.

I have found generally, on further and sometimes casual reflection, that the experiences I—and people I have known living in Nigeria and on the continent—have had are worse than the experiences of protagonists and characters in some dystopias and dark fantasy stories I have read. Our daily lived experiences are sometimes harsher than the sufferings of characters deliberately crafted to be tortured and wrung through great suffering.

In essence, some people experience a reality that is beyond the wildest imaginings of some other people. This is why when people from certain regions that have been dubbed Third World or developing, marginalized people, write dystopias, even non-dystopias, any kind of reflection of their reality that is flavored with a certain harshness, it's considered too unpalatable, unbelievable, too dystopian, especially at the moment, by the global publishing machinery, which is largely Western. The question we should be asking though is: Too dystopian for whom?

You see, our reality is far starker than the dystopia I wrote, which is already too stark a reality for many in a different clime. So when we say fiction helps us escape reality, which reality are we trying to escape? Our own, or knowledge of the lived reality of billions of people from a different place and time? An escape that blinds us as to the true nature of the world and limits or curtails our understanding of it? Fiction can indeed help us to escape reality; dystopias, the dark parts of reality. But they can also be windows to other worlds. Lived, past, and present realities of others.

There is of course reality fatigue, and one may need to step away from it all for the sake of their mental health. And that is an entirely valid reaction. But claiming that all fictional dystopias are redundant because we NOW live in one is a dangerously high level of presumption and an inaccurate assertion. Because we have always lived in one, there has always been a dystopia somewhere in this world that we were only unaware of. And going by the logic of dystopian storytelling being redundant because we are in one, dystopian storytelling should have been redundant since forever, due to the presence of an existing, dystopic reality at some place and time or the other. But the timeline and positioning of Western privilege does not determine the actual position of the world and what is relevant or irrelevant. To assume that is merely Eurocentric hubris.

Beyond Margaret Atwood's *The Handmaid's Tale*, my novella "Ife-Iyoku, Tale of Imadeyunuagbon" examined gender issues women have lived with and continue to face to date. Tlotlo Tsamaase, a Nommo award-winning, Lambda nominated, queer Motswana writer, uses work you can term dark or dystopian to interrogate and come to terms with issues that queer, African, and disabled people can relate to in her works such as, "Dreamports," "Eclipse of Our Sins," "Behind Our Irises," "District to Cervix," and "Peeling Time," forthcoming in the *Africa Risen* anthology.

Tananarive Due, a doyen of Black horror, talks about how Black horror is often a critique of race relations. She often talks about the state of being in alternate realities that speak to a Black American experience. She also cites Jordan Peele and Steven Barnes, with whom she has worked with in shows like Horror Noire in Shudder and AMC; and others, producing works that give Black people a space to examine, confront, and come to terms with the horrors they live with daily.

"O_2 Arena," my Nebula award-winning, Hugo, BSFA and BFA shortlisted climate fiction novelette, interrogates climate crises in the event of neo- and post-colonialism, through the lens of disabled characters dealing with rampant sexism, homophobia, and a vicious fight for the very air in their lungs. While it may be heavy to consume, it is a true representation of Lagos, where it is set, and a story which even some cancer survivors have found representative of their experiences. Sheree Renée Thomas, a Memphis writer, editor, and pioneer in Black speculative literature, also puts out work, like her collection *Nine Bar Blues*, and stories in it like "The Parts That Make Us Monsters" and "Ancestries" reprinted in the *Year's Best African Speculative Fiction* anthology, that though dark, interrogate Blackness on levels that help readers see themselves and their worlds, their realities, in her work.

I have a short story out in the May/June 2022 issue of *Asimov's* and reprinted in *Galaxy's Edge* magazine, titled "Destiny Delayed." In it, a man trades the destiny of his daughter to a firm that offers loans to the destitute, taking the destinies of their young, promising daughters as collateral. They repurpose the destinies for huge profits when the debts inevitably default, and the daughters do indeed become collateral damage. The story was inspired by similar practices in Southern Nigeria that has parents clearing or paying off debts by giving away their young daughters, in child and underage marriages, in Northern Nigeria. It's also a metaphor for the general exploitation and control of birthing bodies that is the order of the day.

What do all these dark, horror, or dystopian works have in common? They are beautiful works of literature that serve a very practical purpose, even in times like these. And it would be remiss and misguided to dismiss them, and indeed, a good number of the most iconic works of literature, to portray them as unfit for consumption because of the "times we now live in."

Part of the argument against reading dystopias in a time of dystopia is that when they too mirror the reality we live in, it can create an emotional overload, a sort of squared experience of the societal breakdowns they examine. But if this were so, that dystopian fiction creates double the effect, then they would also cease to have a strong effect, like a meal eaten too often or a game played constantly will lose its power to delight. Dystopian stories would quickly become redundant. They would become too familiar, too cliché, and lose their power to hurt us. But no matter how often it's created or consumed, dystopian fiction never really loses its power, because its consumption does not just have one effect or purpose. Dystopian stories are not monolithic in effect. While they can horrify, they can also provide catharsis, warnings, and myriad other useful reactions that continue to benefit the consumer and society at large, in any time at all.

We will always need dystopian storytelling. I believe that dystopias in fiction present an alternate, truer view of reality than our actual reality. This is why some stories cause so much outrage and generate such long and intense discussions, when even the things they examine happen daily without causing such a stir or reaction. Take the movie *Acrimony*, for example. It, in my opinion, could be seen as horror, with Taraji P. Henson's character's understandable but scary decline into insanity, stalking, and deadly assault, after a life of mind-bending trauma that many Black women must endure at the hands of Black men and a white society. It is no news that the patriarchy allows men to build their careers off the backs of women, and those women, sacrificial wives, sometimes rebound in tragic ways from the force of their broken backs recoiling. So, what was different between the story and the reality we live in daily but hardly raise an eyebrow to?

I think that these stories are bereft of the bias that lived reality has when they are populated with characters we know, as life so often is. We are unreliable judges in reality's cases and so subconsciously recuse ourselves because of a likelihood of bias and fail to pass appropriate, and often any, judgement. Conversely, true justice is blind, so it's easier to recognize, for example, abuse in a random character in a story than in say, a parent or partner we love.

There is this airbrush effect the mind applies to our lived reality, self-protective perhaps, in a bid to preserve our mental health and sanity. This is why the movie *Don't Look Up* caused such a stir, even amongst people that brush aside climate-fiction dangers and disasters that happen daily. It's like we lose that natural airbrush effect in fiction, making it a tad more accurate and reliable an examination of reality. We don't think it's real, and our defenses are consequently not up. So the full force of the told reality hits us with an impact that the lived one often does not. Doesn't this then make it even more imperative to write dystopias? Especially now? To harness and exploit the window of opportunity they create in allowing us to showcase realities in the most powerful and honest ways, even beyond what lived reality can?

A lot of people cry more from witnessing fictional suffering than from the ones in their lived reality. And I believe that this is one of the purposes of trigger warnings, an attempt to reinstall some of those defenses we lose when we come to a non-lived reality. After all, there are no trigger warnings to events happening in real time. Though, I believe our minds do dull the force of the blow.

The question then should be: Do we really want to escape? Is getting fiction sanitized for Western sensibilities the solution? The realities we live in are harsh. But are we even steeped in them enough? Won't escaping be like plugging into a false reality like *The Matrix*? Shouldn't we immerse ourselves in the multiple realities of others rather than hide from them? Be more *Sense8* than *Matrix*? The problems of the world are myriad, so will it not then take myriad perspectives and knowledge from all the realities they stem from to solve them?

As with all questions, there are multiple answers, like there are multiple realities. May we continue to examine them in a manner that makes our experiences and humanity the best it can be, for us and those around us.

LAND OF THE AWAITING BIRTH

by Joshua Uchenna Omenga and Oghenechovwe Donald Ekpeki

PROLOGUE

Machikwe turned into the road to Atan Cemetery and took a deep breath, glad to have escaped the buzz of the building traffic and jostling crowd on the main road. The noise of the busy roads and streets had effectively faded into the background, and she could hear her own voice when she hummed.

She started trotting, her face fixed firmly ahead without taking any note of her environment. But suddenly, she felt a chill spread over her body. She slowed her pace and rubbed her palms together as if to dispel the goosebumps that had formed on her arms. Then she began to hear murmuring in the background, and she was filled with a premonitory dread.

She looked at the cemetery to her left. She saw no one, and only far ahead did she glimpse the vehicles plying along the University Road. She started walking again, her feet light on the ground, and her ears poised to pick up the anticipated sound. She took just a few steps when she started hearing the murmuring again. This time, the direction was unmistakable: it came from the cemetery. She paused and scanned the graveyard for early morning visitors to graves of newly buried relatives. She saw no one, and although she had stopped walking, the murmuring did not cease. Then her eyes caught some indistinct shapes of mists rising from the tombs.

For all the terror in her heart, she could not remove her eyes from the manifestation. As she looked on, the incorporeal shapes became humanlike and started converging, overlapping into each other. And then their forms seemed to become more solid and white. Breeze started to blow from the dense, overhanging branches of the cemetery, and with it came the unearthly and horrid voices from the gathering. Machi shrieked, covering her ears with her hands.

A cemetery attendant ran to her and asked what was wrong. She did not hear him and was even unaware of his presence until he touched her on the shoulder. She drew back, shouted louder, and opened her eyes.

"What happened?" the man asked.

It took her a while to believe that it was a man standing before her and not the shapes she had been seeing. She shook her head wordlessly and pointed in the direction of the graves. The man looked but did not see anything. "But there is nothing there."

She herself looked again in the direction of the misty forms and saw nothing, not a whiff of the mist she had seen forming into shapes. Even the breeze had stopped blowing, and not a single sound came from the graves. She looked around as if to detect the shapes in another place. She saw nothing.

She opened her mouth to explain but no words came out. Her words stuck in her throat, and she momentarily felt the saliva dry in her mouth. She clutched at her schoolbag and looked furtively about as the cemetery attendant led her out of the cemetery to the University Road. Once along the road, she started running and did not look back once, until she disappeared into the street that led to her school.

The cemetery attendant chuckled to himself. He had never understood why he needed to protect the dead from the living.

CHAPTER ONE

Machi sat on a desk by the corner of the class, lost in thought. The significance of the incidence of that morning shook her, for it was her first time coming in close quarters to the ghosts, and it more than convinced her that it was not her imagination.

The series of incidences started a year ago when she was twelve. She would suddenly, without cause, feel an unnatural coldness all over her body, suddenly miss a heartbeat, or feel an inexplicable palpitation. Then she would start noticing strange movements around her. Sometimes, it would be a black cat crossing the road that no one else would seem to see, and a car or a motorcycle or a hawker passing by the same spot where the cat had crossed would skid or miss his step and come to harm. Sometimes, she would notice among a busy crowd that some people seemed to form a circle around the rest, and that within that period there was bound to be a serious dispute among the people, most of the time leading to a fight in which many people would be injured.

Her first distinctly memorable experience happened at Oshodi when she was returning from the market with her mother. As they were waiting for wheelbarrow pushers to carry their goods, Machi's eyes were suddenly drawn by an overwhelming impulse to the bridge overhead. At first, she did not see anything out of place, but suddenly, she began to notice that the vehicles seemed to be moving in slow motion, and even the pedestrians were walking like zombies, one step at a time, with hands that took seconds between raising and falling, and the sounds seemed muted as if the world anticipated an event.

As Machi continued watching the movements on the bridge, she noticed that among the pedestrians, some of them looked blurry. These set of pedestrians seemed to be passing along the same line, like ants in movement. Then she noticed that they were floating on the ground. She saw a white car coming along the same line. The car, too, was not touching the ground, and did not even cast any shadow on the ground, and she realized with mounting interest that even those who had been walking on that line had cast no shadow either. The people walking along the mysterious line did not give way to the car and it ran over them. But she found them walking on in perfect condition as they had been walking before the car ran over them. She stifled a cry when she saw that the occupants of the car were skeletons!

As the car neared the end of the bridge, it brushed against a danfo bus. The danfo bus skidded, knocked down two hawkers, and hit another danfo bus. The second danfo bus, which was in the process of parking, veered left then right, and hit the embankment of the bridge, running headlong into a car coming from the opposite direction.

The driver of the car, who had noticed the danfo coming, tried to apply his brakes, and had applied them too harshly in order to stop within the short intervening space. The car tumbled, and on the impact of the danfo bus, flew up and rotated three times in the air, then, as if in slow motion, it gradually plummeted to the ground, not too far from where Machi had been standing. The sound of the screeching tires had alerted people to what was happening on the bridge, and everywhere was helter-skelter as people converged at the scene of the accident; the better to observe what had just happened. Everything had happened very quickly, taking everyone by surprise, except Machi. To her, it had all taken hours and had occurred in slow motion, so that she had observed everything in sequence. What most surprised her was that the car, on hitting the bus, had vanished, and with it all the people walking on the line whose feet were not touching the ground.

When later, people gathered to try and find the cause or the beginning of the accident, nobody seemed to know. The two people in the car had died immediately, with one of the two hawkers knocked down by the danfo bus, which received impact from the mysterious car, and about eight people received serious injury. Machi was too shocked at the whole occurrence to tell her mother what she had observed. It was later, when they returned to the shop and were arranging the goods that she told her mother about it.

Her mother paused the moment the last words left Machi's mouth. For several seconds she stared at Machi until Machi became uncomfortable and turned her face away.

"You did not see anything," her mother said at last.

"But I saw it all, mother!" Machi protested.

Margaret placed her hand on her daughter's head and said, like one uttering a benediction, "I am telling you that you did not see anything. And you are not to tell any soul what you have told me, and if anybody asks you what you saw, you saw nothing. Do you hear me?"

Machi nodded.

That would have been the end of the matter, and Machi was quite prepared to believe that she had imagined it all. But when her mother left her in the shop and went to buy food items, something happened to stamp the memory indelibly in her mind.

She was arranging the rolls of sachet tomatoes on the hanging rope when a sudden heaviness came over her and she felt drowsy. She shook her head and stretched herself, but the feeling returned the moment she started hanging the tomatoes again. She put her head on the table and tried to close her eyes. But just as her eyes were about to close, it seemed to her that there was a palpable change in the color of everything around her. The provisions shop opposite her mother's stall seemed flooded with stage light, even though there was no electricity supply. The colors were ever changing, and it seemed to Machi that as the illumination changed, some of the people in the shop transformed too. The only contrast figures were the shopkeeper, his assistant, and two customers who walked out without buying anything.

Sometimes, the people in the shop appeared ashen gray, like images in the negative of a film, their eyes hardly visible from their faces; sometimes they seemed to radiate light by themselves, the tips of their dresses glowing in miniscule blue flames; sometimes they even seemed like skeletons, but only so briefly that she could not see them properly thus. But try as she could, she could not make out one face among the people, even though she saw them very well. They were buying many things, and as they mentioned each item—Machi could not hear them, she could only see the movement of their lips—the storekeeper's assistant gathered the items while the storekeeper packaged them. When everything had been packaged, one of them brought out wads of notes. To Machi, they were only papers cut in the size of money; they were extraordinarily white and plain. However, when these papers reached the hand of the shopkeeper, they turned to currency. He counted the notes, nodded his head, and gave change to the person who had given him the money. The change did not turn to paper in the person's hand. Machi noticed that as his hand neared the purse where the person had retrieved the wads of notes, he had deliberately dropped the change on the floor. Another person among them carried the carton in which the items they had bought were packed, and they walked away from the shop. Just then, the illumination changed in the shop, and it became normal again.

Machi followed these shoppers with her eyes. As they mingled with the crowd, Machi noticed a marked change in the crowd and in the atmosphere around them. She noticed what looked like a ripple effect from the center of the crowd, heads going down and coming up, until the circle widened and petered out at the outer circumference.

In a short while, arguments broke out in the gathering. Voices started rising, then hands waved in the air, and fists flew. A fight broke out, the participants throwing punches at anyone in sight as though they had no particular enemies in contemplation. Some of the fighters, bereft of weapons, lifted items in display for sale and threw them at one another. And amidst the pugnacious crowd, the shoppers emerged without the items they had bought from the provisions shop and walked away as if nothing was going on around them. She saw them enter another shop. She noticed that they were not alone; many other people of their kind were distributed in the market. Two such people passed by her mother's shop, and one of them had looked in as if to browse, but seeing her, hurried away as if afraid. Soon after the people left the gathering, the fight stopped, and people only gathered to commiserate with those whose items had been destroyed in the fight. All attempts to find out the reason for the fight or those who had started it were in vain; even the chief participants in the fight did not know what they were fighting about, or whom they had been fighting.

Machi was inclined to believe the event was part of her imagination. However, before the end of that day, shops which had been patronized by the mysterious shoppers started complaining of either loss of expensive items or of receiving fake currency. Keepers of as many as five shops within the environment raised the alarm. Machi knew these were not mere coincidences; at least from the affair of the fake currency, she could tell that the shoppers had really paid with paper, and the shopkeepers had not realized it at the time. This could only be so if they were under an illusion. All those strange manifestations could not have happened in her dreams.

That night, she was down with terrible fever, and before long, all was blank to her.

CHAPTER TWO

Machi found herself lying on top of a huge log that seemed to extend indefinitely on both sides. She sat on the log and took in the smell that came to her in a pleasing way. The air was redolent with fragrance of wild but odoriferous flowers. The earth under her feet was rich black and moist and sticky and tickled her bare feet. Birds twittered from every direction and insects chirped, and she heard rustling leaves not within her line of vision. But for these sounds, all was quiet; there was no sign of human habitation. Directly in front of her was a green brush with rather aggressive foliage. She stood up and was startled when she placed her hand on the log, for it seemed to her that she felt a movement, and the log had been so soft that it had seemed as if she pressed on foam. But the log was as it had been before and turning forward again, she started toward the brush.

She brushed aside the thick leaves of a giant cocoyam. A swarm of butterflies fluttered over her head before they flew out of the brush in a sequence. Machi followed them with her eyes, taken by the brilliant display of their colors as they reflected the rays of the sun. She looked on until they became dots in the distance and then turned her eyes away. The log from which she had risen was no longer there, but she did not make much of it. She picked her way forward, deeper into the brush.

It was very cool and nearly dark inside. Not one ray of the sun penetrated the thick foliage. She fought her way among the brambles. Her clothes soon became wet with the moistness of the leaves, for although it was high noon and the sun was shining brightly in the sky, the inability of the sun to reach into the brush left the leaves damp from the dews of the night before. The smell here was a mixture of pleasant fragrance and rottenness: the leaves underneath in decay, fruits that had fallen unpicked, and the dungs of unseen animals. She pressed on as if she had a destination in mind and was eager to reach it. Then abruptly, she came to the end of the brush. Before her gaped a void. She stopped short and looked into the bottomless pit, out of which there seemed to come the faint sound of a running stream.

She started hearing distant voices, initially indistinct, like the purring of some domestic animal. Then the voices blended in a harmony, and sweet music sailed into the air right before her. The voices were such as she had never heard—soft, drawn, calm, harmonic, unhurried. She looked in the direction of the song, and her eyes brightened in amazement. Before her rose a beautiful, greenish village. Her eyes lingered on the totality of the village, which at first looked like the work of a naturalist artist—surreal and idealistic and enchanting. She did not believe in the reality of the sight before her until she noticed the movements.

The village was divided into compounds. These compounds were walled by thin poles whose silver color contrasted sharply with the greens of the environment. In these compounds, tiny people moved from one activity to another, their movement as harmonious as the songs she had been hearing. She saw white smoke rising from some of these compounds, and soon her nose was assailed with the smell of cooking meals. Behind the clusters of compounds rose a mountain whose peak seemed intermingled with the sky. The summit was blurry and mist filled. Black eagles hovered around the mountain.

Everywhere she looked, the land was green with grasses that were short and trimmed and uniform. The walkways were delineated by bougainvillea, whose pink petals shone brightly in the sun. At the easterly part of the village, water gushed from a rock and lapped softly on the bank. As she watched the birds that flew down and up from the water, it suddenly seemed to her that the water was flowing upward instead of downward. She furrowed her brow and looked with more concentration. Indeed, the water was flowing upward, and instead of gushing out of the rock, the rock was swallowing the water. She wondered greatly at this. When her eyes returned to the compounds again, she saw, to her further amazement, that the houses had their roofs on the earth. She looked from compound to compound, and all the houses were upside down. How could she not have seen it before? Even the birds were flying with their stomachs to the sky.

Machi started to hear the song again. The little people started congregating, and they started coming out from the different compounds, converging as one group met another. They formed a mass of people. They were walking toward her direction, their voices blended in the song. They stopped at the edge of the village, just before the void that separated the village from the brush in which Machi was standing. One of the little people came forward and bowed to Machi.

Machi noticed that the person who had bowed to her was a child, as were the rest; they were, in fact, babies. But they had the faces of adults.

"I welcome you, Ozoemena, to the great land of the Awaiting Birth!" She bowed again, and all the people behind her bowed.

Machi noticed that they were genderless. The voice of the speaker had sounded like someone talking with a megaphone, and it echoed over and over, long after they had ceased speaking. Machi looked on, curious and flattered that they knew her name, which did not seem odd to her at the moment. She understood the speaker perfectly, although she could not tell in what language it had spoken.

The speaker continued, "We are happy to have you back. Long have we waited for you. May the gods be blessed for finally releasing you from the circles."

Machi understood the words but could not make sense of it at all. Where was this land of the Awaiting Birth? How did these people know her name? What connection did she have with them? Machi was still pondering these questions when she saw them bridging the void with sticks for her to cross. They started chanting again, singing her name, and asking her to come over. She stilled the beating of her heart and stretched one leg toward the bridge.

She felt a sharp and stinging pain on her arm and shouted. Her eyes opened to whiteness all around her—the walls, the ceiling, the nurse who hovered above her with a stethoscope around her neck and a gloved hand holding a needle. She coughed and tried to adjust herself to her new environment. Just then, she saw her mother's face straining to look at her own face. She relaxed her head back on the bed. She could not tell which of her different existences was the real one, but it sufficed that her mother was here.

Margaret felt her daughter's forehead with the palm of her hand. The nurse pulled her gently away.

"She is all right, madam. Just wait a little more. The doctor will soon return with the test result."

Not long afterward, the nurse returned with the doctor close behind. The doctor sat down with them like a counselor and told them that the test disclosed no ailment known to science.

CHAPTER THREE

Three months later, Machi was overcome by a sudden and ferocious fever. She had shown no sign of sickness until about 2 a.m., when she started coughing spasmodically. Her parents woke up and went to her. Her body was already burning. Her mother quickly stripped Machi of her clothes and doused her with water. Machi kept shivering, but her temperature did not decrease. She had taken her medications before going to bed, and Margaret wondered if it would be wise to administer more. Machi trembled when she was fanned, but her body burned when she was covered. Margaret was quite at a loss what steps to take. Even taking her to hospital did not present itself as a very logical step—for what else would they do? Had they not told her to expect the worst? Had they not given her the medications which had not prevented this sudden fever?

Peter Ekuma knew just what to do in this situation when the physicians of the world had failed. He brought his Bible, knelt beside his sick daughter, and launched into a fiery prayer. He praised God. He thanked God. He implored God. He asked God for forgiveness. He asked God for life. All the elements of communications with the Almighty he employed, all the words he had learnt that moved Him, words of praises and eulogy, words of declaration, words of command even. Margaret joined her husband. The two voices shook the room. Other occupants of the building, awakened by the prayer, came to find out what was happening. Some of those who had come prepared to quarrel with the Ekuma family for disturbing their sleep were disarmed when they confronted the scene.

There, on the bed, lay the almost insensate Machi shivering and restive, the whites of her eyes taking dominance every now and then. Some of the neighbors joined in the prayers. Some of the new arrivers were even more fiery than the parents and brought with them another ingredient of imploring the Almighty which the parents lacked: speaking in tongues. Words of prayer rose visibly in the room and bumped on each other. So fervently did they pray that if the Almighty himself had compromised his standard of not sleeping, he would have been awakened that night by the quantity of prayer that ascended to heaven from the room of the Ekuma family, where Machi lay battling for life. Then she passed out.

Minutes passed. An hour passed. Machi still did not wake up. Margaret called Machi's name softly at first but there was no response. "My mother," she said, "wake up now. Machi? Ozoemena? Machikwe? Wake up!"

There was no response from the supine one. Margaret shook her daughter over and over. There was no response. Machi did not even stir. Margaret shook her again. She rolled over like a log of wood. Margaret, alarmed, brought her ears to Machi's heart. She did not hear her heartbeat. She touched her face and the coldness shocked her, and she rose from Machi's body, horrified. For more than thirty minutes they continued trying to revive Machi. They shook her, called her name, poured water on her, pressed her chest, blew into her mouth—they did everything that came into their mind to revive Machi, but she did not respond. Margaret burst into explosive lamentation. All the agonies she had suppressed for her, all the pains, all the tears she had kept unshed—she unleashed them. She threw herself on her daughter's limp body and wept, and her voice echoed beyond the room into the streets.

Peter Ekuma bore his sorrow a little better than his wife. Words failed him. He did not see the logic of it all, but still he held on to his faith. He blamed no one. He found no justification for the Lord taking Machi, but who was he to question the Lord? If the Lord deemed it fit to recall Machikwe at so young an age, who was he to ask of the Lord to withhold His hand? Yet he wept. It was as though someone had scarred his soul. Machikwe had been the one thing he had been using to answer his enemies. She was the answer he put before all those who asked him what his God had done for him for all the time he spent in His service. She was the reward for his faith. And now the Lord had taken her away. The way of the Lord was not like the way of men. Peter would never comprehend the way of the Lord, yet he followed.

He knew he had to inform the members of his family in Lagos about this tragedy that had befallen them. There was no point telling his wife; she would not hear or understand a word at this moment. The intensity of her grief broke his heart, and he wished he were a man to offer consolation. He put on his shoes and walked blindly into the streets, dazed with sorrow.

Margaret refused to let the neighbors cover Machi with a wrapper. She lifted her daughter to the bed, rubbed her face over and over, threw her weight on her body and wept. After a while, she knelt, took her daughter's hands in her own, squeezed them tightly, and wept afresh. Then she started chanting a song of sorrow, calling her daughter by different names, imploring her to return to her, promising her all sorts of things, praising, praising, imploring, imploring, calling her names. The neighbors were sure that Margaret had lost her mind, but no woman dared to pry her hands from her daughter's, for they too imagined her pain. There was no response from Machi.

Still, Margaret continued calling out her names.

CHAPTER FOUR

Machi was there again. Drops of water splashed on her body as she pushed her way through the brush, tickling her with their coldness. She heard sounds like squires mating and turned round to look at them. Two rabbit-sized animals looked up at her, as curious to see her as she was to see them. Their fuzzy tails were lifted to their heads and light shone from the tails, bright enough to illuminate the immediate surroundings. She thought them very cute and reached out to hold them, but they gave some squeaks and disappeared. She turned and pushed her way forward.

She was confronted by the void she had seen the previous visit. Across the void lay the village which shimmered in the sun, brighter than it had been the last time she saw it. She saw the leaves fluttering in the wind, blowing in the village, but they seemed to stop just before the void, as if there was a physical barrier keeping them from crossing and getting to where she stood. The community of the little people of the land of the Awaiting Birth was as lively as it had been before. She watched for a while and was somehow saddened that none of them looked in her direction. Perhaps they had not noticed her presence; or they might be angry at her for refusing the hospitality they had extended to her the last time she was there. Now she yearned to be there. The green lawns invited her. The trees heavy with fruits invited her. The rising smoke invited her. The curvy slopes with green meadows and dandelions and hibiscus invited her. The huge and smooth rocks on the mountain invited her, the sound of the water lapping on the bank, and the enchanted song of the land's inhabitants. But when she looked down into the void before her, she was dismayed. She walked to another edge of the brush to see if there was a way into the village. There was none. It seemed that the void served as a sort of wall around the village.

Then she started hearing the song again, melodious and enchanted and enticing. Like a child seeing other children after a long period of seclusion, she ran to the place where she had been standing before. She saw them now; they were gathering together, and the congregation was proceeding toward her. Her heart beat in excitement. They were coming for her! She threw her hands in the air as if to hurry them. But they kept moving at their pace, their voices rising still in melody, their steps as measured as bearers of a coffin. From afar, they looked like a procession of soldier ants undisturbed. Finally, they reached the void and as before, one of them separated itself from the crowd and bowed. The rest did the same.

"Welcome home, Ozoemena."

She wanted to throw herself into their midst, but the void checked her. It seemed that they had made a provision for her, for just then there was a shuffling among them, and about ten of them came out bearing a huge ladder. They laid the ladder across the void and beckoned her to cross over. She stepped forward, gently, tremulous with curiosity and excitement. She recoiled when she placed her left foot on the ladder; it was cold, as if she had stepped on ice. Still, they beckoned her, laughing at what they must have thought her naïveté. She looked at the whole crowd waiting for her and at the village which her soul yearned to reach, and courage came into her heart to brave the coldness of the ladder. She stepped on it again, then took the second step. It was no longer cold the moment she placed both feet on the ladder. Then she climbed on slowly.

She could not keep herself from looking down when she reached the middle of the ladder and the void. She saw the mists forming into shapes, and the shapes seemed to be transforming into humans, and they seemed to be rising, their claws coming up, seeking her. She shouted and wanted to go back. But all behind her was dark. She could not see the legs of the ladder behind; only forward did the steps lead. And forward she went, buoyed more by the desire to escape the forms below than by the desire to reach the village ahead. She completed the remaining steps in a run and almost fell as she reached the end of the ladder into the village.

She experienced a chill, persistent and rather ticklish. It was unlike the momentary ones she had been feeling before. It was more like the experience of one entering into an air-conditioned room after staying long under the sun. The crowd of small people surrounded her, bore her aloft, and hung a garland on her neck, chanting, "Welcome the Queen!"

Machi was lost in the eerie bliss of the small people of the land of the Awaiting Birth. She had no idea why they called her Queen, but it did not matter at the moment; all that mattered was that she was here, in their midst. What she had seen standing across the border seemed little in comparison to what she saw and experienced in their midst.

The air was filled with fragrance. The breeze tickled the flesh. It was as though the sun had been screened off with glass, so that only the illumination reached the earth, but not the heat. They set her down in a compound where it seemed that the "elders" of the village had been waiting for her. But they too were babies, only with faces more advanced in age. She stood tall before them. Even in her own eyes, she was like a giant, for the tallest of the people of the land reached her waist.

They bowed before her, their heads touching the earth. The elders came forward and drew a circle with chalk around her. Then one of them, raising a bowl, started saying something in a language she did not understand. She looked around. The people were still in their bowed position. When the one giving the incantation had finished, another one of the elders approached her and laid some flowers at her feet. Machi only kept smiling, wondering what was going on. The third of the elders stood up, spread its palms to the sky, and said, "Shamunah hamnea!" The crowd rose to their feet and burst into song.

The song was more melodious than the ones she had heard them singing while she was beyond the border. The whole crowd sang in a synchronized voice, layer upon layer, the sounds resonated, harmonious and melodious, soft and resonant, the words tumbling effortlessly from their throats. As she looked at them it seemed as if their lips were not moving. Those in front formed a circle around her, stopping before the chalk drawn by one of the elders. They moved around her as the rest continued singing. The song continued for what Machi counted as half an hour. When the song was finally over, she was led to a seat which might have seemed huge to the small people, but was just her size, like the stool she used in school. But the stool was not made of wood or any material she had ever known. It looked as if it had been carved out of the earth, with all the greens covering it, yet when she sat on it, it did not feel like grass or foam or wood or metal. It welcomed her as if her buttocks had been used to measure it before production.

The small people were killing goat after goat and roasting them on the fire. Other groups were peeling yams, pouring them into wide pots, and setting them on the fire. The smell of the cooking food and the roasting goats and the fragrance of the flowers and mellowed fruits conjoined to form an irresistible aroma in her nose. She suddenly felt the hunger in her belly. She wished she knew how to ask for food here.

Although she understood them when they spoke, she did not know how to talk to them, for they had spoken in no identifiable language. Presently the food was done, and she saw them ladle it into big bowls. About ten of them carried the bowl and set it before her. They also prepared the roasted goats and brought them in a bowl and set it before her. She looked down with increasing appetite. She knew they were for her, but how did they eat in this land? It would have been easier for her to watch them eat before she ate.

The people gathered around her again, this time in groups. Their clothes were bright yellow. They were all looking up at her. One of them, clad in red as opposed to the yellow garb of the rest, stepped forward and lay before her. "Worshipful Queen and Mother, we thank you for your manifestation in our midst. Accept our sacrifices and bless our land, mother Ozoemena. Protect us from the Dying People. Protect us from the Human Spirits. Protect us from the Sky Dwellers. We pray you, Mother Ozoemena, be our guide in this world and in the world of Humans whenever we may be called upon to go there."

There was a resounding "Shimna!"

Machi lifted her hand to take the bowl. All the small people fell on the ground and prostrated. She opened her mouth to tell them that she was not a goddess, but her throat was dry, and no sound came out of her mouth. Just then, she started hearing another voice, far away and different from the voice of the small people. She raised her eyes in the direction of the voice. She could hear it distinctly. The voice was in a passionate agony.

"My mother, please do not leave me! Ozoemena, do not leave me alone in this world. Ozoemena!"

It was Margaret calling. Machi stood up, much surprised by the plaintiveness of her mother's voice. She walked past the small people, and they made way to her, a feeling of disappointment in their faces. Machi did not heed them. She headed to the boundary from which the voice seemed to be coming. The voice sounded closer and closer and more desperate as she got near.

"I will do anything you ask, my mother, but do not leave me! Come back to me! Ozoemena! Are you not the lonely palm fruit that should not be lost in the fire? Why are you doing this to me?"

Machi walked in frantic steps toward the boundary, expecting to see her mother waiting across. What had she come to do here? But as

Machi got to the boundary, she was confronted by the void. The ladder on which she had climbed to the village was not there. There was no way for her to cross the boundary to her mother. The voice called to her still. She turned around to the sounds of steps and saw the small people gathered around her. She wanted to ask them for the ladder but found, to her chagrin, that she could not open her mouth.

Then she saw them prostrate again and in a united voice started saying, "Mother Ozoemena, do not leave us. If you must ascend to the world, take our sacrifice. Take them as sign of your goodwill to us."

The voice of her mother came more urgently from the other end of the boundary. Machi turned away from the small people. She stepped forward and looked down into the void. The mists were rising again, thick and formless. Then, there was a loud noise and rustling in the brush across the boundary. A huge python reared its head into the open. Machi stepped back. The python moved toward the boundary and whirled around. Machi moved further back. The python stood on its tail and reared its head high above the trees. Machi was too dazed to think of what to do but to watch the python. Then in one swift movement it bounded across the boundary to the village, stopping just before Machi. The small people took to their heels. Machi would have followed had she not lost the use of her legs from shock. And then her mother was calling again. And the python opened its mouth as if to swallow her, but it was speech that proceeded out of it.

"Climb, small one. Do not fear. Your ancestors have sent me."

The python had stretched itself before her. It did not seem odd to her that the python had spoken, and she did not even contemplate what the python had said. More urgent in her ears was the insistent voice of her mother at the other end. She climbed, hardly aware of what she was doing. Seated at the back of the python, she remembered that it was like the log on which she had sat the first time she found herself at the other end of this void. Slowly, the python stretched its head across the void and glided past it, into the brush, and onto the other side, before it stopped and Machi climbed down.

The python whirled round again and said, "I have brought you home." Then it glided away. And her mother's voice came to her again, "My, Ozoemena!"

She coughed.

CHAPTER FIVE

Margaret was resting her head for the umpteenth time when she heard the faint cough. She wiped her own eyes and sobbed again. The trickle of tears left in her glands dropped onto her daughter's body. She lay her head on Machi's bosom, and continued sobbing softly, her eyes vacant. She felt a soft push under her head. She adjusted her head. She felt it again. It seemed as if the bosom on which she rested her head was heaving. Still she pressed her head on the bosom. Then she heard the cough again and raised her head, for the cough had come so close, and she was sure it was not her. The cough came again and again. And it was her daughter, the one who had long gone; it was her Ozoemena coughing!

"Mother," Machi said in a voice that had not changed a bit. "I heard you calling me. Why are you crying?"

Margaret still could not believe that it was her daughter talking, nor that it was not a vision. But Machi stood up and approached her, and when she encircled her in her arms, Margaret was ready to believe anything so long as they were not parted. The neighbors threw themselves on Machi and shouted her name over and over. Then they rushed out and called the other neighbors who had gone. The room was soon filled with people, and everywhere was abuzz with songs and whispers and rejoicing and shouting. Even the little children who had been denied entrance at her death were allowed entrance at her resurrection.

Later when most of the neighbors had gone, and the real parents of Machi were left in the house, they gathered together for a small family meeting. More men had later joined them and more came in while the meeting was going on. The people of Edemma had the tradition that all the members of a family were a unit whether home or abroad. The whole community was regarded as a family, so that whenever a member of the Edemma community in the town had a problem, all the other members of the Edemma community living in the same town were under the obligation to run to their aid as if it had been their own immediate family. That day, as the message spread of the calamity that had befallen the Ekuma family, the people of Edemma in Lagos started coming one by one. Those who did not hear the news at first heard a better version, the resurrection of Machi.

These were the ones whose faces were gay as they approached, and they stood at the door outside and joked and teased Machi before they went into the room for the gathering.

One of the men, who was deemed as the elder because he seemed to be the oldest of the men gathered there, coughed and addressed the rest. "My people, words cannot express my feeling as I talk to you now. God has done the undoable for us. God has turned our sorrow to rejoicing. We have come here with tears in our eyes, but we are leaving here with happiness in our hearts. May God be praised for his great work."

"Amen!"

"This meeting is only for a short while. I know that most of you have left your place of work and your shops and your families to be here to rejoice with us. The good God will replenish your time. But my heart swells in happiness because instead of talking about burial, we can look each other in the face and laugh and drink beer and make jokes because God has turned our mourning to rejoicing. Having said that, I thank all of you once again."

There was an echo of assent.

"The major reason why I insist that we should have this meeting despite the turnaround in events is because of the peculiar nature of the sickness that our daughter is experiencing, which I am sure that most of us are aware of. It is true that we thank God for what he has done. It is true that we hope for the best. But because the hawk has been chased off from the chicken in one moment, does not give the chicken the liberty to roam freely or taunt the hawk. To mention words by name, I am suggesting that we should not relax, but to find a permanent solution to her sickness."

Peter Ekuma greeted everyone present and thanked them for rallying to his support. "My people, I will not say that I do not know what you are saying. No one desires a permanent solution to this problem more than me and my wife. But what is left to be done? Where have our legs not reached? We have gone from one hospital to another. We have bought medication after medication. But the sickness is always coming back. All our money has been spent buying medicine for her, and if not for your support, we would have packed back to Lagos. Just about three months ago, we took her to several hospitals, and even did tests for her. Some of the medicines the doctor gave her were still in the box when she broke down again. Whatever other suggestion you have, please share with us. Thank you, my people."

"Peter, Peter, Peter!" another man called out, and Peter answered three times.

"I called your name three times, not because you are deaf in the ear, but because you are deaf in understanding. My people, I seek your permission to impress some points to our brother here. This is not the first time we are talking about this. I have been called to an emergency meeting of this nature over and over in this family. How many of our sons and daughters from this family would still be alive if Peter had listened to suggestions? When you hunt a ghost, do you do so with bows and arrows? Why has Peter insisted on going to hospitals to solve a problem that has a spiritual origin? My people, my heart bleeds each time I am called here because I know that our brother is stubborn. If anyone knows what to say to him, let him do so. If he insists on going from hospital to hospital, I wash my hands of him."

Peter said nothing in response; he knew better not to.

Another man said, "Thank you, Nweze. I will not say that you are not justified in pouring out your words as they are in your mind. Peter! It is not my intention to speak as Nweze has spoken, but what I have to say is the same thing put in another way. We should have removed the monkey's hand from the soup pot long ago, but you have allowed it to turn into a human hand. But all is well. Whenever a man wakes up is his dawn. Before all our people here, Peter, I am telling you once again, as you no doubt have been told, we are seeking a solution to this problem that inflicts our daughter in the way we know best. We are taking her to the village for proper things to be done, so that the sickness will leave her once and for all. Thank you, my people."

Most of those who spoke afterward were in support. A few people said nothing, either because they were in support and needed not to add their voice, or because they dissented but knew that their voice was in the minority. Margaret watched her husband's face as the men talked. It is the custom with the people at this type of gathering to address him as if she was not there, as if the two of them had not been running the family together, as if she, and not him, had not been providing the money. But these were not the things that occupied her mind now. She was beginning to think seriously of the suggestion the men were giving. She was beginning to think that they had been looking for the cure to Ozoemena's sickness in the wrong direction. She was beginning to think that they had been making mistakes all along, and those mistakes had been fatal, and she was not going to make them again.

Peter thanked the people again. "We are grateful for your support. However, I like to tell you that it is not stubbornness that has made me not take your advice in the initial times this subject has been broached. I know that you make your suggestions out of concern to us, and I thank you for that. But I cannot accept your suggestion to take her to the village to find a cure your own way. I cannot do that, because I will be turning my back from God. I trust in God to do what is best in my life."

"Peter!" the elder called, and Peter answered. "Do not make it sound as if we have come here to tell you to stop serving your God. Are we too not his servants? Who of us here does not go to church? What you must know is that a man must lift his hand to help himself before God will help him. How do you know that God is not helping you with the herbal medicines? Is it not God who has provided the roots and the leaves for the curing of diseases? When you go to a doctor, does that mean that you are refusing the help of God? We are only trying to tell you to go to a different kind of doctor who knows better about this sickness than the doctors you have been going to."

"I appreciate your reasoning, my elder. And I thank you and my people for it. But we all know, my people, that no one cuts up the carcass of the goat without the stench remaining in his dress. We all know that the medicine men you talk about do not simply use herbs. They consult the spirits. I cannot submit to that as it will mean that I do not have faith in my God again."

Some of the men sighed and threw up their hands. Some laughed because they had anticipated this. Margaret raised her hand, and one of the men said, "Our wife wants to say something. Please talk." Margaret stood up to talk, but the men told her to sit down. "You are our wife," one of the men said, "why can we not support in the same bowl?"

"Thank you, my husbands. Thank you for your intervention as usual. I pray and hope that this will be the last time you will be summoned for something like this. Next time you will be coming here, it will be to drink and eat and rejoice over your daughter."

There was a resounding "Amen!" from the gathering.

"My husbands and my owners, I am happy that you have not veiled your words in speaking to us. I wish it was possible to open my heart and show you the pain I have been going through over our daughter's sickness. My mind is never at rest, and whenever she is sick, I fear the worse. My people, it is the tortoise who, believing himself to be wise, packed all his wisdom in a bag and put it before him and tried climbing a tree to hang it from people's reach, only to be reminded by a snail that he was carrying his wisdom the wrong way, and he realized that he did not have all the wisdom after all. My husband and I have done our best, but that is the best we know of. I agree with whatever suggestion you make that will bring a permanent solution to our daughter's sickness. Thank you, my people."

Peter followed Margaret with his eyes. If it was possible, his eyes would have shot her down for the betrayal. His heart seethed in anger, but he restrained himself from expressing it until the gathering had dispersed.

"Our wife has spoken wisely," the elder said. "I am happy that you see reason with our suggestion. As I said in the beginning, this meeting is meant to be short so that we can all go back to where we were looking for sustenance. We will leave Peter and his wife to agree on when to send her to the village for the appropriate cure. We trust that those in the village will direct them best. For we who cannot go with them, I suggest that we give whatever we can to support them."

The youngest of the men stood up and gathered the monetary donation.

The elder continued, "Please call our daughter to come and greet us."

Margaret went out to call Machi. Machi looked at the many people and was at a loss how to greet them all. She knelt from one to the other, and they all patted her on the back, and the women embraced her, and everyone remarked almost at the same time how big she had grown and how beautiful and how they would soon come to drink at her marriage, and so on. At last, the people of Edemma dispersed, and the family of Ekuma were left alone.

Peter confronted his wife, his anger reviving. "Why did you tell them that you agree that Machikwe will go through the heathenish rite of ihiuwa?"

"Is that what I said? I simply said I agreed to a permanent solution."

"But you know that is what they meant!"

"And what of it? What have we to show for all our efforts to find a solution? How many times am I going to be losing children because we are doing things your own way?"

"What are you saying, Margaret? Are we doing things my own way or God's way?"

"Don't come to me with that, Peter. What do you know about God's way? Is it God's way that will be killing my children? Is it God's way that will take Ozoemena away from me? Don't tell me about God's way, Peter. I will not follow God's way if that way is leading to Ozoemena's death."

"Do not tempt God, woman. You ought to be grateful for all he has been doing for us."

"Yes, I am grateful for the things he has done for us. But I cannot pretend that there are things that he has not done for us. Is it not the same God who looked on while she died? With all our prayers and the pastor's and everybody, God was listening, but He did not help! I am grateful to God, Peter, for the things He has done. But for the things he refuses to do, I will find the solution from another place."

"I grieve for you, woman, because you don't know what you are saying."

"Thank you, Mr. Holiness. But I am not letting my daughter die because you want things done your own way."

"She is also my daughter."

"Is she?" Margaret stood akimbo and faced her husband. "Is she your daughter simply because you got me pregnant with her? No, Peter, you know nothing about having a daughter. How much have you contributed to her welfare? How much have you contributed to her upkeep?"

"I do the best I can," Peter's voice was resigned.

"Of course you do. But do you bear the pain of her suffering in your heart as I do? When I am awake thinking about her, do you not sleep soundly? When she tosses in fever, do you not turn here and there in slumber? And you tell me that she is your daughter. Peter, she is my daughter, and I am doing what is best for her. Let me see you stop me."

Peter Ekuma did not stop his wife. He could not stop her.

CHAPTER SIX

"Why did you even agree to return to the village at all?" Amara asked.

It seemed that everyone in the village knew that Machi had not returned to the village for a visit even before Machi herself realized it, having been told and made to understand that she was only coming to the village to receive some treatment before returning to Lagos.

Machi contemplated Amara. What was she to tell her? That she suffered from a disease the doctors could not cure, and that she had come to the village to be cured by herbal doctors? Machi merely shrugged and was happy when Amara did not press the topic.

They were now walking inside a small brush where Amara found the way that led deeper and deeper into the brush, like the trail of some creeping creatures. Machi's sense of foreboding came awake. The bush reminded her of her dreams about the little people of the land of the Awaiting Death. Machi still did not understand why they had passed by the stream to come into the brush. She searched but found no answer in Amara's face.

Amara stopped and brought down her basin. Machi stopped just behind Amara. Before her was a small pool of water, milk white and undisturbed. Machi brought down her basin. Amara bent and scooped the water with the small calabash gourd she had brought with her. Machi expected the small pool to be drained before Amara's basin was full, but as Amara fetched from it, it remained the same, as if an unseen hand fed the pool with more water from beneath. Amara fetched a full basin and also helped Machi fetch her basin. The pool remained as it was. Machi could not contain her wonderment any longer.

"Why is the pool not reducing as you fetched from it?"

Amara smiled, like one in possession of a deep secret. "This brush belongs to the wife of Ede, the founder of our village. The secret of this pool is a long one. It was said that a long, long time ago, there was a war between our village and the Nkazi village. During this war, our people were defeating the Nkazi people. Then one of the elders of Nkazi brought a powerful rainmaker who stopped rain from falling in Edemma for two years. He also poisoned the streams in Edemma so that anyone who drank from it died. Even the goats died when they drank from the streams. The wife of Ede, who loved her people so much, despaired over this affair and forthwith went to her brush, this place, to ask of the gods what to be done to keep the Edemma people from destruction. She supplicated the gods for seven days. On the seventh day, the gods sent a butterfly to give her an answer. To restore the rain to Edemma, she must offer the granddaughter living with her, in sacrifice. Now this was a very difficult and unheard-of thing, because the granddaughter was her namesake, and the only child of her daughter who had died in childbirth and was left to be raised by Ede's wife. She cried and pleaded with the gods to use herself as the sacrifice instead of her granddaughter, but the gods refused. At last, unable to bear the toll of death rising in Edemma with no prospect of end in sight, she brought her granddaughter as sacrifice to the gods. She stood at this very spot while the dragon-messenger of the gods carried her granddaughter away. She wept and wept until her tears, gathered on a spot, formed a pool, then she fell and died. Her tears became this pool, and since then, its water has never, and can never, run dry for as long as there is Edemma, for she sacrificed herself and her granddaughter to ensure that there is always water for the people of Edemma.

"This is the purest of streams. No dirt can settle on it. No one can poison it, for it purifies itself and rejects any poison thrown into it. This is why we come here to fetch drinking water."

Machi was much amazed and throughout that morning thought about the wife of Ede and the sacrifices she had made. But above all, she wondered at how omniscient Amara seemed in these matters. She was like her grandmother; she knew everything she was called upon to talk about.

Machi's bond with Amara strengthened. They went to the streams together and went to fetch firewood together. While Amara climbed the trees to cut dead branches, Machi stood below and gathered them together, after which they divided the wood and tied it up.

One day as they were going to fetch firewood, Amara pointed to a forest and said to Machi, "Look at that forest. Do you see how dense the woods?"

"Yes."

"They are a temptation. Don't you ever fetch wood from that forest."

"Why?"

"Any wood you fetch from that forest will bring down lightning when you put it in the fire."

"Why?"

"It is a forbidden forest. It is said that a long, long time ago, a virgin maiden by the name of Efuloma was stoned to death in this forest for a crime she did not commit, and she cursed the forest to bring death to anyone who touches anything from it. Wild animals roam the forest but not a hunter can catch one. Even a dog cannot go into this forest to hunt."

They passed by the forbidden forest and moved to another clearing where they gathered the stump of burnt wood left after the burning of a field in preparation for hoeing. Machi's eyes lingered on the forbidden forest long after they had passed by it. There were so many mysteries in this village, and Amara, her willing teacher, revealed them one by one as she came in contact with them.

CHAPTER SEVEN

It was a Saturday morning, and Machi had decided to fetch firewood alone without calling on her friends. She walked uncertainly for almost an hour without knowing where to look for firewood. It all looked easy when she was in the company of her friends. Alone, she had no idea where to begin. All the wood was in the trees, and she could not climb as Amara climbed. She searched from farm to farm and found no wood. It seemed that where she passed, the wood had just been gathered with none left for her, except small grasses, which only smoked in the fire and left no embers. After a wearied search, she had only managed to pick some pieces of stick that would not even cook a meal and turned homeward.

Her eyes went to the forbidden forest as she passed by. Even without a conscious effort to search for firewood, she saw them in abundance in every corner of the forest. It was surfeit with it and groaned to be relieved of the excess wood. She stepped close with no rebellious inclination, only the desire for a closer inspection. She saw nothing out of place with the forest. It was like every other forest. She peered inside, on tiptoe. The wickets and foliage and dead branches prevented her from seeing much of what was inside. The wood was even more abundant than she imagined. She could take as much as she needed without actually entering the forest; all she needed to do was to stretch out her hands. Now that she thought about it, it appeared ridiculous to her that she should have believed that wood from this forest would invoke thunder when burnt. How could that happen if she burnt them when there was no rain—assuming even that the woods had any innate propensity to attract lightning?

She stepped forward and started picking the wood. She picked one and then another and another, with deliberation, awaiting a change in her body, awaiting that familiar chill that invaded her in the presence of the spiritual and the dangerous. Nothing of the sort happened. All was perfectly normal. She raised one leg and put it in the forest to see if she had been spared the experience because she had not actually entered into it. Nothing happened. She put in her second leg. Still nothing happened. She brushed aside the trees and entered deeper still. Nothing happened. From where she stood, she saw the sun shining outside. Everything was normal, just as it had been before she entered the forest. The wood she had gathered was lying in the same place she had left them, and no change had come over them, nor had they groaned to be returned to the untouchable forest from which they had been poached.

Emboldened and thinking the story of the forest an apocryphal, believed only because no one had tried otherwise, she started picking more wood, and as nothing still happened, she no longer expected anything to happen. She was even mildly disappointed that she should have defied so great a law without any form of chastisement from the forest.

Underneath the wood, she saw mushrooms. She paused and debated with herself whether to pick them or not. It was a different thing to pick wood from the forest, as wood was not edible, but another thing to actually pick edible objects from the forest; for despite her courage and dismissal of the stories about the forest, Machi still thought that something might yet happen. The mushrooms were uncommonly large and fresh. She remembered how much Grandma had loved the last ones she picked with her friends. She herself had enjoyed them more than she had expected and would have taken it over any meat. She would pick the mushrooms, the most that would happen was that she would throw them away if she came to a contrary decision thereafter. She reached for them and pulled and pulled. They were slippery and stuck tenaciously to the wood. She pulled and pulled until some of them came away. She dropped them and stretched out her hand to pull others. She noticed the blood on her hand and drew her hand back in horror. She checked her hand for a wound. There was none. She had felt none. The blood had not been from her. She saw it now: the mushrooms she had pulled out from the wood were bleeding. She picked them and flung them deeper into the forest. At least she now knew why she could not take them home and why they were forbidden.

A huge snail was crawling away from the wood where she had picked the mushrooms, its smooth and variegated shell glistening as if rubbed with oil. She stretched out her hand to pick it. The snail ran forward, stopped, then continued in its unhurried pace. Without thinking anything odd in the fact that the snail had actually run away from her, she went after it. Each time her hands stretched out to catch it, the snail increased its pace just enough to prevent her from catching it. And the more the snail evaded her, the more Machi was determined to catch it. It would be wonderful to bring home a snail that ran—although at the time, the oddity of it did not occur to her. The snail ran and she pursued. They continued this way until the snail turned the corner of a tree and disappeared. Machi searched around but found no trace of the snail. She raised her head and sighed.

It was dark in the forest, darker than she had noticed before, as though a cloud overhung the earth, or rain threatened, or evening was at hand. She looked about. She could not tell how far into the forest she had ventured, not knowing for how long she had run after the snail. She had no sense of time, for none dwelt in the forest. But in the shortening darkness of the forest, some leaves began to glow and became brighter as she looked on with wonderment. The forest, erstwhile humid and rather repulsive with untrimmed branches, became resplendent. Everywhere she looked, the leaves waved as if stirred by unseen hands, their tips and edges radiating light. The ground underneath her no longer smelled rank but welcomed the feet like a carpeted floor redolent with perfume on which the feet longed to touch outside the soles of the shoes. Machi lifted her hands, whirled around, and bounded forward.

The trees gave way as she advanced; they were like waiting trains, her wish their commands. She skipped about, exploring, touching now this leaf, now another, feeling their smooth spines, her fingers caressing the tips. More awaited ahead and still she moved forward, longing for the increasing luminescence ahead, for the brighter leaves ahead, for the whiff of scented air ahead, for the beckoning woods ahead.

She pushed forward, hardly conscious of what she was doing. Suddenly the luminance of the leaves dimmed, flickered, and went off. She stood still, her heart tremulous. The leaves started shining again, and all was as bright as before. She turned back, indecisive. She took a step backward. The leaves flickered again, as bulbs when the power cables touched and went off, never to come on again. At first, it was utterly dark, but as her eyes adjusted, she began to see the familiar branches again, and the trees and the faint illumination of the outside world seeping in—but it was as if dusk had overtaken the earth.

She knew it was time to find her way back. She looked around. She had no idea from which angle she had entered the forest, nor which way led out, nor which way led deeper. If only she could see a sign, if she could peer through any one corner into the outside world, if she could feel the wind and its direction—but nothing suggested her location. If worse came to worst, she would push forward in one direction, come out in any place, and from there she would find her way home. It would only take her longer. And because it was already getting dark in the forest, she surmised that either it was dusk outside or she had ventured very deep into the forest where the light from outside penetrated only faintly into the forest. None of these prospects cheered her. At any event, she could not afford to waste time.

She moved forward, in the direction she was facing. She heard, simultaneously with her footsteps, a sort of mild groan—from beneath, from the trees, from above, she did not know. She paused in her tracks and listened, but she heard nothing. Perhaps it was just her mind tricking her. She moved forward again, slowly, but as her feet touched the ground, she heard it again. She stopped and looked around. There was nothing suspicious in her immediate environment, but she was sure that she had heard something and that it had not been her heart deceiving her. She turned and continued moving. The sound still came, subdued by her determination. The feel of watchful eyes about her increased, and she turned quickly about. She caught sight of many eyes closing. They had closed so fast that she could not tell from what faces she had seen them. She stared long in the different directions where she had seen the eyes. She saw nothing now, and nothing stirred. She turned slowly to her track and took some steps, then whirled suddenly around. The eyes were there again, and closed when she caught sight of them, but not as fast as before. She saw that the eyes were fixed on the trees but could not tell whether they were the eyes of animals on the trees or the trees themselves, for no matter how long she looked at the trees, she did not see anything. She moved forward again and turned back as she had done before and saw the eyes looking at her. They blinked and closed long after she had been looking at them, as if they had forgotten themselves. The eyes were on the trees, giant yellow eyes, with dark, ominous pupils.

The first indication of fear came over her. She did not look again, even though she felt the eyes watching her as she turned back. She rushed forward, willing herself to hear no sound, not even of her footsteps. But her eyes, seeking direction, could not help but see the trees ahead which had also started looking at her. The eyes remained open even after she paused to contemplate them. She turned back. The eyes at the back looked at her too, unflinching. She stood hesitant for a moment, indecisive about which way to go. Then she heard her name, faintly at first. The voice became louder and discernible. It was her grandmother calling. She strained her ears for the direction, and getting it, turned to it and picked her steps forward, ignoring the eyes. She kept her eyes on the ground; as long as she did not look at those eyes, she would not be frightened by them, even though she knew they were there. She ran, as far as the brambles would let her, she ran. Her steps were fast, and hope crept into her heart as the voice drew nearer and nearer. She hoped, when she looked up again, to be at the end of the forest from which the voice of her grandmother floated to her.

It got darker. She pursued after the voice with determination. She was near it now and looked up to find the relief she had been yearning for, the gleams of light from the outside world, her grandmother's figure waiting outside with worry in her creased forehead—she longed to answer and assure her that she was close to her. She looked up and found not the waiting space of the outside world, but the open jaws of a strange and spiked animal. She stopped short and looked involuntarily into the dark throat of the animal, through grated teeth that seemed made of pulverized ceramics. She saw on the tongue of the beast all sorts of filth—bones and flesh and leaves and rotten fruits. She screamed and drew back, and the beast closed its mouth and opened its eyes. They were red and flaming. Machi turned and fled in the opposite direction, still screaming. Her voice echoed in the forest, over and over, long after she had ceased screaming, louder in intensity with each echo, as if amplified by a great, cosmic amplifier. She closed her ears to keep herself from hearing her own voice, so hollow and strange and tremulous was the voice returned back to her, that it frightened her as much as the beast she was running away from.

She bounded away with great speed, mindless of the little branches that scratched her body. She jumped on a smooth trunk and ran on it for a while before the trunk turned and toppled her. She stood up as fast as she fell. The trunk contracted and turned toward her. It was a python, and its great, ponderous trunk was closing on her. She was on her feet, and with incredible speed jumped and evaded the trunk, then ran without looking back. She needed all the time she could get, and all the distance she could put, away from the python and the beast. In her frantic race, she stumbled on a root and fell. Before she could raise herself, she noticed the roots of the trees gathering in her direction, closing in on her. She dodged them as she had dodged the python, turned in another direction and fled.

All she wanted now was to be away from these grisly beasts and creeping roots, it did not matter if she was not out of the forest. She did not even know which direction to take, or whether she was making progress or going in circles. She saw the beast ahead, grunting and displaying its teeth; she knew she was back where she was coming from. She turned sideways, hoping to avoid the python. She ran, her breath coming in spasms, fear pushing her forward. She ran, heedless of direction, her eyes scanning the ground nearby and the trees around for strange things to avoid. Suddenly the ground sounded hollow. She had no time to pause to contemplate what could be the cause, or to change her direction; she was borne aloft by a huge, somnolent head coming awake and sniffing. Machi had been standing on its nostrils. She toppled and rolled down, falling face down. She turned in time to see the great animal lift itself in full majesty. Trees bent and fell beside it. The trunk on which Machi had placed her hand was in fact the hind leg of the animal. Machi crept cautiously back. The animal had not seen her—she was too infinitesimal for it. It turned its head and sniffed again. The wind coming from its nostrils swayed the branches around it. The great animal shook itself, rolled its baleful eyes about, and seeing nothing worth its effort, gradually sank down in its sleeping position. Machi picked her steps cautiously out of the vicinity of the beast. Inconspicuousness mattered to her more than speed.

Hardly had she found herself out of the immediate reach of the huge animal when she heard the howling of a jackal close behind her. She turned to see the jackal bounding toward her. She ran back to where she'd come from. Faced with the jackal, she forgot the beast from which she was escaping. A twig closed on her legs, and she fell. The jackal rushed toward her. She raised herself and tried to stand up, but the ground was slippery, and she tottered and fell again. The jackal, in one sudden leap, was within biting distance. She closed her eyes in trepidation, anticipating the supreme moment when its jaws would close on her.

Time passed and nothing happened. She opened her eyes and saw the jackal backing reluctantly away, its eyes looking upward. She looked in the direction where the jackal's eyes were fixed. The shadow of the huge animal from which she had lately run away from hovered above her. She lay quiet and tried to think of what to do. The animal grunted and its voice shook the forest. Machi covered her ears. The jackal fled and soon disappeared into the forest. The great animal, unaware that she was under it, returned to its position and almost reclined on Machi had she not swiftly moved herself out from under its belly. The animal did not even notice her as she ran away; or perhaps it did and had only taken Machi for an insect too small to be worth the trouble of catching her. Exhausted and dazed she ran in the direction that her feet faced.

The ground became unusually soft and marshy. Her feet sunk deeper and deeper, and she dragged them with difficulty. She turned back, but not on time. One of her feet stepped into the whirling marsh, and it drew her in. She waved her hands furtively for support but found none. She was drawn deeper and deeper into the marsh. Then she felt a hand, like a witch's hand, with long and dirty claws, stretch to touch her. She gave a wild scream and fainted.

CHAPTER EIGHT

Grandma strode up and down frantically, talking loudly to the throng in her compound, "My god has killed me! What will I tell her parents? What will I tell my ancestors? Better that I had died than to live to see this day!" She brushed aside all the hands that reached to comfort her. She listened to no voice but her own as she strode about talking and biting her fingers.

Grandma's compound was filled almost to the brim. It took just a while for the people to hear of what had happened, and everyone who heard about it rushed to Grandma's compound. Machi had been brought home by a palm-wine tapper who had heard her scream and ran to her aid.

They lay her on a mat outside and poured water on her body. Some people blew a breeze on her with hand fans. Grandma doused her forehead with a soaked cloth. People suggested hot water, and Grandma set off to boil the water, but one of the women took over for her. The hot water was brought, and one of the women soaked the cloth in the water and pressed it on her feet, which had become cold. There was no response. Her heart was not beating. Her forehead was cold. There was no indication of life in her except that she had not stiffened. Her hands dangled when they were raised. Grandma's sorrow was inexpressible with words. As she could not bear to be out of Machi's sight, Grandma sent one of the women to summon the medicine man of the village, Dibịa Agbacha. Grandma recommenced striding about, peering every now and then at the body, and hoping against hope to see Machi move. Machi did not move.

The dangling of metals and bones and talisman and other voodoo articles announced the arrival of the medicine man. People instinctively made way for him as he approached. Even those who had been fanning Machi drew back when Dibịa Agbacha arrived. All eyes left Machi and concentrated on the Dibịa.

Much to Grandma's despair, Dibịa Agbacha took his time to look around before he slowly unburdened himself. Nobody offered to help him, and he would have accepted help from no one. The servants of the gods had no need for human intervention in their service. And no man hurried them either, for no matter how fiercely the bush burned, the chameleon must tread at its customary pace.

Having brought down the various objects he hung around himself, Dibịa Agbacha brought out a mat, spread it close to the mat on which Machi lay, and sat down. He looked at the body for a while, then he reached for his bag, brought cowries, and cast them on the mat. He brought out a chalk and drew on the floor. He shook his head and picked up the cowries, shook them again in his hand, and cast them as before. He observed their position and drew on the ground again with his chalk. He repeated the process once more.

Then he asked for Machi to be taken into the room. One of the men lifted her and took her into the room. Grandma went inside. The medicine man, rising and carrying his implements, told the crowd to disperse or at any rate, to remain out of doors. Then he went inside. Grandma crept to the door and stood irresolute, unable to tell if she was bound to follow the body inside.

Dibịa Agbacha said, facing Grandma, "She is dead, but her soul has not left her body."

Grandma suppressed the lump that rose in her throat. "What can you do, messenger of the gods?"

"Nothing is certain, Nwanyị Eke. But we can implore the gods to return her life to mingle with her body."

"Please great one, do what you can."

"Bring two cockerels, one red and one white."

Grandma was out of the house as soon as Dibịa Agbacha finished giving the prescription. Grandma made the arrangements for the items and returned to the room. The medicine man was bending on Machi and drawing on her forehead with the chalk. Without turning to look at Grandma, he said, "She is a lucky one. She has a strong spirit. There is room for hope."

CHAPTER NINE

But Machi was far away from the land of the living. She was in the land of the Spirit Children where all things were tranquil. She did not know how or when she crossed the great gulf that served as the boundary between the land of humans and the land of the Spirit Children; she could only look back and see the immense chasm and the horrendous creatures with four heads and fearsome, spear-like horns and iron teeth. They were awake, always; they roamed the border day and night, three to each of the six boundaries of the land of the Spirit Children; one border with the land of the Sky People, from which they received messages from the gods; another with the land of humans, through which children were sent at the appointed time to be born; one with the land of the Awaiting Death, for the Spirit Children who were released to spend only a short time on the earth; another with the land of the Ancestors, through which they communicated with the great men who had departed the land of humans; one with the land of the Awaiting Birth, where deviant Spirit Children were sent to inhabit until their reformation, or be doomed to age in perpetual youth; and the last boundary with the Spirit World, where the ghosts of all the spirits of all the lands roam, those whose deeds in their former existence prevented them from being admitted into the necessary place of their sojourn—those doomed to revisit whence they had come. The last boundary was the most fortified.

But in this land of the Spirit Children in which Machi found herself, all was serene. The trees grew tall and wild, and their branches were burdened with fruits that clamored for plucking. The grasses grew as high as a man, and their blades waved in the sun. The earth was soft and greenish, and the inhabitants trod on bare feet, and nothing hurt them, for it was an enhanced land and everything was meant for the comfort of those who dwelt therein. Down every valley clear rivers flowed, and in the bed of the rivers were pebbles like pearls, and they shone resplendently as one looked down. The fishes in the river were golden and transparent and swam peacefully even when people approached; no one caught them, and they too experienced the peace that the dwellers of this land experienced. The rocks on the mountains were smooth and shiny and huge. They were said to have been deposited by the gods at the creation of the world; some of the materials left over in the formation of the earth.

Petals were strewn across the lawn by different plants; petals of different colors, and their fragrance rent the air. The trees flowered and fruited all year-round. The inhabitants of the land ate nothing but the fruits. Their skin was smooth and fresh, and no wrinkles or spots could be found on their body. They neither cultivated the earth nor hunted animals nor kept animals. They only had white little ponies for riding. These ponies were of the most brilliant and smooth curls, and they partook of fruits as their masters. No smoke ever rose in the land; the inhabitants of the land knew nothing about the art of making fire. The sun lighted their land in the day and the moon in the night. This had been so with the founding of the world—on no day had there been no sun, nor night without moon. The rain fell at the appointed time and did not disturb the luminaries. Everything went about in order. That was, for as long as their boundaries held, and nothing was admitted from the outside world to corrupt the working of their land.

Machi was welcomed to the land like one who had long been expected and whose arrival everyone had yearned for. Song burst forth from every corner of the land and the people danced as they conducted her toward the Village Center where important decisions of the land were made. Now these people had neither kings nor leaders, but anyone could call up a meeting and initiate a program for others to contribute to. They brought Machi to a big, igneous rock which stood in the Village Center, and she sat amidst the sounds of jubilation that rent the air. One of them stood beside Machi and addressed the rest.

"Nwefu has come back to us! Let today be a day of rejoicing!"

There was a renewed clamor among the people, and cheering and songs here and there, discordant because different, but pleasing all the same to ears that had not heard them before.

"I am not Nwefu. I am Machikwe."

"We do not know what they call you in the land of humans. Nwefu is what we call you here, since the day you went away from us. Long have we waited for you and mourned for you. We thank the gods you have been restored to us."

Machi made no further protests but watched in amusement as they went about in her service. They brought a crown of polished, transparent stone such as she had never seen and laid it on her head. Its warmth diffused through her hair. Then they placed a necklace on her neck, and its pendant rested gracefully on her chest. The pendant was dark and seemed to have more depth than its size, and it bewildered the eyes as if it held a secret that only deep conjuration could reveal. As soon as the pendant rested on her chest, she felt a surge of power within her. Her eyes were opened to the sovereignty that had always been hers, and she looked upon her citizens and a great love for them welled in her heart.

She rose from her throne and danced with them, swaying to the cadences of their songs.

But as the singing and dancing and eating and drinking and merriment were going on, trouble was brewing in the boundary between the land of the Spirit Children and the land of the Ancestors. The beasts on guard at the boundary were howling. No one remembered the last time such a disturbance had been heard in the land. The merriment came to an abrupt end as they all hurried to the boundary to see what was going on. They all stopped short in amazement at the sight before them, Machi most of all.

Beyond the boundary to the Land of the Ancestors, were dark shadows, shrouded and veiled. Riding on immense pythons, they stood poised with flaming arrows directed at the guardian beasts at the boundary. The beasts, teeth bared, howled at the pythons. But calm was the bearing of the pythons. Here and there they moved their heads with pronounced majesty which seemed to frighten the guardian beasts more than any overt attack could have done. The dark shadows lowered their arrows as the Spirit Children approached. One of them addressed the Spirit Children.

"Spirit Children, may your calm remain with you as always. We have not come to disrupt it. We come only to claim a fellow lately come to your midst who does not belong to you. Hand her over to us and we will make no trouble with you."

The dark, shadowy one pointed at Machi and beckoned, but one of the Spirit Children stepped forward and addressed the shadow.

"In peace have we lived here for hundreds of years. We have known no war because we cause no trouble with any of the lands surrounding us. What is this great cause you have come here to advocate? How do you come here with dreaded pythons, made of the silver god for ruin alone, most deceitful of creatures, and yet tell us that you have not come for trouble? And who are you to tell us who is not ours? Long have we waited for her, long has she been lost to us, since the days of the Red-Haired Goddess. Long have we expected her. Now she has come back to us, and you are here to tell us that she does not belong to us? She has partaken of our food, drank of our wine, and cannot return back to the land of humans."

"Peace I held out to you, on the condition that you release her. I am Ede, the Prime Ancestral spirit of Edemma. This afternoon it was reported to me that one who is undue to pass through the Ancestral Gate had come to the gate, and when turned away, came to your land and you induced her or welcomed her. I do not care what food of yours she had eaten, or your drink, give her up and I undertake to make just recompense as you desire. Tears of wailing from the land of humans have not let me rest since she came to your land."

"What will you do if we hold on to our claim?"

"Blind and foolish you are to ask such a question of me. Have we from our land not protected you when you called for our help? Perhaps you are too young to remember. The fool alone challenges the arms that had borne him. Abundant life you enjoy, but immortal you are not. Resist and I will shoot an arrow through you, and your land will know mourning as it has never known before."

The Spirit Children drew back at the threatening words of the veiled Ancestral Head of Edemma. Machi remained where she was, weighing all she had heard. She liked it here; peace aplenty it promised, and she was loath to leave it. But what would become of the fate of the inhabitants if she refused to go with the ancestors? And if she went with them, where would they take her? Machi did not have much time to think. The shadows had lifted their arrows again and were pointing them at the guardian beasts, which seemed tormented by their flames, for they immediately started roaring and moving restively within their confines. The Shadow which had called himself Ede beckoned to Machi again.

She moved forward, but one of the Spirit Children held her back. Without one word more, Ede released his arrow on one of the guardian beasts and hit it in the forehead. The beast gave a thunderous roar that shook the boundary and both lands. The Spirit Children trembled and held on to each other. The arrow stuck on the head of the beast and caught fire. Its anguished cry as the flame devoured it was horrible to hear; it was like the sound of a thousand voices in agony, multiplied several fold as it echoed in the universe.

Ede took another arrow and pointed it at the gathering of the Spirit Children. They shrank back, and some of them took to their heels. He beckoned to Machi and without another thought, she moved toward him. He approached and the great python on which he rode stretched its head and scaled the boundary. He lifted her, put her on top of the python, and they moved past the boundary into the land of humans.

Behind, the wailing of the Spirit Children assailed her ears, but she did not long hear them, for now she heard her grandmother crying and calling her name, and another voice, deeper and more commanding, chanting and invoking her.

As she tried to answer to her name, she coughed and woke up.

CHAPTER TEN

"Your granddaughter has survived a very great battle. She is lucky and beloved of the ancestors. I do not count on her coming out successful next time. Why have you tarried in destroying her totem? Or do you mean to tell me that you do not know that she is an ogbanje? Her totem must be found at once. And it is better we do it now, when her spirit is still weak from struggle and less disposed to tricks."

Machi, scarcely recovered from the stress of the people who had come to welcome her back "from the dead" was whisked off by her grandmother into the barn where the medicine man awaited, eggs arranged before him, and the mat spread. Without looking up, the medicine man beckoned Machi to sit down on the mat. She sat down. A strange and distrustful feeling came over her when her eyes met the medicine man's.

"Where did you bury your totem?"

"I don't know what you are talking about."

Dibịa Agbacha seemed to believe in the sincerity of her answer, for he did not press her to answer further, immediately. He brought a small calabash gourd, poured in some liquid from one of the bottles he carried about, and gave it to Machi. Then he broke three of the eggs on the mat, dipped his hand in the yolk, and drew on Machi's forehead with the substance. Then he said, "Drink."

The first drop of the drink that entered Machi's mouth sent her retching. She extended the gourd back to Dibịa Agbacha, but he took it and forced the whole content down her throat. Agbacha was so fast that she had no time to resist before the foul content was emptied into her mouth and belly. She coughed several times then became quiet.

"Now tell me where you buried your totem."

At first, Machi made no move. The question sounded as abstract as it had initially. But the Dibịa asked her again. And it seemed as if her eyes were opened, and she was no longer sitting on the mat. She awoke to a new plane of existence, although she could still see Grandma and Dibịa Agbacha. Everywhere seemed changed, and she heard a voice calling her name. Involuntarily she went toward it. She saw a figure like herself as though she had seen herself in the mirror. It was even dressed as she was dressed. The figure held out its hand and Machi took it. It led the way and Machi followed. Behind Machi trailed Grandma and Agbacha. She followed the figure like one in a trance, stepping where it stepped. They walked on, the Dibịa following immediately after Machi, and her grandma coming after. They passed the compound and continued walking. Some of the villagers followed them and the Dibịa did not tell them to go back.

They came into the bush at the back of Machi's father's compound in the village. She led them to the breadfruit tree and stopped. The figure which had been leading Machi pointed to a spot, and Machi pointed at it too.

Dibịa Agbacha said in a very solemn voice, "Is this where you buried it?"

"Yes," Machi said, hardly conscious of the words that proceeded from her lips.

Agbacha sent for hoes, and they were brought, and some young men were told to dig the spot. They dug laboriously, for the ground was stringy, and the small roots of the breadfruit tree impeded their hoes. They dug in turns for almost twenty minutes before they came upon a wrapped object. Machi started when it was lifted. The figure released Machi's hand and moved further from her, its face agitated.

"Is this your totem?"

Machi nodded.

Dibịa Agbacha chanted incantations over it and set it on fire. After a while, the yellow flame turned blue, and the totem started making a hissing noise. Machi felt dizzy. She sank on her heels, and Grandma reached to raise her up, but Agbacha beckoned to Grandma to let Machi alone. The totem burnt some more and then in one flash of white light, disappeared.

Machi fell to the ground. It was as if something was wrenched out of her body. She felt an unfathomable sense of loss. A new sense of being came over her. She slept most peacefully, undisturbed by dreams. Her everyday experiences were most ordinary and eventless. Everything around her appeared on only a single layer: the physical. She no longer experienced an interference of the spiritual world. She felt an immense and unspeakable loneliness. It seemed to her that what had made her whole had been removed and a sense of shame filled her whenever she was in company. She felt naked and unprotected and vulnerable.

EPILOGUE

Three months after the burning of her totem, Machi was at the stream alone when she perceived a wisp of smoke rising from the surface of the water. It was evening and the weather was dry and the air crisp, and only on tall palms did the yellow fingers of the westering sun linger.

As Machi stared intently at the rising smoke, a breeze began to blow over the water, and in that breeze was a voice that sounded both pleasant and harrowing. Machi recognized the voice beyond guessing: it was her grandmother's voice. The cadence of the voice rose and fell, but Machi could not make out what the voice was saying. She stood up and looked about her. There was no one, and if she had not left her grandmother at home, she would have thought she was calling her.

And then, as suddenly as the voice had started, it ceased. The mists cleared. She looked in vain for signs of her recent experience, but she found none. Then she fetched her water hurriedly and turned homeward.

As she neared her grandmother's house, she started to hear murmuring voices. For a moment, she thought she was recalling the occurrence at the stream. But the voices grew louder and then she saw people trooping to her grandmother's compound. Everyone she asked about what was going on turned their faces from her, and none returned her an answer.

Her apprehension grew. She put down her water and rushed to her grandmother's hut. She stopped short at the entrance, for it was barred by a string of white and black cowries arranged in an oval at the entrance of the house.

The door was open, but she could not see inside. An indefinable darkness had taken over the house; Machi caught a whiff of it and felt an otherworldly coldness crawl down her spine. She called her grandmother, but her voice died in her head, and no sound came out. Her head swelled but she could not raise her hands to feel it. And then she began to hear her grandmother's voice, in the same cadence as she had heard her in the stream, but now her grandmother was speaking with others whose voices were like gurgling water—smooth and yet incomprehensible. A voice among the other two sounded familiar, but she could not place it.

Suddenly, three figures emerged from the room: her grandmother with a man and a woman. They were dressed in crimson, and yet the dresses seemed to be not on their body but merely hovering around them. Machi ran to her grandmother, but her grandmother held out a hand and stopped her short. Then her grandmother and the companions walked past Machi into the crowd, but no one seemed to notice them. They faded slowly until Machi could see no trace of them anymore.

Machi turned at the sound of tapping on the ground and saw Dibịa Agbacha emerging from her grandmother's hut. He dug his staff into the ground, and his eyes lingered on Machi before he spoke.

"You may go inside now and see her body. Do not weep for her, for she died in her time."

Machi stared at him uncomprehending, but the Dibịa offered no explanation. He uprooted his staff and left.

Machi went inside and found her grandmother's body already prepared for burial. Then she understood what she had seen earlier: her grandmother had already departed in the company of guiding ancestors, and only her body remained to be committed to the bowels of Mother Earth.

...❖...

Four days after her grandmother's burial, Machi was in the forest fetching firewood when she perceived the leaves whistling from a breeze. She knew it was no ordinary breeze, for it came from the ground and was cold on the body. She turned to run out of the forest but an impulse held her. As she waited, she noticed the dead stumps regenerating and the dry leaves returning to life. And the musty smell of the forest was replaced by a scent of freshness.

Then a single point of light emerged from the ground and grew until it took the shape of her grandmother. She sailed gracefully toward Machi, and when she had drawn close, she opened her palm to reveal a necklace whose pendant looked like liquid pearl. Without a word, she hung the necklace on Machi's neck, and as the pendant rested on her chest, she knew it immediately that it was the necklace she had been given in the land of the Spirit Children.

"I have brought you this from your subjects," her grandmother said. Her voice sounded different, as it must have sounded in her younger days. "Since you cannot come to them, they are coming to you."

Then, as if from the trees and from the ground, there came numerous voices singing in so perfect a harmony that they were like one layered voice. Machi spurn around, but wherever she looked, it seemed as if the voices came from where she was not looking. And then, all of a sudden, she saw the Spirit Children converging around her. As they approached, their words became distinct, and Machi recognized them for the words she had heard them say in the land of the Spirit Children. She knew their meaning, though she did not understand the words.

One of the Spirit Children approached her with the crown they had given her in their land. Machi bent and the Spirit Child placed it on her head, and Machi felt a surge of power and insight come upon her. But as she straightened to look upon her subjects, they were no longer there. Her grandmother had gone, too. The leaves shriveled, the stumps dried, and the musty smell of the forest returned.

For a long time, Machi stood, wondering if she had imagined it all. But the necklace remained on her neck and the crown on her head, testaments of her encounter in the forest. And yet, when she tried to remove them as she came out of the forest, she could not. The people she met on the way looked at her without seeming to notice the crown.

Then she understood that her dominion was only with the Spirit Children, and she had been crowned to govern them from the land of humans. She would be their goddess and guide on the earth. Every newborn was her subject, come on sojourn to the earth, and she would guide them, just as the ancestors guided the spirits of the newly deceased.

THE PET OF OLODUMARE

by Joshua Uchenna Omenga and Oghenechovwe Donald Ekpeki

It was said in the lore of Orisha that in the beginning of time, Olodumare existed alone in the vast uncreated universe. But as the time passed, Olodumare became lonely and yearned for company. He then created a pet which he named "Olutunudumare," and the pet kept him company and brought him comfort from the weariness of primal existence. But after 86,000 years, Olodumare desired the company of beings in his own likeness. So, he created the 401 Orishas, or deities, and they lived with him in Orun, the abode of the gods.

But the Orishas were unlike the Olutunudumare which did whatever Olodumare willed it to do. Being much like himself, the Orishas found it hard to offer devotion to Olodumare, and Olodumare soon wearied of their pretended devotion. Therefore, Olodumare decided to create another being, less sublime than the Orishas, but greater in devotion, like the Olutunudumare. But being too grand to create imperfect beings, Olodumare decided to entrust the task to an Orisha, deeming that an Orisha can only create something less than itself. After observing all the Orishas in their different aspects of life, Olodumare decided to entrust the task to Obatala. So he summoned Obatala to his presence.

Obatala prostrated flat on the ground before Olodumare and said, "Lord of Orun, may you wear your royal crown forever."

"Rise," Olodumare said, waving his fly whisk at Obatala.

Obatala rose accordingly.

"I have a task for which only one with a spotless reputation can be entrusted," Olodumare continued. "I have looked for such one in Orun, and today I recognize your untarnished reputation among the Orishas. Your eyes are perfect. Your fingers are steady. Your muscles are strong. And your mind is healthy. Therefore, I entrust to you the task of fashioning a human body from the clay."

Obatala bowed, and Olodumare waved his fly whisk of blessing over him.

"I grant you the dexterity of fingers and the art of balance, so that the human bodies you create may stand out among other non-celestial beings."

Then Olodumare handed a covered basket to Obatala, and said to him, "In this basket dwells the spirit of artistry and wisdom. It kept me company during the creation of the universe. I give it to you to keep you company while you fashion the human body. Its presence shall endow you with the talent of artistry. But do not open it, and do not let anyone else open it."

Obatala accepted the basket, bowed to Olodumare, and departed to do the task entrusted to him. But first, he built a studio for his work, and the location of the studio he did not reveal to anyone, not even to his wives, for he did not like to be disturbed while at work. In this studio he placed the basket given to him by Olodumare. And then he set about his task of fashioning humans.

After several months, Obatala accomplished his task and unveiled the humans he had created before Olodumare. Olodumare was so pleased with Obatala's performance that he gave Obatala a new and magnificent mansion in Orun. Obatala moved into the mansion with his wives. He kept the basket in one of the rooms and forbade his wives and servants to enter the room.

A long time passed, and none of Obatala's wives or domestic staff ventured to the forbidden room. But after some time, Yemoja became curious of what was in the room forbidden for them to enter. The desire to know grew in her until one day, as she lay in Obatala's arms, she asked him what he kept in the room that he forbade them to enter.

"Why do you seek to know what is forbidden you?" he asked, wrathful at her. "If you are meant to know it, will I not tell you?"

Obatala's reply made Yemoja more curious, but not wishing to clash with her husband over the matter, she bid her time until one day when Obatala went to a feast in the house of Sango. Yemoja knew that he would not return while the palm wine lasted, and when he did return, he would be drunk for days. So she thought the time had come for her to find out what was in the forbidden room.

She was fully ready to enter the room. However, apprehensive of what might be in the forbidden room, Yemoja deemed it unwise to enter the room first by herself. Therefore, she invited Yemowo's servant named Sapaolu and told her to open the door. Sapaolu protested, knowing that it was forbidden of anyone to enter the room. But Yemoja prevailed upon her with promise of ornaments for which human women were fond of.

At last, Sapaolu opened the door, and Yemoja peered into the room. But she saw nothing; there was nothing to see in the room except the basket which lay in one corner. Yemoja was disappointed. Had Obatala forbade them from entering into the room because of a basket?

She turned and would have left the room when it occurred to her that the secret might *be* the basket. So she instructed Sapaolu to bring the basket to her. When it was given to her, she opened it and saw a creature curled inside. It was the most beautiful creature she had ever set eyes upon. Its eyes shone like liquid pearl and its membranous wings showed different colors. Yemoja was enthralled with the creature and was reluctant to part with it. But when she heard Obatala's homecoming and drunken song, she returned the creature to the basket and closed the room.

She fully expected Obatala to discover what she had done, but days passed and Obatala said nothing about it. Yemoja could not stop thinking about the creature. Her craving for it increased day by day until at last she began to create opportunities to sneak into the room to behold the creature. This she did several times until she was no longer content with sneaking into the room to see the creature. She decided to keep the creature for herself, reasoning that if it meant anything to Obatala, he would have missed it.

It happened that Olodumare who had gone on a routine tour of the universe had just returned and desiring some comfort, wanted his pet. So he summoned Obatala and said to him, "Now that your task of human creation is done, return to me the basket which I entrusted to you to aid you in your task."

"Yes, Supreme One," Obatala said, and ran to his abode and brought the basket to Olodumare.

Olodumare accepted the basket and Obatala bowed and turned to go. But Olodumare called him back. He turned and saw that the basket was uncovered and that Olodumare was looking wrathfully at him.

"Where is the creature that I kept in this basket?" Olodumare asked.

Obatala was confused and could not say a word in reply.

"Did I not warn you not to open this basket but to simply stand it in your studio to aid you in your creation task?"

"I did just as you bid me, Supreme One," Obatala said. "I did not open it. And when I finished my task, I kept it in a special room where no one but me had access."

"Then what happened to the creature which I concealed inside it?"

"I do not know, Supreme One. Perhaps someone opened it without my knowledge."

Olodumare's wrath was great, but perceiving the truth in Obatala's words, he simply said, "Go and find the creature and return it to me."

Obatala left Olodumare in sorrow. He was in dilemma. He did not know what had happened to the creature or where to find it. At that time, there was no stealing in Orun and Obatala did not suspect anybody. However, while pondering over the matter, he remembered that Yemoja had once pressed him upon the matter. So he decided to query her over it. But in order not to appear to be suspicious of one wife, he decided to call both Yemoja and Yemowo.

When his wives appeared before him, he asked if any of them had entered into the room which he forbade them to enter. Both denied entering the room.

However, Yemoja feigned to ponder over the matter for a while. Then she came in secretly to Obatala and said, "I remember who could have taken what you look for, husband. Once, I was passing by and saw Yemowo's servant Sapaolu standing in front of the room, holding a basket. I asked where she got the basket and she pointed at the room which you had forbade us to enter. I ordered her to return it. Is that perhaps what my husband has been looking for?"

Obatala thanked Yemoja for the intelligence and promptly sent for Sapaolu. When she appeared, Obatala took her to Olodumare.

"Lord of Orun," Obatala said, presenting Sapaolu before Olodumare. "This human woman stole the creature which you speak of."

Immediately when she heard what she had been charged with, Sapaolu protested fervently that she had only carried the basket to Yemoja as she was bid. Olodumare then sent for Yemoja, and she too came before him.

"Do you know this basket?" Olodumare asked, holding it out to Yemoja.

"Yes, Lord of Orun," Yemoja replied. "I saw it once in the hand of Sapaolu. She took it from the room which my husband forbade us from entering. So I ordered her to return it."

"You did not take or see the creature inside the basket?"

"No, Lord of Orun."

Olodumare saw that both women could not be right, and that the truth must only be on one side. He therefore invited Orunmila, the infallible diviner, to point out where the truth stood.

Orunmila arrived bearing his Ifa in a skin bag. He saluted Olodumare and exchanged greetings with all around him. And noticing the look of discomfort in their faces, he asked of Olodumare what was amiss.

"One among these who stand before me has tampered with the secret which I entrusted to Obatala," Olodumare answered. "But both deny responsibility. That is why I have called you, Orunmila. Tell me where the truth stands between them."

Orunmila smiled and reached into his skin bag and brought out his Ifa board. Laying the Ifa board on the ground, he began to chant:

I sing your praise, Ifa
Oracle of existence
Knower of the past and the future.
The snail does not sleep outside its shell
The viper does not sleep without its poison
The cricket does not sleep without its noise
The chameleon does not move without its colors
Ifa does not exist without its truth.
Ifa does not give gift of rodents
Or hens

Or pregnant goats
Or deer with curled horns
Ifa gives only the truth.
Therefore, I request
Ifa's truth in this matter.

Thereupon, Orunmila cast the sixteen divination palm nuts on the Ifa board. After reading its message, he raised his head and said, pointing at Yemoja, "Lord of Orun, this is the guilty one."

"Orunmila lies against me!" Yemoja protested. "He was not there to see what happened."

But Olodumare rebuked Yemoja in a strong voice. "Do not charge Orunmila with falsehood, for the one who speaks in the voice of Ifa cannot lie. Ifa is founded on truth, and its voice is the voice of eternity and existence. Ifa keeps the record of past existence; it knows the present existence most clearly, and it tells the future without fail."

"But things are not as Orunmila said them!" Yemoja protested still. "It was Sapaolu who opened the door and took the basket."

"She says the truth in this," Orunmila said, and hope entered Yemoja's eyes. "But Lord of Orun," Orunmila continued, "truth does not consist in slices of facts. Sapaolu did enter the room first and carried the forbidden basket, but she did all at the bidding of Yemoja. An act is not done by the doer, but by the one who authorizes its doing."

Olodumare thanked Orunmila for his service, and he departed. Then Olodumare commanded Yemoja to return the creature she had stolen. Shamefacedly, Yemoja went to her room and brought the creature and gave it to Olodumare.

Then Olodumare said to her, "Because you have stolen the Olutunudumare, a creature of primal existence, I banish you from Orun. Your abode shall be in the ocean below and there you shall exercise dominion. I shall have nothing to do with you henceforth, for you have chosen the path of ignominy."

Yemoja bent her head in shame and departed from Olodumare's presence.

Then Olodumare turned to Obatala. "And because the humans you created have seen the secret of their creation, death shall come upon them, and they shall no more dwell in Orun. Therefore, a habitation shall be found for them in the ocean below."

"But, Supreme One," Obatala protested, "I did not create humans to live in water."

"I am well aware of that, Obatala. And I do not propose that they should live in the water. But they shall live on the earth that shall be formed out of the ocean. Therefore, I am sending a delegation to create the earth, and you shall be at the head of the delegation to ensure that the earth is created with all the specifications needed to sustain human life in the fashion which you have created them."

Obatala bowed and returned to await Olodumare's instructions.

As for Yemoja, she returned in bitterness to her abode to prepare for her departure from Orun. And recalling that the truth would not have been revealed but for the intervention of Orunmila through his Ifa, she decided to punish Orunmila by stealing the Ifa. This she accomplished and hid the stolen Ifa among her property which she took out of Orun.

Meanwhile, Olodumare was greatly unsettled by the incident, and he was eager to have the earth created and humans relocated to it. He formed a delegation of the Orishas and sent them forth to create the earth.

The delegation met with fierce opposition from Yemoja when they reached the ocean to carry out their task. Yemoja still bore the grief of banishment in her heart, and she vowed that the earth would not be formed in her domain for the habitation of the humans whom she deemed to be the cause of her woes. So she formed league with the creatures of the ocean and baffled the efforts of the delegation sent to form the earth. They returned without success to Orun.

Olodumare sent another delegation. This delegation included Sango with his lightning bolt meant to conquer Yemoja. But with the aid of the Ifa, Yemoja foresaw the plots of the delegation and countered them. Olodumare sent still another delegation, and Yemoja baffled it also.

When it seemed that Olodumare's plan would not be realized, Yemowo sought Olodumare's audience.

"Lord of Orun," she said, kneeling before Olodumare. "I wish to make amends for the wrong which my servant Sapaolu has done to you."

"How do you propose to do that?" Olodumare asked.

"Send me among the delegation to the earth."

"To what end?"

"To distract Yemoja while the delegation performs its task."

"How do you intend to distract Yemoja when no deity has succeeded in gaining access to her domain?"

"With the Olutunudumare, Lord of Orun," Yemowo said. "Give me the Olutunudumare, and with it I shall distract Yemoja while the earth is formed."

Olodumare pondered upon her request, for it troubled him to part with the Olutunudumare again. However, as he could not refuse aid to one who wished to accomplish his task, he reluctantly released the Olutunudumare to Yemowo.

Having been granted the Olutunudumare, Yemowo traveled with the delegation toward the ocean abode of Yemoja. When they were near the ocean, Yemowo instructed the delegation to wait until she gave them sign to meet her. Then she went alone to Yemoja.

Yemoja was surprised to see that Yemowo had come alone and not with a delegation as the Ifa had revealed to her. She was unsettled to find out that the Ifa could be wrong. But Yemowo soon put her mind at rest.

"I have come in courtesy and not to intrude in your domain," Yemowo said, perceiving the distrust in Yemoja's eyes. "I have come to commiserate with you and make amends for the injustice done to you in banishing you from Orun."

Yemoja laughed in mockery of Yemowo. "Do you imagine that I desire any commiseration or amends from you or from any of your lot in Orun? I am more than content with my new domain. You speak of commiseration because you have not seen the glory of my domain. When you see it, you would not think me missing anything in Orun!"

Then Yemoja led Yemowo into her domain in the ocean and showed her all its glory. It dazzled Yemowo and she deemed it fairer than Orun. Thereafter, Yemoja took Yemowo to her chamber and showed her the store of jewels. Then Yemoja wore a different jewel one after the other, and her beauty dazzled Yemowo as Yemoja had intended. Yemoja was a proud Orisha and ever sought to display her beauty and opulence even before her enemies.

"Do you see," Yemoja said in satisfaction upon seeing the wonderment in Yemowo's eyes, "that I do not need your commiseration or the amends of Orun? I have all in my domain that Orun cannot give me."

"Your domain is truly glorious," Yemowo said. "I came bearing a gift from Olodumare, but now I see that it can mean nothing to you."

"What gift can you possibly bring to me from Olodumare?"

Yemowo brought out the Olutunudumare which she had erstwhile concealed in her bosom. Yemoja recognized it. She stared at it, pretending to be unmoved. But soon her desire overtook her, and she reached out to hold it as she was wont to do. But Yemowo drew back the Olutunudumare.

"You said you have brought it for me!" Yemoja said.

"Yes," Yemowo said. "I brought it to you in exchange for something."

"What would you have in its place?"

"The construction of earth on a portion of your ocean."

"Have you then come at the bidding of Olodumare?"

"Yes, Yemoja. I have come at the bidding of Olodumare."

"Then leave my domain at once! It is my pact with Olodumare that we should have nothing to do with each other."

"I do not doubt that you may be right. But please, let me rest awhile. My journey was long, and I am weary. Tomorrow I shall return to Orun."

"You may have your rest and return tomorrow."

But Yemowo had not asked the favor out of tiredness. She knew that her proposition festered deep in Yemoja's mind, so she sought to buy time for its fruition. When morning came, she made a show of departing from Yemoja's abode. But Yemoja implored her to stay awhile, and she feigned reluctance. Meanwhile, Yemoja asked to hold the Olutunudumare once more. And when she held the Olutunudumare, she found it even more enthralling than she had in Orun, and she was loath to part with it.

"The ocean is vast," Yemoja said condescendingly to Yemowo. "I shall grant you a portion for your earth project in exchange for the Olutunudumare. But do not exceed the portion which I grant you."

"Thank you for your generosity," Yemowo said, secretly rejoicing at the success of her ploy. Then she signaled the delegation, and they descended to the ocean and created the earth. Thereafter, Obatala brought the humans he had created and settled them on the earth.

Now that their task was done, the delegation prepared for their return to Orun. As she packed her bag, Yemowo called the Olutunudumare and it ran into her bosom.

"You cannot go with it," Yemoja protested. "We had an agreement that it should be mine in exchange for the portion of the ocean for constructing the earth. I have yielded a portion of the ocean, so the creature is mine now."

"No," Yemowo said. "We only agreed that you shall have it in exchange for the construction of the earth on a portion of the ocean. Now the earth is constructed, and our agreement has elapsed."

Yemoja saw that Yemowo had deceived her in the wording of their agreement. But she would not let herself be cheated. She lunged at Yemowo and gripped her by the throat. As Yemoja's grip tightened on her throat, Yemowo felt her celestial essence diminishing and her strength ebbing with it. She began to choke on Yemoja's grip. A cough started in her belly but it could not pass through her throat. Then she felt her consciousness receding.

Suddenly, the hand let go of her throat, and she staggered back, gasping. Yemoja was staring at her hand and looking more infuriated. Then Yemowo felt the soft touch on her neck and saw that the Olutunudumare had come out from her bosom where she had hidden it and had bitten Yemoja.

Yemoja's eyes shone with new fury. "Return it to me and I will consider you relieved of your obligation under our pact."

"I owe you no obligation, and I cannot return it to you. Olodumare kept it in my custody and only to him will I return it."

Yemoja lunged at the Olutunudumare, but Yemowo had anticipated her and sprang away like a deer. Yemoja did not chase after her. She merely gave a prolonged laughter, but as she laughed, water gushed out of her mouth and became a stream, and the stream overtook Yemowo. As Yemowo struggled to keep herself from drowning, Yemoja floated toward her and snatched the Olutunudumare from her bosom. Then Yemoja brought out a tiny vial from her hair, dipped it into the water, and the water was sucked into the vial.

"Now that I have retrieved the Olutunudumare, I consider your pledge fulfilled, and you may return to Orun," Yemoja said, returning the vial to her hair.

"I cannot return to Orun without the Olutunudumare. What will I tell Olodumare?"

"Then you may remain on earth. But I warn you, do not enter my domain henceforth. Any day you enter any river connected to my domain, I will drown your body so fast that your spirit will have no time to escape to Orun."

"Obatala will find me if you dare use the ocean against me."

"Will he?" Yemoja said in a mocking tone. "Where has he been all these years that you were been trapped in my domain?"

"He did not know where to find me, but now he does."

Yemoja seemed about to talk but considered it unnecessary and turned to go. Just then, there came the sound of a whirlwind overhead, and a blinding column of light descended from the sky. For a moment, the shaft of light blinded both of them. But gradually the light dimmed to reveal the magnificent figure of Olodumare.

Yemoja and Yemowo bowed simultaneously, and said, "Lord of Orun, may you wear your royal crown forever!"

Olodumare motioned them, and they stood up and faced him. His face was fierce as he looked upon them.

"Shameless Orishas, vain fools!" Olodumare said in the thought-tongue of Orun. Yemowo bent her head penitently as Olodumare's words poured forth, but Yemoja stared ahead in defiance, her hands folded backward where she held the Olutunudumare.

Olodumare swung his staff as if he would smite one or both of them. "Now, what is the matter between you?"

There was a moment of silence as both Orishas stared at each other. Then Yemowo started to speak, but Yemoja interrupted her, and both started quarreling. Olodumare planted his staff on the earth, and a wave of vibration rippled through the earth.

"Do you think I have come here for your quarrels?" Olodumare shook his head before he continued. "You are unto yourselves masters over your own affairs. If you desire to destroy each other, that is your affair. I shall not interfere, but I shall not receive report of your ignominy either. I have come here for the sole purpose of retrieving my pet. Now Yemowo, where is the Olutunudumare that I committed to your care?"

Yemowo pointed at Yemoja and said, "She took it."

"Hand it over," Olodumare said, turning to Yemoja.

"I cannot, Lord of Orun. It was pledged to me in return for the use of my domain to construct the earth."

"When did I make such pledge to you?"

"Yemowo brought your words of pledge."

Olodumare turned at Yemowo and she said in embarrassment, "Lord of Orun, who am I to make any pledge on your behalf? I merely promised Yemoja that she might play with Olutunudumare while the earth was constructed."

"Liar!" Yemoja shouted into Yemowo's ears. "You promised the Olutunudumare to me in exchange for the portion of my domain to be used in constructing the earth."

"Silence, both of you!"

The two Orishas ceased talking instantly.

Olodumare turned to Yemowo and said, "Who makes a pledge of what they do not own?" Then he turned to Yemoja. "As for you, how can you presume that I would pledge to you the victim of your atrocity? Now, give me the Olutunudumare!"

Reluctantly, Yemoja produced the Olutunudumare and handed it over to Olodumare. As the Olutunudumare touched Olodumare's grasp, it glowed in full glory in its panoply of colors. He caressed it gently and a smile came upon his face.

"But I was deceived!" Yemoja grumbled. "I was told that only the portion I granted would be used for constructing the earth. Now humans are filling the ocean with sand and raising their buildings and polluting the waters. You looked on and said nothing, but just because I want to enforce my agreement with Yemowo, you came to reprimand me."

"I have not come to reprimand you, Yemoja. Now that I have reclaimed my pet, you may go on quarreling with Yemowo as you wish. As for humans, you determined the boundary of the ocean upon which the dry earth was formed. If they trespass into your domain or pollute it, deal with them as you wish, but do not complain to me about them. I have washed my hands of the control of humans. And what is more, I am also washing my hands of the affairs of Orishas too. Humans may, out of the weakness in their creation, prove foolish, but what weakness drives you whom I created perfect to your perfidious ways?"

Olodumare looked upon the two Orishas, his eyes blazing with reproach. But when he was done reprimanding them, he looked upon the Olutunudumare and caressed it again, and his face glowed with joy. Then he lifted his staff, and the Orishas knew he was about to depart.

"Lord of Orun," Yemowo said, bowing. "Permit me to return to Orun with you."

Olodumare looked at Yemowo for a while, then held out his hand, and Yemowo took it. Then, lifting his staff, Olodumare blazed forth like a column of light and shot skyward out of the earth, and Yemowo and Olutunudumare were like tiny stars holding onto the sun that was Olodumare.

It was said that thereafter, Olodumare was embittered by this affair, and he decided to retire from the affairs of his creations. But not desiring humans to be entirely without supervision, Olodumare assigned the Orishas to be gods unto humans and supervise their affairs accordingly. Then Olodumare retired to his special abode in Orun where he found the peace he wanted in the company of his pet Olutunudumare. Thereafter, he no longer intervened in the affairs of humans.

THE AUTHORS

Oghenechovwe Donald Ekpeki is a highly acclaimed, award-winning African speculative fiction writer, editor, and publisher in Nigeria.

He has won the Nommo award twice, and an Otherwise and British Fantasy award. His novelette "02 Arena" won the Nebula award, and is a Hugo award finalist, making him the first African to be a Nebula best novelette winner and Hugo best novelette finalist. The thought-provoking piece was also a finalist for British Science Fiction, British Fantasy and Nommo awards.

He edits *The Year's Best African Speculative Fiction* anthology series, of which he's the first African Hugo award best editor finalist for Volume One. He's the first BIPOC to be a Hugo award finalist in fiction and editing categories in the same year, and *The Year's Best African Speculative Fiction* Volume One anthology he edited and published is also a Locus, British Fantasy and World Fantasy award finalist.

He co-edited the *Dominion* anthology, *Africa Risen* anthology, and was a guest of honor at the 2022 Cancon and 2023 International Conference on the Fantastic in the Arts (ICFA).

He currently resides in Lagos, Nigeria.

Joshua Uchenna Omenga is a Nigerian editor and writer of African speculative and literary fiction. His story, 'The Deification of Igodo' appeared in Tor.com (*Africa Risen* anthology) and in *The Year's Best Fantasy*, Vol. 2 (edited by Paula Guran). His 'Pet of Olodumare' (co-written with Oghenechovwe Ekpeki) appeared in *F & SF magazine.* He has also appeared in *Obsidian* with his story, 'The Phial of Olodumare'. He copy-edited *Dominion: an Anthology of Speculative Fiction from African and the African Diaspora* (Ekpeki & Knight eds.). He was a participant in the 2nd edition of the Mawazo African Writing Workshop (2018-2019). He resides in Nigeria where he combines literary writing with legal practice.

Printed in the USA
CPSIA information can be obtained
at www.ICGtesting.com
JSHW022104050324
58641JS00001B/1

9 781647 100841